LAU
GI

"Do you believe in magic?
You will when Gilman's done with you."
—*New York Times* bestselling author Dana Stabenow

"Readers will love the *Mythbusters*-style fun of smart,
sassy people solving mysteries through experimentation,
failure and blowing stuff up."
—*Publishers Weekly* (starred review) on **Hard Magic**

"Layers of mystery, science, politics, romance,
and old-fashioned investigative work mixed with
high-tech spellcraft."
—*Publishers Weekly* (starred review) on **Pack of Lies**

"Innovative world building coupled with rich
characterization continues to improve as we enter
the third book of this series."
—*Smexy Books Romance Reviews* on **Tricks of the Trade**

"Gilman spends a good deal of time exploring—and
subverting—the trope of the fated-to-happen relationship.
Readers will find this to be an engaging and
fast-paced read."
—*RT Book Reviews* on **Dragon Justice**

"Gilman delivers an exciting, fast-paced,
unpredictable story that never lets up until the very end.
There's just enough twists and turns to keep even
a jaded reader guessing."
—*SF Site* on **Staying Dead**

heart of briar

LAURA ANNE GILMAN

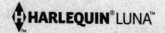 HARLEQUIN® LUNA™

Recycling programs
for this product may
not exist in your area.

ISBN-13: 978-0-373-80355-2

HEART OF BRIAR

Printed in U.S.A.

www.Harlequin.com

For Jenn. With thanks.

Chapter 1

Tyler Wash had pulled off another miracle at work today. There would be another crisis in the morning—there always was—but for this one day, good had triumphed, evil had been banished, and the world—or at least, the university's intranet—was safe from bad coding.

His lips twitched as he imagined his girlfriend's reaction to that stream-of-consciousness ego trip. She'd roll her eyes, even as she smiled, and ask him if he had a cape and long underwear hidden somewhere, probably. SuperTy, she'd call him, until he distracted her enough to forget....

"You're not drinking your coffee? Do you not like it?"

His companion looked at him, her lovely face creased with worry. Even though they'd only just met, it seemed a shame to cause any wrinkles on that face, and so, to appease her, he lifted his cup and took a sip.

"That's better," she said, the frown easing, and she reached out to touch the back of his hand, her long fingers stroking his skin in a way that would have made even a eunuch think dirty. She wasn't sex on a stick, exactly, but there was something about her that made him feel a little bit like a bad boy, the kind of guy mothers warned their daughters about, instead of being the one they urged the girls to catch.

He kind of liked that feeling.

That was why he'd agreed to meet her tonight, to feel that way. Not forever, just a little while, a chance to be someone other than Tyler Wash: ordinary, reliable, predictable. Not that he had a problem with his life, his life mostly rocked. But sometimes… Sometimes he looked in the mirror and all he saw was *boring*.

So when a woman like this offered to buy you coffee, and you had nothing else on your schedule, why the hell not?

Tyler took another sip of the coffee, and his nose twitched. The steam was still rising, and the coffee tasted thicker and heavier—more pungent—than he had been expecting. Were they trying out a new blend? If so, he wasn't sure that he liked it: the smell was less coffee than spice, not unpleasant, but different. He liked different, but…

Her foot touched his under the table, and then he felt it slide, slowly, up his calf, a touch that couldn't have been accidental. He managed not to startle, acting as though women did this to him all the time, no big deal. He'd tell her to cut it out in a minute, or maybe two. Or if her foot went any higher.

Her foot lingered just below his knee, a warm, pleasant weight, and his thoughts drifted off, spiraled around, the faint memory of the song he had been humming earlier tangling with the hiss-and-chunk noise of the espresso machine behind him, the low conversations of the people around them. What had they been talking about?

She was talking again, her voice a pleasant murmur, but he found it difficult to focus on the words. He put his coffee down, tried to shake off the disorientation, but his eyes were filling with the steam, his mind equally clouded, and when she touched his hand again, pulling him toward her across the table, he did not resist.

Her lips tasted like spice, cool and firm.

This was wrong. This was further than he'd planned to go—wasn't it?

What else did you come here for? What did you think—hope—would happen?

He stared at her, unable to answer the voice in his own head, the mocking, cool tone.

"Come," she said, and they rose from the little table, her hand still on his, leading him to the door. He followed, obedient, his coffee and coat, his wallet and phone, left behind at the table, forgotten.

Outside, the air was clearer, the smell of the coffee fading, and he blinked, shaking his head slightly to clear his thoughts. The song came back to him, the notes more clear. He had been singing it in the shower this morning, thinking about…what? About the day, the job, the night before. Her? No. Someone else. He tried to grab hold of the music, the memory, as though it would lead him out of the fog. "Where…?"

"Come," she said again, her fingers curling around his, tugging him gently forward. The sound of her voice was honey and spice, her skin soft and cool, filled with promise and suggestion, and the song— and the memories—faded under its intrusion.

They walked through the night, heading away from downtown and the university campus, onto streets he should have recognized but did not. His skin prickled, uneasy. "I don't…"

"Shhhhh…" Her voice had less honey and more spice now. "You came to me, joined your hand with mine. Of your own will do you come, Tyler Wash?"

He shouldn't. He couldn't. There was something he had left behind…. But the hint of promise and suggestion lured him on; the male ego impulse—stupid, but irresistible—pushed him over.

"I do," he said, and she smiled, teeth too white, eyes too sharp.

Around them, the air crackled, a faint familiar smell overlaying the normal odors of the city at night. Something twisted inside him, hard enough to hurt. He managed to lift his eyes from her face, force them to clear enough to see something ahead, dim lights swirling like a corona, the static fizz of noise on the wire, and then it cleared, creating a massive oval of cold white, filling the entrance to an alley, and obscuring what was beyond.

He stared, fascinated. "What?"

"Yours. Yours and mine, together. We will make it stronger." That too-white smile disappeared, and her face went still. "Come," she said again, her fingers hard against his own, and together, they stepped through.

Jan was dreaming. She knew it was a dream: it wasn't a nice dream, it was the same dream she always had when she was stressed, about not being able to breathe and nobody hearing her call for help, but she let it carry her along, anyway, unable to stop it until the alarm went off, and she woke up.

Over the years, she had perfected a basic morning routine, Monday through Friday. Roll out of bed two minutes before the alarm went off, take the litany of pills waiting on her nightstand—birth control, asthma meds, iron supplements—then stagger into the kitchen and pour herself a glass of grapefruit juice while the coffeemaker—set to go off exactly at six in the morning—started its spluttering little song. Pour that first cup of coffee, feel her neurons start to fire, and head back across the apartment to her office. Flip open the laptop, start the email download to see what fresh hell her office had sent her overnight. Sometimes she missed having a commute, an office, coworkers to gossip with. The rest of the time she thanked god for telecommuting. She could start work at seven and get a head start on whatever was going on.

And for the past three—almost four—months if she had woken up alone, she had added another early morning routine. The first words of the day, typed into the small text box in the upper left hand of the screen: Hello, lover.

Normally, her screen would show a reply almost immediately. But today, the text box on her screen remained blank, save for her words.

She waited a minute, then another. Nothing.

Well. Maybe he was in the bathroom. Or dealing with a work thing. Tyler did contract work for the university, which meant there was almost always a crisis happening—academics were worse than corporations for wanting something changed and then not understanding why it couldn't be done. But it also meant he wasn't away from his monitor, when he was on the clock. Not for long, anyway.

They'd met in one of those dating-site chat rooms, ironically self-conscious and, she admitted, a little desperate. She hadn't expected anything; so many of the guys would chat, email, they might even call once or twice, and then disappear. But Tyler had suggested they meet for coffee, almost immediately. They'd both been awkward, almost shy, for about ten minutes. Then…magic.

It wasn't because they were so alike—they weren't. And it wasn't because they were total opposites, either. There was just enough overlap that they didn't run out of things to talk about that night, or after, for that matter.

Jan frowned at the screen. Maybe he had gone onto campus today, rather than working from home? He hadn't mentioned anything about it yesterday, but something might have come up after he left.

He'd gone home the night before around eight o'clock; they both were busiest in the morning, so Monday through Thursday they tended to sleep in their own beds, work until around two in the afternoon, and then hook up again. She might have liked waking up with someone snuggled against her more often, but Jan admitted that she liked her space, too.

So, yeah. That was probably it: he was on the bus heading toward campus, and he'd check in later. Reassured, she opened her work in-box and got hit with an urgent email from a client in Ireland whose site had apparently gone FUBAR, "and she swears she didn't touch it, didn't do anything," according to the email from the project manager.

"Yeah. Sure you didn't." Jan shook her head and got to work, digging through the code.

By the time she'd restored the site, finished her first pot of coffee and refilled it, there was still no message from Tyler in her text box. She frowned, chewing on her thumbnail, then—after glancing to make sure no new mail had come in red-flagged for an emergency—typed again.

You there?

No response. She looked at the time display: 10:40. More than enough time for him to have gotten into the office—maybe it was a really massive crisis?

She opened another browser and brought up the university's site. It seemed to be running fine, although god knew what was going on with the intranet, which was Ty's baby.

"Okay, then," she said, and typed, catch up with you later, then, mmmkay? It wasn't as if he had to check in, after all. She was just used to it. Spoiled, after three months. Odds were, the project he'd been working on yesterday had gotten more panicked, and he was head down in that. He'd resurface later, apologize, or just show up, filled with news of how he'd licked the problem. The vague sense of disappointment she felt was silly, and she pushed it aside.

The worry didn't set in for another six hours, when he didn't show up after work, and nobody in the campus office had seen or talked to him all day.

By twenty-four hours, the worry had become panic.

The next morning, Jan needed to talk with someone, preferably someone who could talk her down off her nerves.

"Come on, come on, pick up…." Jan drummed her fingers on the desk and stared at the monitor, where the icon was circling around, the faint, antiquated noise of a phone ringing accompanying the visual.

Finally, it stopped, and the screen cleared. "Hey, there. You rang?"

Glory's tousled black curls suggested that she'd just gotten out of bed, and her accent was a blurred version of her usual clear tones.

Jan frowned at the screen, taking in the backdrop. "It's lunchtime there. You should be at work now, not just waking up. Oh, Glory, did you get fired again?"

Her friend lifted her coffee mug in salute. "How'd you guess? Yeah, guess calling the boss's pet a puss-bucket wasn't the best thing to do."

Jan was momentarily distracted from her own woes. "Glory…"

"Ah, don't lecture me, Janny-girl."

Glory worked in the UK; they had met through a "women in tech" mailing list back when those were the hot thing, and when the list died, they stayed friends. That didn't mean they always approved of each other's choices, though.

Jan couldn't help herself: "Some day you're not going to find another job." The economy still hadn't entirely recovered, and she knew Glory didn't have any savings left.

"Ah, I'm too good at my job to not find work, and hiring a black woman fills two slots on their to-do list. But you, you're not looking good, and you're doing that keening thing again. Sweetie, stop it, it makes my stomach hurt watching you. What's wrong?"

Saying it made it real. "Tyler's missing."

"What?" Glory's coffee mug slammed down on her desk hard enough to slosh the liquid over the side, unnoticed. "Did that SOB dump you? I swear..."

"No! No, I mean, he's missing, he's gone. He didn't go to work, and it's been twenty-four hours, and I haven't heard a thing from him."

Jan leaned forward, and then back again, unable to stop the slow rhythmic rocking motion that bothered Glory. "He's never not responded for this long. We talk every day, Glor, every day we're not together. And he's never once missed a good morning."

"Yeah, I know. But, sweetie, you've only been together, what, three months? Guy's what, thirty-two? He probably has a lot of bad habits he hasn't shown you yet."

Jan tried to still herself, focusing on the screen where her friend's image was looking out at her. Miles away in distance, but Glory was still one of her best friends, the person she'd told about Tyler, punch-happy from their first date, when she'd finally thought that maybe, just maybe, she wasn't doomed to go through life alone. And then again after the third date, when he'd told her he'd felt the same way.

Glory had always given her good advice.

"Janny, listen to me. One day? That's nothing. Boys will be boys, and Tyler-boy is probably just fine. If you spank him when he comes back, he'll promise never to do it again. He'll be lying, but he'll promise, and you'll feel better. That's how happy relationships stay happy."

Jan rocked back and forth again, but more slowly. "Says the woman who's been single for how long now?"

"Thirteen years, and loving every minute of it. Look, sweetie, give him a little space, then call his mom, or something, see if he's been in touch with her."

"He hasn't talked to his stepmom in two years. His dad is dead, his sister's off somewhere on a fishing boat or something…."

Their lack of any real family had been one of the things to bind them: her mother was gone, her father was in a nursing home, didn't even recognize her anymore, and she'd been an only child. "Us together against the storm, Jan," Tyler had said after one of his sister's infrequent phone calls, holding her while they'd listened to a thunderstorm rage overhead. They had fallen asleep tangled together on the sofa, her last conscious memory him humming contentedly under his breath.

Jan felt her body sway forward again and tried to halt the backward motion without success. It normally calmed her, the back and forth almost a meditation, but no matter what she did, the thready feeling of panic wouldn't subside. It was like her dream the night before: no air, and nobody coming to the rescue.

"Jan! Sweetie, breathe. Where's your inhaler?"

"No, I'm okay." She held up a hand, then patted the inhaler on her desk by the keyboard to reassure Glory. "I'm just...I'm okay."

"All right." Glory regrouped, focusing on the problem at hand. "So he skipped work, isn't answering his phone. You need a guy's take on this—what did Steverino say?"

"The same thing you did," Jan admitted, not surprised that Glory knew she'd already asked him. Steve worked out of her company's main office down in New York and had been the one to hire her. He was somewhere between big brother and mentor, and she'd asked him last night, via email, for advice. "He said that I was suffering from early onset relationship jitters, and not to freak out for at least forty-eight hours."

"Uh-huh. But you're still worried. Did you call the police?"

Jan nodded. "I called last night, and they pretty much told me to chill. I'm not a relative, I'm not a long-time companion, and Tyler's well over eighteen, so I can't file a missing person's report without cause." And the local cops had more important things to worry about than one adult who hadn't checked in with his girlfriend; that vibe had come through loud and clear. Considering the scandals that had rocked the local P.D.s in the three years since she'd moved to the New Haven area, she wasn't surprised.

"And you've gone over there and hammered on his door, demanding that he come out and explain himself?" Glory said.

Jan shook her head, biting her lip.

"No? Janny…" Glory leaned forward so that her face filled the screen. "Girl, if you're that worried, why not?"

"I called his super—I met him once, when there was a problem with the heat. I asked him to check." She hadn't felt comfortable going over there, not if he hadn't called; it was too…stalkery. She could worry in private, but letting him know she was worried…

"Oh, Jan. And?"

"And Tyler wasn't there, and there was no sign of any forced entry, so…"

"So." Glory sat back and idly twirled a pen in her fingers. "Back where we started, then."

Jan reached out and touched her inhaler again, the way someone might touch a good-luck charm or a worry stone. "Yeah, I know, I know. Everyone's giving me the same advice. You don't think his silence is worrying, you don't think there's anything odd in someone going off-line for an entire day without calling or texting his girlfriend. And you all think I'm overreacting."

"Janny..."

"No. I'm not pissed. Normally—normally I'd agree with you. I'd say, oh, he had something land overnight that he needed time away to deal with, and he forgot to email me. Maybe there's an unsent email on his laptop, that says 'going off-line for 24, dinner when I get back.'" She forced a smile for Glory's sake. "You're all probably right. Once I make him properly apologize, I'll let you do all the toljasos in the world."

"Damn straight," Glory agreed. "Go back to work, girl. Let me know what happens, okay?"

"Yes, Mother."

Jan ended the vid-call, and ran her hands along the surface of the desk, noting that new email had landed while she'd talked to Glory. One was from Steve, asking if there was any update.

All right, maybe she had overreacted a bit. Clicking on that email, she typed in a response.

Not yet. He so owes me dinner for this!

She studied her response, decided that it had just the right tone of aggrieved but not-worried girlfriend, and hit Send.

The other two emails were follow-ups on projects she'd closed out last week, her name on the cc list. She didn't have any websites going live this week, and nothing else seemed currently to be on fire, so she had room to breathe.

Except she couldn't. Despite what she'd said to Glory and to Steve, Tyler's continued absence—the worry about his continued absence—was almost like an asthma attack, closing up her chest and making her feel a little weird, off balance and dizzy.

"It's silly," she said out loud. And it was. Everyone was right: she knew that. She and Tyler had only met four months ago, and, yes, they'd pretty much fallen into each other's lives without a hitch, like the true love neither of them had claimed to believe in, but there were always surprises, bumps and revelations along the way, and twenty-four hours wasn't all that long for an adult to be out of touch, especially since there wasn't any indication there was anything wrong.

Except Jan knew. Deep inside, in some skittish reptile part of her brain, she knew. Something was wrong.

The rest of the day, Jan tried to take the excellent advice she had been given. She closed the text box in the corner of her monitor and cleared her in-box down to zero, then worked on a project with an extended deadline until she was actually ahead of schedule.

And if every ping of incoming mail or text message made her heart speed up in anticipation, she didn't let it distract her. Too much.

She even left the apartment to have dinner downtown with a friend, didn't mention anything to her about Tyler going missing, and tried not to think about going to bed alone. But when she woke up to a second day of silence, that sense of something being wrong began to chew on her nerves.

By midmorning, her nerves had gotten so bad, it was almost impossible to focus on her work. She opened the text box, closed it, and then opened it again, afraid that she would miss him when he did check in.

"Obsessive, much?" She clicked on the text box, closing it again. "Let it go." But she couldn't.

When afternoon rolled around, and there was still no word, Jan couldn't just sit and wait and try to be patient. Sending an email to let the folks at the other end of her projects know that she would be off-line for a bit, she shut down her computer, shoved her cell phone, inhaler and wallet in her daypack, and headed across town. Glory was right, and she was a wimp. If the cops wouldn't investigate, then she would.

It was only a twenty-minute bus ride downtown from her apartment building—but it took almost that long for a bus to actually show up. Jan tried to stay calm and not over-anticipate what she might find there.

His building was older than hers, without a digital security box. If you had a key, you could go right in; if not, you had to wait for someone to buzz you through the lobby door. She had a key. He'd given it to her, two weeks after they'd met, on a little keychain with a vintage Hello Kitty on it. If she hadn't already been pretty sure she was in love before, that would have sealed it for her. Hello Kitty wasn't his thing, it was hers, and he'd known that.

She took the elevator up to the fifth floor and walked down the hallway to his door. Once there, though, all of her resolve fled. She'd never been here before, without him. He hadn't called and said "get your ass over here, I miss you." He hadn't said anything at all, not to look after his plants—he had none, he was the original black thumb—or pick up his mail. The super might have come in at a bad time and missed him. Tyler might be inside, just not checking in, might be blowing her off, or…

If he was that much of a coward, she could hear Glory saying, then he totally deserved to be caught at it.

Jan agreed. She just didn't want to be the one doing the catching.

"He gave you a key," she told herself. "If anything is wrong…standing out here isn't going to find that out, is it?

She was worried. No matter what anyone else said, this wasn't like him. He never went offline this long. He couldn't—he had clients and email, and even if his connection was down, he would have called and told her. If he was breaking up with her... No. He wouldn't do it this way.

And it wasn't as though she was breaking and entering. Okay, it was entering. But not breaking. She had a toothbrush there, and an extra emergency inhaler, and knew his super, and where he kept the spare change for when the ice cream truck came around and he had a craving for an ice cream sandwich.

So why was she standing in front of his door, key in hand, terrified to go in?

Because she wanted to find something to explain it...and was terrified of what she might find. Because maybe everyone was right, and she was a ninny. Or worse, they were wrong, and he was on the floor, dead, or dying, or...

She swallowed, trying to deal with the conflicting urges, half-ready to turn around and go home without even putting the key in the lock.

"Ma'am?"

She turned, her heart in her throat, and saw a cop standing in the hallway a few steps away from her. She had been so focused on the door, she hadn't even heard the elevator open or anyone come out.

"You a friend of Tyler Wash?"

"I'm his girlfriend." It still felt weird saying it out loud. Three months. What was three months?

It was forever, when you knew, she reminded herself. And they had both known, so fast, never any doubt...right?

The cop looked her up and down, as if he was trying to memorize her to pick out of a lineup, later. "Have you heard from your boyfriend recently?"

"No. I came over… I haven't heard from him in a couple of days, and that's not like him at all. Are you… Did someone hear something? Is he okay?" Panic swamped her, cold and hard. Why else would the cops be here? Had the super heard or seen something, and not told her?

"He resigned his position but failed to return his equipment. I'm here to get it back."

Her eyes focused on the badge on the shoulder of his uniform: not a cop, campus security. Then the words he'd spoken registered with her.

"Resigned?"

The security guard gave a shrug, as if he didn't really care either way. "Polite way of saying he blew a major deadline, and hasn't responded to the boss in three days, so they terminated his contract. Didn't tell you, huh?" The look the man gave her now was filled with pity.

Jan swallowed, hard. The panic had subsided, leaving her too drained to move. "No."

"Well, he did. People think that working out of the office means they can do whatever they want, they get an unhappy surprise. His choice. But the school wants its equipment back." The guy wasn't being mean, just matter-of-fact. He stepped forward, moving around her when she didn't get out of the way, and knocked once, hard on the door.

Jan wanted to defend Tyler—he wasn't like that!—but she couldn't. Because that was just what he'd done, wasn't it? Just disappeared, dumped all his obligations, responsibilities. And that wasn't like Ty, wasn't like him at all. But he wasn't sick, he wasn't in the hospital, so where was he?

There was no response to the knock, not even the sounds of someone trying to avoid visitors.

He knocked again, and then Jan spoke up.

"He's not there. But I have a key."

It was as much stubborn pride, a reaction to the way he'd looked at her, that made her say anything. *See? I have a key. I'm not some fly-by-night chickie he just forgot about.* Plus, if she was helping someone else get their property back, it wasn't breaking and entering. Or being stalkery. Right? It was just keeping Tyler out of trouble. Out of more trouble, anyway.

The guy stepped back and let her have at the door. Her hand trembled a little in the locks, then she heard the dead bolt snick free, and the handle turned, opening into Tyler's apartment.

There was no body lying sprawled in the main room.

The apartment looked…exactly the way it had the last time she was there. A lot of open space, and the whitewashed furniture with denim upholstery that looked as if he'd stolen it from some WASP's vacation home. He'd always laughed and shrugged; he liked to confound expectations, although he'd never admitted it.

If the super had poked around, he'd not disturbed anything.

The apartment was also weirdly silent. She couldn't remember it ever being that quiet. Tyler always made noise, muttering to himself as he worked, occasionally singing under his breath, in constant movement. She would sit, her legs crossed under her, and not move for hours, while he buzzed around the space, the activity in his brain echoed in his actions.

Nothing moved. Even the two of them, once inside the threshold, seemed frozen, as though something held them back.

"All right. Where would his tech be?" The security guy's voice was too loud; it didn't belong in this quiet space, and Jan shuddered in reaction, as though he'd said something vile.

"In the office." She led the way across the floor to the small room in the back that, for someone else, would have been the bedroom. Two glass-topped desks filled the space; one laden with monitors and decks, the other at a right angle to it, holding only a laptop and a three-level filing box that was stuffed to overflowing with papers.

The security guy went over to the first table and started unplugging one of the decks from the monitor. She watched him, making sure that he only was interested in the ones with the university's name stenciled on the side, and then went over to the laptop.

The rest of the tech was for work. The laptop was where he'd done all of his personal stuff. If there was a message for her, or some clue she was supposed to follow, it would be here. She put her pack down on the floor and sat down in his chair. And then she didn't move, staring at the fifteen-inch silvery square in front of her.

"All right, that's it. Thanks for your help." The guy had the deck under his arm and was having trouble meeting her gaze. "I…hope everything works out."

She stared at him, not quite able to parse his comment, and then just nodded absently. "Yeah, thanks."

She heard him leave, the door closing firmly behind him, while she stared at the laptop. Taking a deep breath, she lifted the lid and woke it up.

The wallpaper was the same it had been the last time she'd seen it: the two of them, heads together, trying to fit in front of the webcam while he hit the button, smiles bright and about to break into giggles. If he was going to break up with her, he would have changed his wallpaper, right?

"Dammit, Ty.…" The security guy's pity was like salt in the wound she'd been trying to ignore, and her worry ignited into anger again. "What the hell are you up to? If you're secretly working for the CIA or something and went off on a top-duper-secret mission, I'm so going to kill you myself."

The idea of Tyler—gawky, geeky, *gentle* Tyler— as a CIA anything made her close her eyes against sudden tears.

"You've been reading too many thrillers, Jan," she said, trying to channel some of Glory's tartness into the scold. "This is real life. In real life, the CIA doesn't recruit quality assurance tech-heads who can barely handle English, much less any other languages."

Although, yeah, he could have been hiding a facility for Arabic and French and Chinese from her…but she didn't believe it. Tyler could strip down a webpage and rebuild it to be fabulous, and put together a gourmet three-course dinner out of whatever was in his kitchen, and he was pretty damn inventive in bed. But sneaky? Sneaky wasn't in him.

"So, then, where is he?" He wouldn't have gone without a word, unless he was hurt, maybe had been injured somewhere else? But he always carried his ID with him, his photo ID and emergency contact, ever since he'd gotten hit on a bike when he was a kid, he'd said, so if he were in a hospital the cops would have known….

She was dithering. Jan straightened her back, aware that she'd fallen into an uncomfortable slump over the laptop—she was five-six, he was five-ten, so his desk was the wrong height for her comfort— and opened the most obvious place to look: his personal calendar.

Typical organized Tyler: work events in blue tabs, social in green, and their dates were in red. Her finger traced the weeks, stopping when she came to the day he disappeared. Then she backtracked one. There was a yellow tab.

A doctor's visit, maybe? Tyler didn't like doctors,

hated going to the dentist.... Maybe he'd not told her because he was trying to avoid thinking about it, and something had gone wrong....

No. If he walked away from his job, that wasn't...

The thought stopped her again, as if someone punched her in the stomach. He'd left his job. Without a new one being offered? Another thing that wasn't like Tyler: he worked remotely because that's how the job was, but he liked the familiar aspects of it, the steady paycheck and security. He wouldn't just walk away without a new job in-hand.

Had he gotten another job and not told her?

Thoughts of the CIA surfaced again, and to push them away, she clicked on the yellow tab.

Stjerne, 10pm, l'coffeehouse

She didn't know any Stjerne. She hadn't known he'd known any Stjerne, either. Not that that meant anything. It was an odd name—Norwegian, maybe?

"Steh-gerne," she said out loud, and shook her head. She didn't remember Tyler mentioning anyone like that, either.

Still, working remotely the way they both did in the tech field, they met a lot of people from around the world; maybe it was a coworker who was in town, and they'd met up for a late-night coffee when he'd gone off-shift? That would be the kind of thing he wouldn't mention until after the fact. "Oh, met this guy, Stjerne, works for an outfit in Holland. Drinks beer for breakfast…" Yes. That made sense. And maybe…

What had happened, when he'd had coffee with this guy? What if this Stjerne was a serial killer? Had other people gone missing recently? Had the cops been alerted? Would they even notice, or care?

Even in her worried state, that was too much for Jan. "If there was a serial anything in town, the cops would have paid more attention when you called about someone going missing—and every local news-feed would be screaming, and the university would have held a press conference, or something. Get a grip. Losing your boyfriend is no reason to become an idiot."

Switching tabs, she went into his email program, scanning for anything from someone named Stjerne. A contact point, she needed a contact point. Who was Stjerne?

There. A dozen or so of them, all recent, the past week or so. Probably a coworker then, arranging a meeting while he was in town…she clicked on one at random, calling it onto the screen.

I want to feel your hands on my skin, gripping me, pulling me, holding me like you'll never let me go. Your mouth on me, moving lower, until my legs open, helpless, as you lap at me, tongue and fingers making me writhe and moan, calling your name to stop, never stop, Tyler, oh Tyler, until I fall over the edge… and then come back to return the favor for you, my mouth red and wet against the darkness of your skin, taking the length of your....

Jan closed the email with a hasty jab of her finger, and closed her eyes. No. She hadn't just seen that. It was a mistake, or someone had forwarded porn—she had nothing against porn, as a general rule, although it didn't do much for her. That was it. He'd forwarded it to himself, maybe, or...

His name had been mentioned. Specifically, and with lurid detail.

That punched-in-the-gut feeling came again, harder this time, and Jan thought she was going to throw up. She fought it and stared at the laptop's screen, the photo of the two of them, laughing like nothing in the world could ever be wrong. Her mouth worked, and she was finally able to voice her reaction.

"You son of a bitch."

Chapter 2

Jan left the keys to the apartment on the desk, right next to the still-open laptop. When Tyler the son-of-a-bitch finally wandered back from whatever had kept him three days with his online porn-partner, he'd be smart enough to figure it out.

Or not. Right then, she didn't give a damn. Rage and betrayal made her body shake, and once in the elevator she reached for her inhaler out of habit, although the pain in her chest was nothing like an asthma attack.

"Son of a bitch," she said again. "You slimy, sneaky, no-good, two-timing son of a bitch."

The man in the elevator with her gave her a sympathetic look but didn't say anything, and Jan clamped her own jaw shut, determined not to let that son of a bitch get one more outburst from her.

When she left the building, the bright blue sky and crisp autumn wind felt like a betrayal. It should be darker, rain clouds scudding across the sky, thunder booming and wind swirling, people scurrying for cover, not strolling along as if they didn't have a single trauma in their lives.

She stood on the street and thought about going to his office, demanding someone tell her something. The thought of the fuss that would make, probably getting her escorted off campus, certainly making it harder for Tyler to get his job back, if—when—he came back…. She thought briefly about going into one of the bars that lined downtown, catering to students and professionals, and tying a few on, but booze had never been her thing.

No. The only thing to do was go back home.

The bus came eventually, and she got on, paying her fare and finding a seat toward the back, where fewer people sat. The last thing she wanted right now was some wannabe Romeo in her space. Or any human being, actually. She wasn't sure she could be civil to anyone, just then

Sitting down, she shoved the fare card into the side pocket of her pack, and her fingers touched the keys she'd put there, the cool smooth texture of the Hello Kitty key chain. She'd left the keys, but the key chain was hers, damn it.

Tyler hadn't just run off with some cyberslut; he'd left his job, too. That still didn't make any sense to her. It wasn't as though he had piles of cash hanging around, that he could quit like that. Or did he? What did she really know about him, anyway?

Jan pressed her hand against her stomach, trying to calm the knot there. There was a feeling as if she wanted to throw up, even though she knew there wasn't anything in her stomach. Nerves and anger. She had never been very good with either. Conflict wasn't her thing.

"Let it go. He's not your problem," she told herself, her voice an unexpected, oddly unfamiliar noise, hard and mean. "Tyler Wash is no longer ever again your problem."

"Problem is, you're his only chance."

"What?" She twisted in her seat, knocking the pack to the ground. The person who had spoken sat down next to her, way too far into her personal space, then reached down and picked up the pack, handing it to her. She took it, numbly, barely even noting what she was doing.

"He has been taken. And you are his only chance to return."

Those words, like the security guy's, didn't make sense at first. Unlike earlier, they didn't resolve into anything that did make sense.

The man—his dark blue hoodie up, but not quite enough to hide some kind of deformity around his nose, shaggy dark hair obscuring his eyes—made a strangled, frustrated sort of noise. "Listen to me. You must listen, and hear. Your leman needs your help."

"My…what?" She just sat there and stared at the speaker, her earlier anger washed away by the certainty that she should not be talking to this man, and an equal certainty that, if she tried to move, her feet wouldn't support her.

He growled once, as though annoyed with her denseness. "Your lover. He has been taken."

The words were in English, and they still made no sense. She shook her head and shifted in her seat, as though that would be enough to make this crazy person go away. She'd been told, ever since she moved into the city, that crazies would come right up to you, but she'd never had it happen to her before. It wasn't as if this was New York, or Chicago…. Of all the days, though, it seemed inevitable that it would happen today.

The next growl was definitely one of exasperation, and he raised his head to look directly at her, swiping some of the hair away from his face. His nose was too thick, almost more a muzzle than a nose, and his eyes—they were dark, but they looked almost red under the bus lights. Was he wearing contacts? A mask? It wasn't anywhere near Halloween yet, but—

"Woman, you must listen," he insisted, and she started to get pissed off.

"I don't have to do anything, buddy. Back off."

She should have started carrying mace, or a whistle, or something. Not that she'd ever have the nerve to use it—she was more likely to apologize to a mugger than fight back. But still, this guy was giving her all the creeps.

"I told you that was the wrong approach," another voice said, even as someone sat down heavily in the seat on the other side of her.

Jan swiveled around, feeling her body shrink in on itself as the frozen sensation of fear intensified. She might not have been city-raised, but she knew better than to let two strangers bracket her like that, so close.

The second stranger put his hand on her arm, gently. "It's okay."

What? She almost laughed. None of this was okay, not at all. Jan stared at the hand, not sure why she hadn't knocked it off, gotten up, and found somewhere else to sit. It was a normal hand, skin smooth and scattered with fine brown hairs, the nails painted black but well-groomed, and when she looked up, his face was just as ordinary, wide-set brown eyes in a long, sort of blocky face. Easier to look at him than the other man, with his odd face and disconcerting eyes, even if it was a mask, and why was he wearing a mask?

Her heart was racing, but her brain felt like sludge, unable to understand what it was seeing, unable to react the way she knew she should, to make them leave her alone.

"Please," the second stranger said, his voice smooth and soothing. "We want to help Tyler, too."

They knew Tyler's name. They knew Tyler. Somehow. She clutched at that thought. Had they followed her from his apartment? They thought something had happened to him, too. Had that bitch…

"Who are you?"

She had almost asked "*what* are you" but had resisted at the last instant; if she looked, she'd stare, if she stared, she'd have to acknowledge that it wasn't a mask probably, and it wasn't polite to stare at people with disabilities, anyway.

"Friends. If you'll have us."

Something about the smooth guy's words was too smooth. Jan's instincts jangled again, the anger and panic mixing with her natural caution, almost overwhelming her desire to not make a fuss. She slid her arm out from under his hold, thankful he didn't resist. "I'm choosy about my friends," she said.

"Huh. She's smarter than she looks," the first one said.

She turned to glare at him, and he *grinned* at her, that nose, yes, it looked like a muzzle, and the jaw hung open showing sharp teeth and a red tongue visible. Not a mask. She shuddered and looked away— then looked back and stared at him, politeness be damned, this once.

They locked gazes as her heart went thump-*thump* thump-*thump* a dozen times, and the bus swerved around corners, hitting one of the inevitable potholes and making everyone bounce in their plastic seats, but she refused to let herself look away from that awful red gaze until he blinked and looked away first.

"Satisfied?" The guy with the black nails wasn't talking to her, but to his companion.

Hoodie-guy shook his head. "No. But it's not like we've got any choice, is there?"

The squabble, a clear continuation of some longer debate, didn't make Jan feel better—especially since the suggestion had been made that she somehow might not have been acceptable. Bad enough she'd just been cheated on by the love of her life. Now this crap?

She could make a bolt for it—they didn't seem to be violent, but you couldn't always tell, right? Only they were both bigger than she was and looked as if they were in shape; two against one, there was no way she could get away if they tried to hold her. Jan looked toward the front of the bus, to see if anyone was sitting nearby who might be willing to help her get away if things got ugly. An old man with a shopping bag on his lap looked at her uncomprehendingly, and two girls sitting farther down were too busy giggling with each other. The others were too far away; they didn't notice anything was wrong.

The black-nailed man put his hand on her sleeve

again, and she shivered a little under his intent gaze. Having a guy look at you like that, as if he wanted to carry you away somewhere... Her skin prickled in warning. Black Nails might look more normal than his companion, but he gave off seriously weird vibes, too.

No. She was not going to fall for any creepy stalker maybe-rapists, maybe-cannibal tricks or mind games. "Look, I don't know what the hell game you're playing, or what this has to do with Tyler, who by the way is a bastard and you can tell him that next time you see his skanky ass, but—"

Black Nails interrupted her. "Is there somewhere we can go, somewhere, private, to talk?"

"Are you kidding me? I'm not going off anywhere *private* with you two," she said, her voice rising enough that people might have taken notice, if they weren't all carefully not paying attention.

"Oh, for the love of Pete..." Hoodie-guy slapped his hands on his knees, the noise making her jump slightly. "Listen, we don't have time for this. There's no way we weren't noticed, following you, and—"

The bus went over a particularly bad pothole and jolted them out of their seats. Something scraped along the bottom of the bus, making both guys flinch. Jan tried to use the distraction to get up, get away, but Black Nails grabbed her again, hauling her back, pulling her toward the back exit.

"We have to go *now,*" he said.

"What?" She tried to free herself, but his grip was painfully strong. Should she scream? Would the bus driver help her? There were reports of drivers who didn't do anything, even when someone screamed, but those had to be urban legends, right? Stuff that only happened in big cities, not here, not—

"Off the bus, now!" Black Nails sounded worried suddenly, and that scared her all over again, although she couldn't have said why. *The bogeyman of my enemy is still a bogeyman?*

The one with the messed-up face had already pulled the yellow cord that called for a stop, and the bus driver was jockeying through traffic to pull to the side at the end of the next block, even as she was being yanked toward the exit.

"What are you— No!" She finally pulled away, drawing breath to scream, when Hoodie-guy glanced at the back of the bus and swore. Jan couldn't help herself; she looked, too. The bus jolted again, there was another shrieking noise underneath, as if the bus had run over something sharp and metallic. Then the metal floor buckled once, twisting weirdly, as if it was melting. The old man stared at it, then looked away, and Jan wondered if she were hallucinating… except the guys hauling her out kept looking back, worried, too, hands flat against the door, waiting for the bus to stop so they could get out.

"What is—" she started to ask, about to pull herself loose from their grip and tell the bus driver something was wrong, when the floor buckled one last time, and something shoved its way through, a long arm with small fingers, skin the gray-white of old bread streaked with mold, stretching as though to grab at whatever rested above.

Right where she would have been sitting.

Suddenly, getting off the bus seemed like a damn good idea.

The hand sank below the metal again, the fingers creeping around the opening, as though searching for something. Or someone.

"Off," Black Nails said, and with a shove from behind, they were out, even before the bus had come to a stop, and the three of them were standing on the street. "Keep moving," he said, and pulled her forward, away from the curb. "Don't look back."

Jan felt her chest clench and grabbed her inhaler out of her pack, even as they walked too quickly for her comfort. "What…what was that?"

The other one, the one with the snout, answered. "A turncoat."

"A what?" Her fingers curled around her inhaler, and she took a hit from it, feeling her chest ease slightly.

"A—" He growled, and this time it was a definite growl, the skin on her arms pricking again with goose bumps. "There's no time, now. They'll figure out we're gone in a minute: we have to get you somewhere safe."

"But...the others on the bus..." Jan waved her free hand vaguely back at the street. "We can't just—"

"Once you're gone, it'll leave, too. The damage will be blamed on metal fatigue, or something. Worry about yourself, not them!"

"Where did we leave the truck?" Black Nails asked.

"Down there, back in town, a couple—five blocks." They switched direction, walking too fast, almost dragging Jan between them. She looked over her shoulder and saw that the bus was out of sight; was whatever had broken through still on the bus right now? Or were these guys right, had it left, was it after them?

"What the hell is a turncoat? And who the hell are you? And where is Tyler?" Jan's usual tolerance had taken a hard blow today, and she wasn't the most patient of people even on a good day. But this...this was beyond enough. She coughed and then, despite the inhaler, started to wheeze.

"I need to sit down," she told them.

She must have looked as bad as she felt, because they swung around and plunked her onto a bench in the Green, away from the inevitable gaggle of teenagers hanging around the fountain. She bent over and tried to calm down, waiting for it to pass.

"You okay?" Black Nails asked.

"Stupid question," Hoodie-guy snapped.

"No, I'll be okay." She was able to speak, and her

chest was starting to ease, now that she'd stopped moving.

Black Nails sat down next to her while Hoodie-guy prowled back and forth, clearly looking for… something. His gaze flickered everywhere, the nervous energy pouring off him, just like it did Tyler when he was wound up by an idea.

His nerves got on her nerves, which were already ragged, and she wished that she had something heavy to throw at him, to make him stop pacing like that.

Black Nails tried to take her hand again, but she pulled away and glared at him, horrified to feel hot tears prickling in her eyes. She rubbed the heels of her hands against her jeans, hard, trying to drive the tears away.

"I swear, tell me now or I'm gone." She didn't care about Tyler. She didn't. But that thing on the bus…. "What the hell was that, on the bus?" she asked again.

"Turncoats. They're…" Black Nails hesitated. "They're rooting for the ones who took your leman, they want to prevent you from rescuing him. They will do anything to ensure that—and the easiest way is for you to…"

"Die." The growl was back. Hoodie-guy stood in front of them, his hands fisted on his hips, and scowled. Not at her, Jan noted, but at the other man. "If you're too delicate to tell her, I will. They'll catch her and tear her apart and eat her for good measure. They've always liked human meat."

"AJ…"

Jan latched on to one word out of all that. "Human? What do you mean…"

"Of all the moon-washed idiocies…we don't have time for this." The one called AJ reached up and pushed his hoodie back. "Human. You. Not us."

Not a monobrow. Not a misshapen nose. This close and clear there was no denying that it was a real muzzle, short but obvious, with the jaw hinged oddly, coarse dark hair overrunning what would have been a hairline to trace down to the end of his nose. Round dark eyes set too far back stared at her, waiting for her reaction. Not red, but she thought they would glow in firelight, a bright, dancing red. Like a wolf's.

She stared, and then turned to the other man, studying him more carefully. He *looked* human. Face normal, if a little long to be attractive, and his hair was a neck-length tousle of black that a supermodel might have longed for. The right number of fingers and limbs, his skin tone normal for someone who was maybe Indian or South American, she thought, even as a part of her brain shrieked *run, you idiot, run!*

"No," he said, his voice still silky-smooth and soothing, his hands taking hers between them, holding her still. "I'm not human, either."

She jerked her hands away and tried to stand up, but they had her effectively trapped. She should have listened to her gut, back on the bus, she should run, she should scream…but she didn't.

Her heart raced, but her mind was oddly clear. Or maybe she'd gone into hysteria already, and this was what being crazy felt like.

She'd stared down muzzle-boy—AJ—once already. That memory gave her just enough courage to ask again, "And that thing under the bus...it wasn't human, either." She had known that already. Mostly. Guessed it, at least, even if she hadn't let herself acknowledge the insanity of it.

"Gnomes," he said. "Nasty little bastards, all teeth and greed."

"Gnomes." All right, then. "And Tyler? He's been taken, you said. By..."

"Not by us, or ours," AJ said. He watched her carefully, not the staring contest of before, but cautious, judging. "Our enemies. Yours now, too."

"This is a joke, right? Tyler set this whole thing up. That's some kind of costume—a good one, you got me, but the joke's over." She looked between them, shaking her head. "Is this being filmed? 'Cause it's not funny anymore and there's no way in hell I'm going to sign any kind of release form for you to use the footage. And Ty's *still* a shit for pulling this."

AJ growled again. "For pity's sake, Martin, you show her."

"Me?" Black Nails sounded...worried?

AJ had pulled his hoodie back up and looked up at the sky, as if that was supposed to mean something. "I can't, you idiot."

"And you want me to—" He—Martin, Jan reminded herself—waved his hands, the black-painted fingernails catching light and sparkling slightly.

"We're running out of time. And so is her Tyler. Come on, you swish-tailed wuss. I know damn well you can control yourself when you want to."

Martin sighed and heaved himself off the bench and— There wasn't any warning, just a drawn-out groan and the sound of things crackling, the sound you'd hear when you stretched after sitting for too long, bones protesting and muscles stretching and the urge to close her eyes as though water was pressing against them, swimming underwater, and when she opened them again, Martin was gone.

And a solidly muscled pony, russet-coated with a black mane cropped short, was regarding her with deep brown eyes that were disturbingly familiar.

Jan had been the normal horse-mad kid, but that stage had worn off years ago. Still, she couldn't help but reach up to touch that nose, then slide her hand along the side of its neck. The pony lowered its head and turned slightly, as though inviting her to continue. Without meaning to, she found herself standing by its side, contemplating how difficult it would be to tangle her fingers in that stiff brush of a mane and haul herself onto its back.

AJ let out a harsh, rude growl. "Martin, stop that. I swear, we should have left you behind, if that's how you're going to behave."

The pony shook its head and whickered, and Jan stepped back, the spell broken.

She stared at it, and then at AJ, who was suddenly, bizarrely, the lesser of two weirdnesses. "That's... oh, my god."

"No, just Martin." AJ still sounded disgusted. "Don't get on his back. He really can't help himself then, and we need you intact."

"What?"

"We're— Oh, so help me, swish-tail, if you relieve yourself here, I'm going to pretend I don't know you. Go do your business elsewhere if you can't wait."

The pony—Martin—gave an offended snort, and the crunchy-snapping noise made her close her eyes, and when she was able to open them again, he looked human again.

Looked. Wasn't.

Jan thought she might pass out.

The next thing she knew, she was sitting on the bench again, with Martin on her left and AJ pacing again, looking up and down the street and occasionally stopping to scowl into the gutters. Keeping guard against those...things from the bus, she guessed. Or whatever else was about to come bursting through the sidewalk, or popping out of a mailbox. As insane as it all had to be, as insane as she had to be, somehow Jan couldn't doubt it, not any of it. Not after Martin had done...what he had done, and not with the memory of those moldy-looking fingers reaching up to where she had been sitting, forcing their way through metal to get to her....

"They've always liked human meat."

Neither of her two rescuers were exactly knights in shining armor, but they had to be better than that.

"No knight, but the steed," she said, and a slightly hysterical giggle escaped her. Shock. She was in shock.

"What? Oh. No." Martin smiled, picking up the joke. "A sense of humor, that's good. You're going to need it."

As unnerving as the transformation had been, she still felt herself lean toward him, moving like a flower to follow the sun. AJ was unnerving and dangerous. He…AJ said Martin was dangerous, but instead she felt comforted. Protected. Safe.

That was insane. Not human. Hello, not human!

A were-pony? Jan closed her eyes, shook herself slightly, opened her eyes again. Martin was still there, watching her.

Jan had always been a practical sort: she worked with what she could see. There was no way to believe—no way to convince herself to believe that this was a hoax or a prank, not anymore. She had seen Martin change form. She had seen AJ's face, heard him growl, a noise that couldn't have come from a human throat. She had seen…*something* tear through the bottom of a city bus as if it was cardboard.

God, she hoped everyone on the bus was okay. There hadn't been any sirens or screaming, so she had to believe her two rescuers—captors—were right, that it had abandoned the uptown bus the moment they left....except that meant that thing was looking for *them*.

Why? What had she been yanked into?

"Okay." She breathed in and out once evenly, the way her doctor had taught her, calming her body, telling it to relax and stand down, and sat straight-backed on the bench, watching a squirrel balancing on the bike rack opposite them, nibbling at something. "Not human."

Martin nodded once, approvingly, and she heard a muffled snort coming from AJ, that they both ignored.

"You know Tyler. You said something had taken him.... Something like those turncoats?" The thought made her cringe inside—maybe they were hurting him, maybe... Oh, god.

"No." Martin shook his head this time, the thick black hair falling over his eyes exactly the same way it had done in his other form. Somehow, that small detail made it make more sense in her brain. "Not them. We could have stopped them, if that were it. Or, we could have tried to stop them, anyway. They're just...turncoats." The way he said the word made it sound like a curse. "They've sold out their own kind."

"You...your kind...?" She made a gesture that was

meant to indicate him and AJ, who was pacing again, but instead came out as a wimpy hand-circle.

"Us, and you." AJ's muzzle twitched. "Look, there's natural folk, you humans, and us, the super-naturals. That's…there are different species, all scattered around the world. Some you've heard of, some you haven't, some don't come out much anymore. Mostly we get along because we ignore each other. And humans like to pretend we don't exist, at all. It's better that way. Safer."

Safer. Jan wondered if he used the word the same way she did. None of it mattered; she only wanted to know one thing. "What happened to Ty?"

"Your leman…he's…." Martin stopped and considered her, as though gauging how much more she could take. "Not much" was the answer, she suspected, but she'd do it, she'd deal with it. Her hand slipped down to touch her inhaler, reassurance, even though she didn't need it just them.

"We didn't know about him specifically," AJ said, his pacing taking him away and then back to stand in front of Jan. "We were tracking the preter, found her in time to see your leman being taken, two nights ago. We were too late to interfere, but we backtracked from there, found his wallet, and waited outside his apartment, to see who would show up. Three days, we waited!" He sounded annoyed. "We were just about to give up when—"

Jan wouldn't let herself be distracted. "Who. Took. Him?"

Martin sighed. "For lack of a more useful term... Elves."

Chapter 3

Tyler didn't know how long he had been there, or
even where there was. There were birdcalls in the
distance, sweet and high. He tried to focus on them,
reaching for the music that had always come naturally, but the voices in his ear were too loud. He did
not know this language, although he tried to pick
out words; when he was clearheaded he knew they
did not want him to understand, that they were talking about him.

He was not clearheaded most of the time.

The chair was too soft, the air too thin; it all felt
wrong, but he couldn't say why, couldn't put a finger
on what bothered him. He tried to remember. He had
been somewhere familiar, the smell of coffee thick in

his nose, laughter and clatter around him, and then *she* had taken his hand, drawn it across the table, and spoken to him…. And then nothing, a sense of time passing but no details in the void.

He was not supposed to be here. He was not supposed to be in this place; it was morning, and every morning he…he… What did he do? The memory glided out of reach, taunting him with the memory of pale green eyes and soft skin, lighter than his and soft as a peach….

"Eat, sweet."

He ate, although he couldn't have identified what he was eating. Not a peach, although it was sweet, and soft, like overripe fruit, but without any juice, and the moment he finished it, the taste was gone, nothing lingering in his mouth or throat. He felt languid, drained, his usual energy faded to nothing.

A hand took up his, sliding against his fingers, the tawny skin almost translucent…did it glow? He could not trust his eyes, he could not remember his name.

They had hurt him, until the pain was too much, and then offered him a way out. All he had to do was let go, let go of…what?

"Walk with me."

He walked, although he could barely feel his feet, unable to resist that voice. The path they followed was plush with pale green grass, and the trees reached overhead, blocking any view of the sky. It was night, he knew that—or thought he did, anyway. He had left his apartment at night, drawn by urgency, a fear that she would not wait for him…. He had…

What had he done?

There was a low, steamy-sounding hiss and a dry, metallic rattle somewhere behind him, then the low sweet voice whispered something and the rattle went away, fading into silence. The rattle-voiced ones were everywhere, but they never came close enough to see.

He shook his head as though bothered by a fly, and his feet stopped moving. He looked up at the branches, trying to see beyond them. This…wasn't right. He had left his…apartment…. Why? What had he left behind?

Skin like a peach, sweet and succulent. Eyes like leaves. But who?

"Easy, sweet. Do not worry. All is well."

The soft voice wound around him, bringing him back.

Stjerne. The voice was Stjerne's.

The name brought memories to fill the gray void. Her hand in his, her lips on his skin, solace and cool comfort against the unbearable pain. She had brought him here and given him food to eat and wine to drink, and now she walked with him, her fingers laced in his own.

"Come. Walk with me." It was less a request than a command, this time. The fingers were cool against his skin, her voice soft and heavy in his ears.

Tyler was not certain he wanted to go anywhere

but could not resist. He breathed the air and smelled the same sweet scent of the food he had been given, the perfume that floated around Stjerne herself, and then exhaled. Chasing after a worry had never helped; whatever he'd forgotten couldn't be that important, or he'd remember it soon enough. And a walk might help, yeah. It certainly couldn't do any harm.

She led him through the garden, to a building made of silvery stone, where others waited. He tensed, the faded memories telling him what would come next.

"Do you trust me, sweet?"

Of course he did. He nodded, and she handed him over to those others. They took him, took his clothing, dripped too-sweet water into his mouth, and forced him to swallow, and left him naked and shivering in the odd light, his skin both cold and too warm, unable to move, feeling the clank-and-whir of things settling over his skin.

They had done this before. Before, and again and again...

"Stay with me," she said. "Feel me. Give in to me. It will all be over soon."

It would never end. He knew that, a split-second of clarity before the feel of tiny claws digging into his skin intensified, burning like drips of acid down through to bone. They held him down on the chair of feathers and thorns, the one that Stjerne said was his throne, built just for him, to sit by her side, and impaled him and burned him, a little more each time.

"Can you feel me, sweet?" Stjerne, just out of range, just beyond touch.

Tyler would have nodded, but he could not move. "Yes."

He could. No matter what they did to him, he could feel her there, like the sun that he could never quite find anymore, the only warmth in this world.

Sometimes, he could remember another voice, another touch…brighter lights and different sounds, different smells. But they faded, and there was only her. She protected him. She took care of him. She would make them stop this, silence the voices and take him by the hand and lead him along the path that ended in a warm soft bed and cool hands stroking him to incredible pleasure. Everything she had promised. And all he needed to do was…what?

He focused, trying to remember, and her hands touched him again, calling him back.

"Open to me," she said, her voice spice and smoke, swirling around him. "Let me in, and we will be together forever, you by my side, never aging, never dying. Sweet days and sweeter nights, and everything you could dream of, I will give you, once you let me in."

The feathers swept and the thorns dug, and he could feel the things the chair was doing to him, scouring out what had been. Agony. Stjerne's lips touched his, her scent filling his nostrils, and all he wanted to do was please her, so that she would make the pain go away.

But something resisted, held on. If she were in him, where would he go?

"There's no more time to dither, or wait for you to make up your mind. We have to go. Now." AJ was getting more agitated, his muzzle twitching with every breeze. A middle-aged woman pushing one of those wheeled shopping bags in front of her slowed down and stared, then sped up again when he growled at her.

"AJ." Martin sounded scandalized.

Jan was now pretty sure that she had lost her mind. Or the entire world had been insane all along, and she was only now realizing it. But even if it was mad, it was real—and the mad ones were the only people who were taking her seriously. Even if what they were saying was impossible, insane, crazy. Even if what she knew she had seen was impossible, insane, crazy.

Maybe she was hallucinating all this: Tyler was actually asleep in bed next to her, snoring faintly, and she had dreamed it all, his disappearance, and everything since then....

It was real. She was stressed, and tired, and tearful, and afraid of that thing she had seen on the bus, more than even AJ's teeth, or Martin's...whatever it was Martin was, but she couldn't deny that it was real.

"Go where?" she asked.

"Somewhere safe," Martin said. "Where we can protect you. And explain things better, not…so out in the open."

"Now," AJ repeated, practically shoving them into movement.

Martin frowned, clearly trying to remember where he had left their vehicle, and then pointed back toward town. "That way." They walked four blocks away from the park, to a street lined with old Victorians in various states of repair, and stopped in front of a small, dusty, dark red pickup truck.

Her lips twitched, looking at it. "I thought you nature types were all supposed to be environmentally conscious?"

"Funny human," AJ growled. "Get in."

AJ drove, while Martin sat on the passenger side, Jan squeezed between the two of them. Martin took her hand again, the way you would someone on the way to the doctor for surgery, to reassure them—or to keep them from bolting. She stared down at the black polish on his nails, then past him out the window. Neither of them tried to talk to her, or to each other, for which she was thankful. Anything more, and she thought her head might fly apart, or she might really throw up this time.

She needed time to take it all in, to figure out… No, there was no figuring out. She just had to roll with it until something made sense again.

They had an answer to what had happened to

Tyler. She clutched that thought, warmed herself with it, soothed her uncertainty and the awareness that getting into this truck might have been the last, stupidest thing she'd ever have done.

Somehow, she didn't believe they would hurt her.

"Last words of every dumb, dead co-ed ever," she said to her reflection in the window, and sighed. And then, in self-defense, and because she couldn't do anything useful, and neither of them seemed inclined to explain anything yet, Jan let her brain drift into white noise, her gaze resting on the rows of storefronts and apartment buildings as they drove farther out of town, trying not to think at all.

And, despite everything, or maybe because of it, she fell asleep.

Martin woke her with a gentle nudge with his elbow as they pulled off the road and parked, the engine turning off with a low cough. Jan, blinking, sat up and looked around. The sun had slipped low enough that streetlights were starting to come on, but half the posts were burned out. They'd gone east, toward the waterfront, but she didn't know where, exactly.

She looked around as they got out of the car. They were in a small parking lot next to a warehouse that looked as if it had been abandoned for years. The nearest sign of life was a strip mall a little while away, the lights barely visible, and the sound of traffic on the highway a little beyond that. There were two beat-up pickups in the parking lot, which was cracked through with weeds and a sense of desolation beyond merely being abandoned.

"This way." AJ started walking toward the warehouse, and Martin waited until she followed, then fell in behind.

Jan had the feeling, as they walked from the truck to the building, that they were being watched. The question—watched by *what?*—flashed through her mind. Not human. Whatever was going on, wherever Tyler had gone to, she was getting the feeling that getting him back wouldn't involve sitting in front of a monitor fixing other peoples' mistakes or listening to excuses. That might be a nice change.

Or it could get her killed. That would be a less-nice change.

Up close, the warehouse was in better shape than it seemed at first; the windows, set high up in the walls, were intact, and the cement walls had been repaired recently. The cargo-bay doors were padlocked with heavy chains. They walked around the side of the building to an oversize metal door with an "all deliveries to front" sign over it. The door looked heavy as hell, but AJ pulled it open without hesitation. It was unlocked, which surprised Jan. Why padlock the front, and leave the side open?

Inside the warehouse, the first thing she saw were remains of old cars, clearly cannibalized for parts, and workbenches filled with power tools. She took that in, letting her eyes adjust to the dim light, and saw, farther in the back, the huge lifts that you saw in repair shops. Off to her side there was a long metal table covered with license plates from a dozen different states.

Her eyes went wide, even though she would have sworn that nothing else could have surprised or shocked her then. "You guys are car thieves?"

"It's a living," AJ said tersely.

She was not given time to gawk, but led away from the machinery and cars to a corner of the warehouse that had been set up to look slightly more homey, with seating and a small kitchenette jerry-rigged against the wall.

AJ disappeared, and Martin indicated that she should sit down on the battered couch that looked as if it had been pulled from someone's garage. It was like someone's cheap college apartment; all it was missing were the milk crates up on cinder blocks.

"You want something to drink? I think we've got coffee, tea…."

"Tea would be nice, thank you." The politeness made Martin smile, and he went off to fuss at the kitchenette, finally returning with a mug of tea that smelled like mint.

Jan hated herbal tea. She took it, anyway.

Martin sat down next to her while AJ returned with someone else he introduced as Elsa.

Jan blinked, and then laughed, the sound escaping her like a sob. "I'm sorry. I just thought you'd have—" Jan gestured a little, helplessly, sloshing her tea on the concrete floor "—more unusual names."

"Some do," Elsa said, not taking offense. Her voice was a rough, grating noise that matched her appearance perfectly. Jan understood better now why AJ and Martin had been sent to find her, if the newcomer was more typical of...what had AJ called them? Supernaturals. AJ's face might be unusual, but nobody could avoid noticing a moving pile of rusty brown rocks shaped—vaguely—like a woman.

"I'm a *jötunndotter*," Elsa said. "It's all right to stare. I prefer it to those sideways looks people use when they're trying to be polite."

Jan, who had been trying to not look at her directly, blushed.

"You don't want to meet the ones who insist on old-school names," Martin told her. "They're... difficult."

"What swish-tail means," AJ added, "is that they're isolationist, and would just as soon humanity went a tipper over the edge into annihilation. Or went themselves, which is more likely."

"There aren't many of them. Not anymore." Martin took her hand again, the one not holding the tea mug, and Jan pulled it away out of reflex. He was way too touchy for her taste, even if he was sort of homely-cute. "Humanity used to be good at getting rid of threats. The rest of us…well, there aren't that many of us left, either. But we adapt. We try to blend."

Elsa was not about to blend anywhere.

"Most of 'em aren't blending so much as they're sticking their heads into caves and leaving their asses hanging in the breeze. And good riddance to the lot of them."

"We don't play well with others," Elsa said, almost apologetically.

"We don't play well with ourselves, either," Martin said, and AJ snorted agreement.

The sense of curiosity from earlier was tipping into panic again. Jan kept her life on an even keel. She *liked* her even keel. This was leaving her distinctly unkeeled. "You're all… How many different… No. You know what? I don't care." Jan reached for her inhaler, just to have something real in her hand rather than because she needed it. "This is all insane, and the only reason I'm even here is that you keep telling me that Tyler's been taken, that I'm his only hope—that those *things* are out to get me because of that… but nobody's actually told me what's going on!"

"We were too busy trying to save your life," AJ snapped. "In case you've already forgotten."

"My life wasn't in danger until you showed up!"

Elsa shifted her weight, a crackling noise accompanying the movement, and glared at AJ until he looked away.

"It's a lot to take in," she said to Jan. "We know. But they had to get you here, safe, and even now there's no time to answer everything, or explain things you don't need to know. The clock's been ticking ever since your boy was taken, and you waited too long to show up and claim him."

"Excuse me?" Jan was, weirdly, relieved to feel angry. She didn't like anger, but it beat the hell out of being scared and confused. She put the tea down, having only taken one sip from the mug, and glared at all three of the…whatever-they-weres ranged around her. "If you knew what the hell was going on, whatever the hell *is* going on, why didn't you do anything? Before I was in danger—before Tyler was in danger?"

The *jötunndotter* lifted her hands, each finger a smooth length of brown stone, the palms like congealed gravel. "We couldn't. Not without—there are ramifications and limitations to the natural world, and—"

"Elsa, stop." AJ stalked back from the perimeter, which he'd been pacing, and crouched in front of Jan. He'd pushed the hoodie back when they'd come in, so she couldn't avoid seeing the strange wolfen features, or how his oddly hinged jaw moved when he spoke. "We didn't because we can't. It doesn't work that way. What's going on caught us by surprise, too." It hurt him to admit that, she could tell. "We're trying to play catch-up."

"So you're not…." She didn't know what she was going to ask, but AJ laughed. It wasn't a nice laugh.

"Humans veer between thinking they're the only ones here and assuming that there's this malicious cabal of woo-woo, messing with their lives at every turn. Both're crap. There's the natural, that's you, and the supernatural. Us. We all belong in this world together…you people just take up most of the room. Mostly, we ignore you. Occasionally, our paths cross. It doesn't end well for us, most of the time."

Jan spoke without really thinking about it. "Fairy tales."

AJ spat on the ground, and Martin sighed.

"Humans call 'em that," AJ said. "Humans don't have a clue. They revile what they don't recognize, demonize what they fear, simplify it so they don't have to deal with reality." He sighed, his muzzle twitching, and then shrugged, as though deciding it didn't matter.

"Like I said, we try to ignore humans, the same way you ignore us. Most of the time when our people meet, it's just…skirmishes. Awkward moments and bad relationships."

"But not always?"

"Not always. Sometimes it works out—not often, but sometimes. But that's when it's us, natural and supernatural."

"There's something else?" Jan felt her body tense, as if a fight-or-flight reaction was kicking in, although nobody'd said or done anything threatening in the past minute, and wasn't that a nice change?

"Yes…and no," Elsa said.

"Seven times that we've recorded," AJ said, "something else gets added to the playground." He held up his hand, not even trying to hide his claws now. Three fingers ticked off: "Naturals, supernaturals, and preternaturals."

"Preter…"

"Humans call them elves," Martin said. "What we call them isn't so pretty."

Elves. Jan thought of Keebler elves first, baking cookies, then the slender, coolly blond archers of the *Lord of the Rings* movies, and suspected AJ wasn't talking about anything like that.

"Why two names? Aren't you both—?"

AJ didn't roll his eyes, sigh, or make any other obvious sign of irritation, but he practically vibrated with it. "Supernatural, above nature. Preter, outside nature. One belongs here, the other does not. Nobody teaches Latin anymore, do they?"

Jan had gone to school for graphic design, not dead languages.

"Supernaturals are part of this world," Martin said. "The preters…come from somewhere else."

"Fairyland?" Jan laughed. Nobody else did.

"And they…took Tyler? Why?" If they didn't belong here…where had they taken him? How had they found him?

AJ settled in on his haunches, resting his elbows on his knees in a way that she would never be able to balance. Another reminder that he wasn't human, that his body wasn't what it looked like....

Jan tried to focus on what he was saying, now that they were finally *explaining* things.

"Preters have a history of stealing humans. Used to be, they'd slip through and steal whatever took their fancy. We didn't know why they liked humans so much, but they do. Babies, especially."

"Changelings," Martin said.

"Right. Only sometimes they take adults, too. Males mostly, but sometimes females. And they never let 'em go."

"And they took Tyler.... why?" Jan knew she was repeating herself. She was trying to process all this. All right, she'd accepted—mostly—the fact that there was more than she knew, more to the world than she'd ever dreamed, after what had happened on the bus. But this? Changelings and kidnappings and elves from another world, some kind of parallel universe or something? Seriously?

Tyler was gone. These people—supers—were here, and they were the only ones giving her any kind of explanation, no matter how insane it sounded. Unless ILM or some other Hollywood effects company was involved, there was no way this was any kind of prank.

Then her eyes narrowed, and she looked first at

Elsa, then at Martin, and then back at AJ. "But why do you care?"

A werewolf's laugh was, Jan discovered, a particularly atavistically terrifying thing, like a harsh howl that echoed against the roof and raised the hair on her arms. Almost instinctively she turned again to Martin for reassurance. He shook his head, his long face solemn, and looked back at AJ. So she did, too.

"Smart, yeah. You're smart. And quick. Good." AJ was serious again. "You're right. We're not all that fond of humanity overall. Sometimes we have periods where it's bad, sometimes when it's hunky-dory, but mostly, we *don't* care. But this isn't about you. It's about us. Like I said, this world is our home, too. We both *belong* here. The preters…don't."

"They are not part of our ecosystem," Elsa said, moving in closer. Jan shifted, uncomfortable, and the *jötunndotter* stopped. "They come in like invaders—"

"They *are* invaders," AJ said. "Never forget that."

Elsa nodded. "They cross borders that should not be crossed, and take from us. From this world. Humans, and livestock, and whatever else strikes their fancy. In the past, only a few have been able to pass, and only in force large enough to be noticed. Troops, they were called, and we could find them, and force them back.

"That has changed, Human Jan."

Elsa seemed at a loss for what to say next, and Martin took up the narrative. It was almost a relief to turn to him, even though Jan knew damn well—intellectually, anyway—that he was no more human than the other two.

"It used to be, they had to wait until the moon was right, or some other natural occurrence, um, occurred. Then they came through either one at a time, or in a troop. Even with the natural world cooperating, it was an iffy thing, unpredictable. The portals shifted, moved. The damage they could do was limited, and if they stayed too long, we found them."

The implication was pretty strong that, when found, they weren't invited in for tea.

"The past year, maybe more, that's changed. They're coming in during times that the portal should not be open, in places they should not have access to—cities were never their domain. Even cities that were built on old sites: over time the pressure of naturals wore the access away, broke down the ancient connection." Martin looked over at AJ, as though waiting for permission to continue, and then said, "The preters have found some way to open the portals that we don't understand, move them to places they should not be, and they're raiding us like an unguarded vegetable patch."

"Taking humans…" Jan was still—understandably, she thought—stuck on that.

"Taking a lot of humans," AJ said. "And that's just in the three months we've been aware of it."

"You didn't know, before?"

"I told you. Mostly, we—supers and you naturals—
ignore each other. And whatever use preters have for
humans, we don't fill it. None of our people disappeared. So, no, we didn't notice that your species was
disappearing at a faster than usual rate.

"Not right away, anyway. The dryads…they've always been fond of humans. No idea why, but…they
like to listen. And they love to gossip. And they heard
whispers. Those whispers reached us."

Somehow, Jan suspect "us" meant him, AJ. For
all his cranky manner—or maybe because of it—he
reminded her of her first boss, a guy who'd known
everything that was going on in the office, even the
stuff they'd tried to keep from him.

"And then we discovered why. Or rather, how."
Elsa sounded almost…frightened. "The barrier between our worlds shifts, and can be influenced. We
knew this, but never cared overmuch about the whys
or hows…but the preters cared. Very much so. Before, it required, as AJ said, a natural turn, some con-
junction to open a portal large enough to be useful.
Now they have discovered a way to…thin the barrier.
To create an unnatural portal that they can control,
and not depend on the whims of nature or the tides
of the moon."

"How?"

"If we knew that…"

"It's because of your computers," Martin burst out.

"What?" Jan was suddenly lost again—her brain

having slowly twisted around the idea of werewolves and trolls and elves, roughly hauled back to technology.

"Back then, it was all environmental. We could feel when they came into the system, when something shifted. Like an earthquake, or a storm coming in off the ocean; something changed. But it's been quiet for a long time now. And then the whispers started, and we realized that quiet didn't mean dormant."

"They're using technology, somehow." Martin got up and paced this time, while AJ stayed put and continued explaining. "We know that much; once we started looking for it, we can feel it around their portals, the aftermath of them, like a static shock in the universe. It's the same feeling that hovers around some of your labs, the major scientific ones. CAS, Livermore, CERN, *Al-Khalili*..." He shrugged, as though knowing all those names was unimportant. "But we don't understand how. We don't...that's something humans do. Technology. Computers. But the preters have figured it out, and it's giving them access—giving them control of where and when a portal opens."

Martin touched her shoulder, drawing her attention. "That's your world, Jan, not ours. Technology is a human invention. We wouldn't know where to begin."

Jan started to laugh. "So, what, you want me to shut down everyone's computers? Set off some kind of virus to kill the internet? I can't, I'm a website tech, not a hacker, I can't do something like that, and I wouldn't even if I could!" She worked with tech; she didn't make it—or break it. Not intentionally, anyway.

AJ snarled at her, and this time it was a purely human—human-sounding—noise of frustration. "We're not idiots. No. We can only find them after a portal opens—and that's too late for us to do any good. We need to find out how they're using it, learn how to shut it down. The only way to do that is to catch one of them. And the only way to do that is to play their game. But we don't know what it *is*."

"And you think that I do?"

"You can help us find out," Martin said. "We need one of their captives, to find out what was done to them, and how. But they don't take supers, only humans, and the only thing that can reclaim a human from a preter's grasp is the call of their heart. Only a mother, or lover, has ever been strong enough. You're the only one who can save Tyler…and Tyler is the only one who can save the rest of us."

Jan officially overloaded. "You're all insane. This is insane, this is…he wasn't abducted! He went off with some hot chick, that's all. He quit his job, just walked away from everything…."

"Not walked. Was led. The preters…" AJ was reduced to waving a hand at her—his fingers were tipped with short, blunt claws that looked as though they were designed to tear flesh off bone, so it was an effective swipe, making her scoot as far back on the sofa as she could. "Come on, woman, have you read no stories in your entire life?"

Jan stared at him, utterly at a loss. Then, slowly, the bits she needed surfaced from her memory, taken less from stories than role-playing games and movies, but enough that she began to understand.

"They seduce," she said, slowly. "They lure...all of you do. Fairies, and mermaids, and will-o'-the-wisps.... You drag humans off..." Like they had done to her, she thought but didn't say. Although, really, they'd used less seduction and more strong-arming. Was that better, or worse?

"Why do you care? Why not just let the preters drag humans off and good riddance? I mean, you're all—" She waved her hand, as though to say "all the same, not-me, not human."

Elsa looked at AJ, who looked at Martin, who looked up at the ceiling. Jan followed his gaze, as though there might be an answer. All she saw was a tangle of cables and industrial lights, most of which had burned out and not been replaced.

Something was going on that she wasn't privy to, that they didn't want her to know about. Jan opened her mouth to demand an answer when AJ cut her off.

"We're not going to pretend to be saints," he said. "But humans have a history of bad behavior, too, and they tend to use more violence. So let's just call the past the past, okay? Like I said, we all belong here. We're part of this world. So we have to deal with each other, even if dealing looks a lot like ignoring.

"That's the difference. A thousand years of history show that preters don't deal, they don't compromise. This isn't their place, it's a…a storeroom they can raid. They don't care about you, or us, or anything except themselves and what they want—and whatever they want? It's bad for us. All of us."

Jan shook her head. "You still haven't given me any reason to trust you. How do I know that anything you've told me is true? You could be lying, this could all be some giant, impossible, stupid sick joke…."

The tickle in her throat got worse, and her chest closed up, the warning signs of an asthma attack kicking in. Too much dust in the warehouse, and with her luck she was allergic to supernaturals. She grabbed her inhaler, hitting it hard until things eased again. Two in one day; that wasn't good.

Martin got up, shoving AJ aside and going down in a crouch next to Jan.

"Are you all right?"

What do you care, she wanted to retort, but the concern in his face was real, or *looked* real, anyway. His black-tinted nails glinted even in the dimmer light of the warehouse, and Jan thought of the tar-black hooves of his pony-form.

She waited until she could breathe normally, then

shook her head. "Asthma. It sucks, but I'm okay. That's not nail polish, is it?"

He ignored the question. "Jan. I'm not going to ask you to trust us. Trust is earned. But *believe* us."

His voice was smooth and soft, especially after Elsa's granite rumble and AJ's growl. More, his touch was soothing, his hands on her bare arms, stroking down from elbow to wrist. The sensation eased the pressure in her chest even more, as if it was enhancing the drugs in her system. If so, she wanted to bottle that touch and make a fortune selling it.

"We're selfish and we're secretive, but I swear, on the river I was born to, I swear this: everything we've told you is true."

Jan's practical side fought its way through. Preters seduced. But so did supernaturals. The way he touched her... "Tyler was taken by elves?" Her voice was too high, as if she'd sucked helium instead of albuterol.

"I know what you're thinking. That that's crazy. Too crazy. You can see us, feel us, so you know we're real, but we're...strange. Monsters maybe, even. Elves? Elves are the good guys, the graceful ones, the moonshine and stardust ones. But they're not. They're predators."

Behind him, AJ snorted, and Martin winced.

"They're predators without an off switch," he amended. "The only thing that's kept us safe until now is the barrier between our world and theirs. A barrier they couldn't control. And now they can.

"Jan, humans aren't people to them, they're toys. Things they take, use, break, and discard."

Jan looked him straight in the eye, but included AJ—and all the others—in her question. "And you? Okay, fine, we're all in this world together, woo, that has never stopped humans from beating the crap out of each other, doing horrible things. So, tell me, what are humans to you?"

He hesitated, although the motion of his hands never stopped. "Neighbors. Family. Extended family, yes, but… We're all of the same soil, the same air, the same waters."

Jan didn't know if that was truth or bullshit. She didn't know if any of this was truth or bullshit. But if it was true…her faith in, her love for Tyler was being validated. He hadn't abandoned her, hadn't been untrue, not willingly. Something not-human had taken him. She clung to that and nodded. It might all be insane, but the only other option would be to accept that everything she had believed in was a lie, to walk away, to give up on Tyler, to never trust her own instincts about love ever again.

"What do I need to do?"

There was a change in the air around her, as though the warehouse itself had exhaled in relief, and Jan had the sudden feeling that she'd just signed on for more than they had told her.

* * *

The feeling of being watched out in the parking lot had been real: while only three of them had come out to convince her, once she agreed, the shadows around the edges of the warehouse pulled back, and other figures began to emerge. Most of them looked human enough, like Martin and AJ, and she had to look carefully to see the scales or the horns, the slight hint of a tail or fur. Ten, maybe a dozen; they came and went around the auto corpses and workbenches with the air of people—things—people—on important missions, although none of them seemed interested, just then, in power tools or tires.

Someone shouted and waved an arm at AJ. He snarled in annoyance but got up and walked over to the shouter. After a hesitation, Elsa did the same, her body moving more slowly than AJ's brisk lope.

That left her with Martin.

"What do you expect me to do?" she asked again, trying to ignore the flow of activity, knowing that they were all staring at her freely enough. "If you can't find them until they're already here, can't trace them once they are here, how do you expect me to do any better?"

"You won't. You can't. But you can figure out how to lure them to us. Offer them what they want— a human who is willing to buy into their promises, give them what they want. And when they think they

have you…we have a way to figure the portal out—
and you can take back what is yours."

Jan stared at him, and then laughed, a harsh exhale
that didn't sound amused. "I'm bait, in other words."

Martin hesitated, just a bit. "Yes."

"You know that I know what happens to bait,
right?"

Martin tried to take her hands again; that seemed
to be his thing. "We will protect you."

She moved her hands out of his grip. "Uh-huh."

Jan had a very strong suspicion that it wasn't as
easy as Martin was making it sound. But if they were
right… If this had been going on for months, maybe
longer, then she wasn't the only one to have a loved
one stolen away. But she was the only one who could
do something about it.

"And the others…they're part of a normal carjacking ring? Or…?" She made a vague gesture to include
the entire warehouse.

"We're all volunteers. The car thing, it was a small
operation AJ's pack ran. We're using it as a cover, a
place to gather. Whatever we need—whatever you
need—they will provide."

That was comforting, she supposed. Although she
had no idea what she might need….

"Wait." She reached out to touch Martin on the
shoulder, but something—some memory of AJ's
words, warning her not to touch him in pony-form—
made her stop. She had never been the hero type,

never been asked to step forward, or picked first for any team. "I'm not the only one you've tried to convince, am I?"

Martin looked as if he wanted to escape, which made her eyes narrow. "Tell me, or I'm walking, right now." He had sworn to her that he wouldn't lie.

"No. You're not." His voice was full of regret, which made her not want to know what happened to the others.

"What happened to the others?" she asked, anyway, with a suspicion she knew already.

This time, when he took her hands, she let him. "The turncoats came after them, too. We don't know how, don't know how they knew, how they found them, unless the preters told them, but by the time we figured out who had the connection we needed, the gnomes were already there, and—"

Her throat hurt, suddenly. "And had eaten them."

"Yeah." He looked as nauseated as she felt; if his other form was a horse, then maybe he was a vegetarian?

"We found you in time, got you away from them. We'll protect you," he said again. "We need you to be safe."

There wasn't much more she could say to that.

Eventually, AJ and Elsa came back, their faces grim. Well, AJs face was always grim. Elsa's craggy expression didn't seem to change much.

Jan had never been to a council of war, only what she'd seen in movies, but she was pretty sure their version was pitiful: the four of them sitting on old furniture in an old warehouse, with supernatural creatures stripping cars in the background.

"We've been trying to predict where and when, with no success," AJ said. "There doesn't seem to be any pattern or logic to it, except that they always go back to where they came through, so the portal doesn't move, and they can't just open another one by snapping their fingers. But they never reuse one, either. Our old ways of finding them are useless, and we can't wait for a portal to open and hope that you're nearby. You need to tell us what to look for."

"Me?" Jan was already tired of asking that. "I'm not the one who—"

"They are coming out of phase, at a time and place of their own choosing, and returning with their prey almost immediately. How?" Elsa leaned forward, the sound of gravel crunching with every move. "How did they find your leman and catch his attention?"

"Sex." Jan heard the bitterness in her voice, thick in that one word. Elf—preternatural—or no, they'd used the most basic lure, and he'd fallen for it. Apparently she hadn't been enough for him, that he had to fuck around, too.

"Yes, obviously." Elsa gave her an odd look. "But how? In the past, their victims have stumbled upon their portal-circles, or been caught at transition times."

"The dark of the moon," Martin said, coaching Jan. "Fairy rings. The change of seasons. Times and places a human might come in contact with them, intentionally or otherwise."

Jan tried to remember what he was saying while still focusing on Elsa's questions. He was too close, and she was noticing things like the way he smelled, a green, musky scent, instead of what was happening around her.

"But they no longer need such things, if they reach directly into homes and draw their prey to them, or go directly to where their prey already waits. If they have found a way around the old, physical, temporal limitations...how? That is what we need to know, to lure and trap them in kind."

Jan stared at her, completely out of her comfort zone, or any zone she recognized. Her daypack rested at her feet, and she clutched at it now, the only remnant of reality left. Her wallet, her cell phone—but there was no one she could call. Nobody who could get her out of this, or throw her a lifeline. "I... How am I supposed to know?"

"Think, human. If this man was in your life, you know his habits. You know where he went and what he did, yes?"

"Yes." Her response was immediate. Of all the things they had asked, this she had no doubts about.

"But he didn't go anywhere. I was the one who had to drag him out and be social. The only thing he did was…"

She stopped, and Elsa leaned forward.

"Yes?"

Jan dug her fingers into her hair, trying to massage some of the stress out of her scalp, but all that did was remind her of the times Tyler had done the same thing, the fingers that danced so quickly over the keyboard going slow and steady through her curls.

"We…we do a lot of socializing online. Digital networking, vid-conferencing, that sort of thing. But that's people you already know. Tyler wasn't much for chat rooms, said they were overrun with noobs and trolls— Oh, sorry. It's a Net term, it's not—"

Elsa stared at her, not taking offense, waiting for her to get to the point.

"The thing is, we met on a dating site. It's a…a place where people go, when they want to meet someone else, outside their usual social group. You put your profile into the system, and you look at other profiles, and you decide who you want to talk to after you check them out, see if you share interests…."

Jan swallowed hard, remembering the email she had found in Tyler's in-box. "It can get pretty racy there, if you want."

Elsa's eyes didn't widen—Jan wasn't sure her expression could change, at all—but it was obvious that she understood. "This site, it allows others to find sexual partners?"

"Yeah. Some of them are looking for marriage, some of 'em are just wanting a hookup...the one we used was more casual." Saying it made the tips of her ears flush, as if she was some kind of slut, but that was silly: so she didn't want to get married, that didn't mean she had wanted a bunch of one-night hookups. And neither had Tyler—she thought. But if he had stayed on the site, kept his account active after she closed hers... The bitterness stuck in her throat, like heartburn.

"If you were using sex, seduction to lure some-one—" wasn't that how they said a lot of serial kill-ers found their prey? "—then a dating site like that would make sense. People are open to it, not suspi-cious, or wary. We *want* to be seduced."

She had to laugh, had to say it. "On the internet, nobody knows you're an elf."

The others looked at her, clueless, and she sighed. "Trust me this time. It's a breeding ground of des-peration and hope."

"So that is where we will start." Elsa nodded, sat-isfied with her pronouncement, and then tilted her stone-gray head curiously. "How do we do that?"

Jan would have been happy to set them up and leave them to it, but AJ hadn't been exaggerat-ing when he said supernaturals didn't use much modern technology—despite the machinery scattered throughout the warehouse, not a one of them there had a laptop, not even a netbook. Worse, Jan couldn't get a signal with her phone, even outside the warehouse—wherever they were, there wasn't a tower within clear range.

"You couldn't have found somewhere actually on the grid?" Jan said in disgust, sinking back down into the sofa, interrupting a group of supers who were apparently on their coffee break. They all gave her moderate hairy eyeballs and she—having tossed good manners out the window by now—gave it right back. She'd just spent half an hour walking around the perimeter of the warehouse—followed by AJ and Martin acting as bodyguards, or to make sure that she didn't bolt—trying to get a signal. Not even a single bar flickered, much less enough to load data.

"It was large enough, defensible enough, and cheap enough. You want some coffee?" The offer came from a man who barely came up to her waist, dressed in black jeans and a black button-down shirt, black sneakers on his feet. His shoulders were too large for the rest of his body, but otherwise he could have been any height-challenged human, even if you noticed that his ears were slightly pointed, unless you looked into his eyes. Jan did and had to resist the urge to back away. There was nothing human about those eyes.

"No. Thank you." She desperately wanted some,

actually. It had been a long time since lunch, which had been a yogurt on the bus over to Tyler's place. But the thought of letting one of them make it…wasn't there some story about eating the food of fairyland? Did that apply here?

"There's soda, too." Those yellow-ringed eyes didn't blink. "Still factory-sealed."

"What, she doesn't trust us?" A voice came from above them. Jan didn't look up, pretty sure that she didn't want to know where that snarky, snide voice came from.

"Would you?" Yellow-eyes responded, not looking up, either. "Come on, girlie, it's just a soda."

She was thirsty—extended bouts of fear and panic did that to her. "What kind?"

"We got Coke, Diet Coke, Dr Pepper and Jolt."

She realized suddenly that he had a small, sharp beak rather than lips, giving him a faint, sharp lisp. That…was weird. Weirder than a werewolf, or a woman made of rock, or a guy who turned into a horse? Yes, she decided, it was.

"Gotta love that stuff," he coaxed. "Twice the caffeine, all the sugar."

"Do I look like a programmer?" she muttered. "Diet Coke. Please."

Something swooped over their heads, a shadow of wings, and Jan ducked instinctively.

The owl-faced being chuckled at her reaction. "Ignore it, and it'll leave you alone. Don't take that as a general rule, though; sometimes ignoring things can get you eaten. My name's Toba. I'm the closest thing to a geek we have, so I guess that makes me your aide-de-camp."

He had a nice laugh. "How much of a geek are you?"

Toba shrugged. "I use a cell phone, and I know how to send email."

"Oh, god." Not that she had been expecting much more, at this point. "All right, that'll have to do. If I'm going to get online to anything, I need my laptop, and a signal. That means I can't work here." She didn't *want* to work here, more to the point. "I need to go back to my apartment."

Where it was safe. Familiar. Not filled with… things swooping overhead, changing shapes, or looking at her with wide, golden eyes.

Toba shook his head solemnly. "Can't do that. The turncoats've marked you. Ten minutes outside, out of our territories, and they'd track you down."

The matter-of-factness finally got to Jan, where everything else hadn't. "The hell I can't go back to my apartment! My gear is there, my clothes—my medication!" Her inhaler would only last so long, especially if they kept throwing stress like this at her. And the dust—god, between the dust and noise, warehouses were not high on her list of places to be. "If I stay here much longer, I'm going to get sick again," she said. "Maybe bad enough to need the hospital."

"You don't want to lead the turncoats back to your apartment," Martin said, coming to join the conversation, obviously having overheard everything. She wondered, a little wildly, how good their hearing was, could they all listen in, even from across the warehouse floor? Did she have no privacy at all?

"They're slow thinkers, but determined, and vicious; if they figure out where you are… You have to stay here, where we can protect you."

"No. Oh, no." Jan shook her head, determined on this. "I can't stay here. I can't work here." The warehouse was large, but at that moment she would have sworn that the walls were closing in on her. "If I'm going to do anything at all—"

"We will send someone for whatever you need. Elsa is finding somewhere you can work, somewhere safe. And then—"

"No." It was his voice, that calm, soothing voice, that made her snap, suddenly.

"What?"

"Look, you don't get it at all, do you? I have a life! I have a job, and friends, and a family. I took the day off, that's all. I can't just disappear, the way Tyler did. No."

They stared at each other, and Jan willed herself not to back down. After all of the crap that had already happened, this shouldn't have been so important to her, but it was.

"Fine." Toba broke the stalemate. "She's right: to do anything online, she needs to be connected, and reception's shit out here. So we'll move in with you, set up protections there. Don't give me that look, kelpie. You don't have to come. Not like you're good for much, anyway."

Martin drew himself upright, making the most of the full foot of height he had on the other supernatural. "I swore I would keep her safe."

Toba seemed to find that hysterical. "You? Right."

Jan looked back and forth between the two of them, confused. If anything, Martin—twice the height and stronger—would be able to protect her better than Toba, slight and hunched over, whose sole weapon seemed to be his wit.

"Look, I—" Martin took the shorter being by the shoulder and led him away, not gently. They started to argue, their voices lowered so that she could not hear them, no matter how she tried. After a minute and some emphatic gestures from Martin, Toba looked over his shoulder once at her, then shrugged. Whatever Martin was saying, it seemed to not impress the owl-faced being much.

Finally, they called AJ over, and the whole argument started again.

Jan curled up on the sofa and closed her eyes, weary

beyond belief. Standing up for herself always took so much energy, even when people didn't get mad.

Where was Tyler? What was he thinking just then? Were they…were they hurting him? Or was the seduction that had stolen him continuing? The thought burned, but she forced herself to face it. He might not *want* to come back.…

And then, suddenly, the argument in the corner was over, and she was being bundled back into the SUV. Martin drove this time, with Toba perched on the other side of her. They drove back into the city, following her directions, headlights picking out landmarks, the streets slowly becoming familiar again, until they pulled up outside of her building.

By then, night had fallen with a definite thud, and there was a chill in the air that made her wish she'd been wearing a sweater that morning, instead of a long-sleeved T-shirt.

Had it really only been that morning that she'd left her apartment, intent on finding out what was really happening with Tyler? Since then…the world had turned upside down and inside out. She was worn down and exhausted, and wanted only to stagger up the stairs, check her email, and pass out facedown on her bed. Maybe when she woke up, this would all be a terrible dream.

Chapter 4

"Hey you. Sleepyhead." His breath was warm on her bare shoulder. "Wanna go for a run?"

"Are you kidding me?" She didn't run. She walked at a nice steady pace and did all her exercising at home, on a yoga mat. The only time she wanted to run was if something was chasing her, and even then she though she might let that something catch her, rather than die in a gory coughing-up mess. "I'll keep the bed warm, how's that?"

"Yeah, that's good," Tyler said, leaning over her, and she turned slightly so she could see that familiar, slow, so-sexy smile on his face, until she realized his lips, usually so soft and full, had narrowed to hard lines, pointed like a beak, and then his face changed,

*eyes glowing gold, the beak opening to reveal double
rows of sharp teeth as though he was going to bite
her entire face off—*

And Jan sat up in bed, not really awake yet but
shocked out of the dream, her eyes wide-open and
her heart racing.

"Holy shit on a shamrock."

Just a dream. *It was just a dream, you idiot, and
what did you eat yesterday that gave you a dream
like that?*

Operating on routine, she rolled out of bed, took
her pills, and headed for the coffeemaker, where her
sleep-dazed awareness took another jolt at the sight
of Martin, wearing only a pair of low-slung jeans,
standing in front of the coffee machine, already adding coffee to the filter.

"Hey," he said over his shoulder. "Good, you're up.
I didn't know if you liked it strong or not."

She looked at him, not quite certain what he was
talking about, and he blinked back at her. "What?
Coffee? We like it, too."

It took a minute before her brain caught up with
the rest of her. Yesterday. Tyler's apartment, the bus,
the warehouse, coming home with two men who
weren't actually men, who wanted her help to save
the world….

No wonder she'd had bad dreams.

Unable to deal with the realization that it had all
been real—or at least true—just yet, Jan looked down

at her feet. The polish on her toes was starting to flake off. Her gaze flicked away, like her brain, unable to settle on anything for too long, and caught sight of Martin's feet, instead. He was barefoot, which wasn't surprising, and his feet ended, not in five toes, but a single wedge with one dark nail, like…like the tip of a hoof.

That alone should have sent her screaming out into the hallway, or at least back to bed. Instead, she simply said, "I like it strong," and went past him to the refrigerator, pulling out the carton of orange juice. Out of deference to her houseguests, she poured it into a glass, rather than taking a swig from the carton the way she usually did.

The thought struck her, then, that she was only wearing her nightshirt, which barely covered her ass. It struck her immediately after that she didn't feel the slightest bit of embarrassment, standing there in front of Martin, both of them half-dressed.

"Shock," she diagnosed. "Yesterday was… This will all hit me later, and then I can have a nervous breakdown."

Martin either didn't hear her or decided to ignore her. "Did you sleep well?"

Jan put the juice back and closed the door. She had to stop and think about the question. "Yeah. Weirdly enough, I did." Despite the dream waking her up in a cold sweat, she felt rested, as if she'd had a full eight hours of sleep.

He went back to measuring coffee into the coffeemaker. "Good. You had a busy day yesterday."

"Yeah. You could say that." Hysteria would be appropriate but useless, she decided. "You? I mean, how'd you sleep?" She had been so tired by the time they got back last night, she'd barely had time to throw extra pillows and blankets at them before retreating to her bedroom and closing the door. She didn't even know where they'd bunked down: there had been no trace of pillows or blankets in the main room when she'd wandered across. She would have noticed that. Probably.

"I did. Toba doesn't sleep much. And we had… There was… A third…" Martin floundered a bit, then pushed the start button on the coffeemaker, and turned to face her. "AJ sent someone else to join us, to help set up the protections. He doesn't think what we set up last night was enough, especially if we're here, too. Just… Ignore it. The…the other, I mean."

"Ignore it. Uh-huh." Considering what she'd already seen, that wasn't particularly comforting. Nor was the fact that Martin looked a little uncomfortable even talking about it.

She decided to change the subject. "So, what exactly are these protections? Spells?"

He seemed just as happy with the change of subject. "No. Or, not really. A kind of glamour, sort of, to make it seem as though you're not here. It's hard to explain. Toba's better at it than I am. I tend to make a splash."

The coffeemaker spluttered to life, and the first hint of aroma filled the kitchen. Jan inhaled deeply. Maybe the world wasn't entirely FUBAR'd, after all.

"If you really want to understand it, you should ask him," Martin said. "Do you need breakfast? Because we really should get started. Your leman's been missing for four days now; if we're going to have any chance of reclaiming him, it will have to be soon."

Jan's stomach clenched into knots again, and the coffee suddenly didn't smell as appealing. "Is fifteen more minutes going to make a difference?"

"I— No. Probably not."

"Okay. There's something I need to do, first."

First, she put herself under a very hot shower, scrubbing hard enough to wash everything that had happened yesterday—the past week—off her skin, then towel-dried her hair until it started to curl. She went back into her bedroom and stared at her closet, finally putting on a pair of jeans and a long-sleeved T-shirt. At the last minute she added a silver cuff bracelet and chunky silver earrings to the mix. Silver was supposed to be protective, right? Or was that only against vampires?

She walked back out into the main room, picked her cell phone off the desk, and dialed a number off the Post-it stuck to the left of a slightly bedraggled-looking house plant. While she waited for the call to go through, she picked up a half-empty glass of water from the desk and poured it into the plant, imagining she could hear it whispering a dry thanks as she did so.

Something moved in the corner of her vision, and she turned to see a too-thin wisp of a creature with pale blue skin and a thin, lipless mouth staring at her. She managed not to jump or shriek, although her hand gripped the phone hard enough that she could almost feel the plastic casing crackle under her fingers.

The creature—the "other" Martin had mentioned, who had arrived while she'd slept—closed its over-large black eyes once and turned away. Jan let out a faint exhale of air and carefully eased her fingers loose, before she broke the damn thing.

"Fort Wood Precinct, how may I direct your call?"

"Hi. I, um, I'd like to talk to Office Jarvis, please? It's…it's about Tyler Wash." She chewed on the edge of her thumbnail, trying to ignore the three beings taking up space in her apartment—an impossible act. Martin came in and handed her a mug of coffee, then settled himself on the sofa, watching her as if she were the newest must-see show on cable. Toba and the one who had arrived after she'd gone to sleep, who hadn't been introduced, had started walking through the apartment, poking at the walls and staring out windows as if they were expecting something to stare back at them.

If something could hover outside her fifth-floor window… Jan remembered the swooping thing in the warehouse and restrained the desire to tell them to board up the windows as if a hurricane was coming. The turncoats had gotten through the floor of a bus—did she really think wood or brick was going to stop them?

The image of those creepy-as-hell hands reaching for her, where she'd been just a second before, made her shudder.

"I'm sorry," the voice on the other end of the line came back. "Officer Jarvis isn't available right now. Would you like to leave a message, or speak with someone else in that department?"

"Oh. No, I understand." It wasn't as though the cop was suddenly going to be more sympathetic, after all. "I just…I'm still worried about him. Tyler, I mean. My boyfriend. He disappeared a couple of days ago, and I tried to file a missing person's report, but…." She was babbling, and tried to rein herself in before she really made a fool of herself.

"But you're not a family member, and you're frustrated because nobody seems to be doing anything?" The voice was sympathetic, not sarcastic, and something inside Jan crackled a little; she hadn't realized she was expecting to be ridiculed or patted on the head and told—again—not to fuss over it.

Toba and the other super went into her bedroom, and Jan tried to remember if she'd left anything embarrassing out in plain sight—then wondered what would be considered embarrassing to them and why she cared.

The voice at the other end of the phone line was still talking. "I'm sure it was explained to you about the logistics about a missing person's report, and why we can't respond immediately to every one."

"Yes, I just…" She thought about what the others had said, about seasons and moon phases. "I'm wondering how many people—adults, I guess—go missing. If there's a cycle, or a seasonal pattern? And what happens to the people who aren't reported? What if their family just assumes that they're being flaky, or not answering the phone?"

"That's an interesting question. Two questions, really." The voice—another cop, a city-hire receptionist?—sounded intrigued, not annoyed. "I'm sure that there are organizations that track seasonal disappearances, but we don't officially compile anything like that. Generally, people get reported more often than they actually go missing—that's why we ask so many questions, because a lot of missing-person reports are simply that someone was out of reach for a while, and their loved ones panicked. But, yes—with the homeless population what it is, and people living on their own, especially people who came here from somewhere else and haven't established a support system…there's always people who disappear and we don't know to look for them. But that's not the case here—your friend had you."

Jan nodded and then glared at Toba, who had appeared in front of her, his body language saying that he was about to ask a question. Apparently, they were done installing the protections, whatever they were. "I just…" She couldn't tell this person what she knew, she couldn't even *hint* at the fact that there were people gone missing—people in danger—who didn't fit their damned profile and weren't going to be reported. Not without sounding like a crazy person.

She had three supernaturals in her living room—one of them eating the melon she'd been saving for breakfast—and her lover was being held captive by evil elves. Yeah, that would get her official attention, but not the kind she needed.

"Thank you," she said. "You've been very…kind."

"I know it's hard," the man on the phone said. "You keep checking in with us until your friend comes home. Okay?"

"Okay. Thank you."

She hung up the phone and raised her eyebrows at Toba, who was still waiting, expectantly. "All right. What?"

"The police will think you're crazy if you tell them anything."

"Yes, I already figured that out, thanks. But I'm not going to abandon the possibility that they might have new information—either on Tyler or anyone else who disappeared. Relying on only one source is crap research."

The pale blue creature, who had been hanging back as though it were unwilling to approach Jan too closely, made a noise that might have been a breathy laugh or a scoff, she couldn't tell.

"Shush," Toba said to it. To her, he said, "Right now, we don't have time. Your leman doesn't have time."

"Yeah, so everyone keeps telling me. But I needed to sleep, okay? I don't think well on less than a solid seven. I want to find him, more than you do, but if they're using dating sites, this isn't going to happen immediately."

Trolling for elves. Jan shook her head. If she thought about it for too long, her head might explode. But, oh, the urge to tell someone—Glory, probably—was nearly overwhelming.

She took a sip of the coffee and felt her brain kick in a little more, then frowned. "All of you keep using that word. What the hell does it mean?"

"What, leman? Your beloved. Your lover."

"So why not say that?" She was being a brat, she knew, but a sudden need to establish some kind of control—even over words—drove her on.

"Fine. Your lover. Does it matter what we call him, if he dies?"

That stopped her cold.

"If he…" She had accepted that Tyler was missing. She had accepted that there was danger. But even the comments about the turncoats eating humans hadn't... "Dead?"

"Not yet." Martin was off the sofa and on his knees in front of her, his wide black-brown eyes holding her attention, so she couldn't look away. "Maybe not ever. The preters...they are not as we are, they are not as you are, but it has never been said that they are killers. Not needlessly. And they have a need for your Tyler."

"But they have no care for flesh, as we do," Toba said. "Martin, stop sugarcoating. You're not here to get in her pants. They'll use him until they get what they want, and if he dies while they're getting, they'll just steal another.

"More, the longer they have him, the more they'll own him. That's how they do it—they put a glamour on humans, lure them away, and consume them, bit by bit, until their pets will do anything they ask, believe anything they say."

"Brainwashing." That, out of everything else, she understood. Sort of.

"More. Worse. Human, listen to me." Toba's voice managed to draw her attention away from Martin. "If you believe nothing else, believe this. If you do not get your leman—your lover—back soon, you will get nothing back but a shell. A heartless, soulless shell."

She licked her lips, which had gone dry and cracked. "The legends say that you guys don't have

souls, either." She had remembered that, before she
fell asleep last night.

Toba clacked his beak together, the sound clearly
one of exasperation. "I can't speak for pony boy here,
but I'm not going to steal your soul. I have no interest
in it, no use for it. All I want is to keep my home safe,
keep preters on their side of the divide, not messing
with the balance of what should be, what is. That's
my incredibly self-serving, self-centered motivation."

"That's what we're all motivated by," Martin said.

The blue thing didn't say anything.

Jan thought of Tyler. She thought of all the others who might have gone missing. She thought about
creatures that would do that, steal people away and
suck them dry, and thought about them having access to everyone, without any barriers or hesitations.

"All right. Let's get started, which means figuring
out how they're finding their targets. If this Stjerne
is one of them, then she probably met him the same
way I did, through a dating site. That's where we're
going to look first." She paused, frowning. "Men,
or women?"

"What?"

"Do they prefer men or women? That's going to
influence what we're looking for."

Toba blinked, his yellow eyes going even wider,
and looked over his shoulder—his head swinging
too easily to even pass for human—at the blue thing
lurking by a window before turning back to her. "I

don't know. Men, usually—they're easier to lead by their dicks."

She tried to ignore the head-turning-owl-thing, because thinking about it made her queasy. "No argument there. But dating sites aren't just about sex. They're about making contact, about not being alone, or lonely."

"Manipulating emotions, coaxing those in need onto…into their grasp." Martin's smooth tones sounded a little hoarse, she thought, and then winced at the unintentional pun.

"Yes."

"Much easier than wandering the countryside looking for someone randy enough to fall for their glamour, hey, Martin?" Toba said. "Technology must be like candy to them, if that is what it does."

"Still, more likely men," Martin said, glaring at Toba. "They are shallow things and have never spent overmuch time with their wooing; they use glamour to entrap, and a man is more prone to react without thinking of danger. But we cannot overlook a female, no." He frowned, his annoyance fading as he thought. "Preters are matriarchal, always led by a queen. I wonder if that is why they usually take men. She may object to women being brought into her realm."

"Great. So we need to sort through the profiles on both sides— Oh, hell. What about gay sites?"

Martin snorted, and for an instant Jan saw his pony-shape superimposed over the two-legged form, but when she blinked, it was gone. "The preters like the pretty on either side, but most are narrow in their preference, by all accounts."

"Unlike you, who'll do anything that moves," Toba said, almost but not quite under his breath.

Jan decided that she was just going to ignore whatever was going on between the two of them. "Fine. That makes it a little easier, for really relative values of easier. We set up accounts, figure out what's a tip-off, and then go trolling for someone who might be a…preter. And then?"

"And then we bait the hook," Toba said.

Jan—being the human bait, was pretty sure she did not like that particular metaphor.

Setting up a dating profile was a torturous process when doing it for yourself. Doing it as bait, to lure someone—or something—specific, Jan discovered, was considerably easier: she could make things up without hesitation or guilt.

While she developed a quick portfolio of online personas, Toba and Martin drew up a list of key words they thought might be indicative of a preter looking for a human servant—Jan shied away from using the word slave, even in her own head.

"If you're boosting cars for a living, I'm going to take a wild guess and say that the stories about fairies and the like having pot-loads of gold aren't entirely accurate?"

"That would be a good guess," Toba agreed.

"Great. Then we're only going to do the free sites, or the ones that let you sign up for a trial membership, 'cause I don't have the cash to pony up, either. Let's hope, lacking fairy gold, the elves are doing the same." If they'd been human, she would have assumed they had phished credit card numbers, but that took a bit more know-how than, allegedly, the preters had.

Allegedly. As far as they knew. There were holes in what they knew large enough to drive a Zamboni through.

Martin got up, stretching his arms over his head, and wandered to where Jan was sitting, reading over her shoulder. His hand kept touching her shoulder, stroking, and every time he did it she shuddered, as though something cold had touched her—but she didn't tell him to stop.

Seduction. But she got the feeling he wasn't even aware that he was doing it. Somehow, that made it easier to ignore.

"Say they're lonely," he said.

"That's so clichéd."

"For humans, maybe. I told you, the preter're shallow. They don't feel the way we do. They're cold, calculating…."

"Speak for yourself, kelpie," Toba said. "I'm plenty cold."

"Compared to a preter? You're an outpouring of warmth and compassion," Martin said.

"Never having met one, can't compare. And neither have you."

"Wait—you guys have never... You don't...?" Jan got a grip on her thoughts. "You've never actually run into a preter?"

Martin tilted his head back, thinking. "AJ did, once, during the last invasion. He's older than we are."

"How much older?" She thought about that question for a second, and then shook her head. "Not important. If none of you have ever met one of them, then how do you know they're so bad?"

Toba clicked his beak once. "How do you know Nazis are bad?"

Jan shook her head. "I can't believe you just went there...never mind. Point taken. They steal people and want to overrun our world, and generally are not nice and do not play well with others. That's enough for me."

They had taken Tyler. That was enough for her. Even if the supernaturals weren't telling her everything—and they had admitted they weren't—they had saved her from the things on the bus and...

How did she know the things on the bus would have hurt her? Maybe they were trying to save her from AJ, and...

"No. Brain, stop it. Shut up."

"What?" Martin's hand stilled on her shoulder, and he was looking down at her again, his shaggy hair falling over his eyes exactly like a pony's mane, enough to make her want to giggle.

"Nothing. Never mind. I talk to myself a lot." She looked at the on-screen form she had filled out, and sighed. "Now, we need photos. I don't want to use people I know, that's seriously rude and could get me into a lot of trouble if they complain. You guys do appear on film, yes?"

"You're going to use our pictures?" Toba seemed dubious.

Jan looked at Toba, then looked back at the computer screen. "Not for you, no, sorry. My Photoshop skills are not up to the task. I have a few old pictures of my dad when he was younger that should work." Even if he'd still been around, she doubted he would be roaming the internet to notice.

Toba snorted. "That'll do."

The slender blue thing by the window shifted, and she shook her head. "Not using you, either, sorry."

It was impossible to tell if it was disappointed, or if it even noticed. It was difficult to focus on, which—now—perversely made her more determined to actually look at it. Manners seemed less important than knowing what she was dealing with. It was tall, taller than Martin, taller than Tyler, who was almost six feet, and skinny, and she had originally thought that it was draped in a pale blue cape of some kind. Now, with coffee in her, and more awake, she realized that it was actually skin, that the creature's arms were actually wings wrapped around itself, and what she had taken for a hood was...

"Don't." Martin's voice in her ear, soft and cool, his fingers gripping her shoulder tightly enough to leave indentations through her shirt. "Don't look. You'll make it uncomfortable."

And that, she gathered, would be a very bad idea. Nobody seemed to be giving a damn about her comfort, but whatever.... She pulled her gaze back to the computer screen and sighed. "All right, that leaves you as poster boy for the other profile, I guess."

Taking Martin's photo was more difficult than she'd expected: he kept trying to look at his own image, rather than into the camera, and trying to strike a pose.

She attempted to catch him not mugging it up, and failed again. "No, dammit, just look into the camera—the little red dot there, right. No, don't look at the screen... Jesus, Martin!"

He looked at her, his dark eyes wide with utterly manufactured hurt, and she lowered the digital camera in disgust. Maybe she would use an old photo of a college buddy, anyway. It wasn't as though she were using their names, too, and she could claim plausible deniability if anyone caught it, because really, why would she be setting up male dating profiles?

"Once more," she said. "Try to just…look natural, okay?"

Martin's idea of "natural" apparently involved channeling Rudolph Valentino, or maybe Burt Reynolds, so over the top he went from sexy to, well, stupid.

"Oh, god. Martin…" She was trying not to crack up. "No."

"Kelpies," Toba said in disgust, turning away from the interrupted would-be camera shoot. "Yes, you're gorgeous. Now, can you get this done so we can start the hunt, already?"

"Huh." Martin was sobered for a moment, remembering that they were there for a serious matter, and then turned his head to look slyly sideways at Jan. "Do you think I'm gorgeous?"

"I think you know damn well what you look like," she said tartly, resisting the urge to smile back at him. He oozed charm too easily. She might not know much about kelpies specifically—and she hadn't had time or breath yet to look anything up—but she knew enough to be suspicious of any male that charming, human or otherwise. "Look, just look straight ahead and smile for the camera, and let's get on with this, okay? Or are your looks more important than saving the world?"

"And do you want us to have to tell AJ your screwing around cost us time?" Toba added.

That got Martin to behave, and he managed a few shots that Jan was able to crop into usefulness.

"Some of the sites like to match you up with people based on their own algorithms. We're not going to worry about those—it would take too long and I'm guessing the preters figured that out, too."

Also, they tended to be the ones that cost. She thought again about adding them, for fear of missing where the preters might be hunting, and then thought about how quickly that could add up. Somehow, she didn't think they were going to fly as business deductions, and "saving humanity from preternatural slavery" didn't have a check box on the tax forms, last she'd looked.

The scattershot approach across the free sites would be enough to start. She hoped.

Jan finished up the accounts and hit Send for each of them. Three accounts male, three female, one each to three different sites. This way, they could each run two, and split the work. She was assuming that skinny, silent Blue wasn't going to be much help. Then again if he—it—was working the protections they were talking about…

Yeah. Leave it alone, let it do its damn job.

"Now what?" Martin looked over her shoulder again, fascinated. "Do we have to wait?"

"Oh, no, you get to play right away." The thought of turning Martin loose on a dating site was both horrifying, and hysterical. "First, though, I want to check something."

Bracing herself, she opened the male-based IDs and went searching for "Stjerne."

Some of the sites didn't let you search for someone specifically, but the freebies were less discriminating. Stjerne apparently got around: she, or someone with a similar name and email—was on all three sites, with the same profile.

She read the profile out loud. "Am tired of sitting here alone, looking at everyone else having fun. Looking for a guy who is ready to take a risk and live dangerously.... I'll make it worth your while."

"No, seriously?" Jan shook her head, even as she studied the picture on the site. Redheaded and glamorous, like a human Jessica Rabbit. "That's not real. I mean, even more than airbrushing or enhancing, that's so obviously not real. Not that any guy is going to stop and think about it. Not the kind of guy she's trolling for, anyway."

Her Tyler had fallen for that. She supposed that if she, with her green eyes, had been exotic to Tyler, a redhead would have been even more so.

"She's got her prey," Martin said, his hand resting on her shoulder. "She's not hunting right now. There's no point in baiting the hook for her."

Jan tried to imagine Tyler's reaction. Had she approached him? Had he contacted her? "How faked is this? What do the preters look like?"

"Human, mostly," Toba answered. "Most of us do, like Martin, here. There's a theory that we're all from the same clump of genetic goo, all the supernatural species, and humans, too, and just evolved differently."

"You believe in evolution."

"You don't?" He mimicked her surprised tone perfectly, to the point of mockery.

They stared at each other, and she let out a little surprised laugh, and then Toba followed suit. Martin rolled his eyes.

The creature standing in the corner, seemingly staring through the walls at what might lurk outside, ignored all three of them.

He was starting to lose track. Of time, of self, of everything. When Stjerne was with him, that didn't matter. There was nowhere else to be, no one else to be with, nothing else to think of; she filled his senses, awake and dreaming. But she left, occasionally. Not for long, never without a sweet-whispered promise to return, draping a thin, heavy chain of silver around his neck, the length of it resting against his heart, to remind him of that promise.

But then she would be gone, and he would be alone in their rooms, the lack of her like an abscess, or a sudden lack of pain where it had filled him to satiation, the aloneness weighing against his skin like humidity, thick and wet, making it impossible to find comfort. Then he would note how quiet their rooms were, the wind muted outside the windows, not a single voice lifted in either a shout or laughter, even the birds perched on stands outside brightly colored but silent.

She was gone now, had left while he slept, and the silver itched against his skin, leaving a pale bruise. He held it in his hand, away from his skin, and while the itching faded, other thoughts tried to slip through, cold slivers under his skin, into his nerves, into his brain.

He remembered, then, that he had forgotten things. Fleeting memories, vague, too distant to be disturbing, and yet they left him…disturbed.

He let the silver chain drop back against his skin, preferring the itching to that strange sense of loss.

Their rooms were large, well-furnished, with chairs and a wide, soft bed, a gaming table, where they would move stones across a board when Stjerne wished to play, and a bathing chamber scented with warm oils, but there was little else. When Stjerne was there, he felt no need to wander, content to stay by her side, wherever she led and whatever she did. When she was gone, she did not tell him to stay, and so he left their rooms and wandered.

There was little more to see beyond their chambers. There seemed to be no end to the structure where they resided: smooth, unadorned walls of silvery stone, rose-colored tiles underfoot. The halls seemed to go for miles no matter where he walked, great stone windows open to the air, looking out over gardens and groves, the world wreathed in the ever-present mist that lifted and swirled and then descended again, like breath.

It made him nauseous to watch it for too long, and so he learned to keep moving. The movement of his body, the stretch of his muscles, soothed him, the sound of his bare feet against tile creating an almost-music that made him pause to listen, trying to capture it, but the music faded when he stopped moving, and silence filled him again.

The missed sound caused him pain; silence brought a cool, numb sensation. After a while, he learned to tune out the almost-music and listen more closely to the silence, to choose the softer, quieter garden paths, rather than the stone hallways.

There were others in the structure, too; like Stjerne, they were graceful, seductive. They would nod to him, solemn bows as they passed in the tree-lined paths, or in the cool stone hallways, but they did not speak to him. They never spoke to him.

And, on occasion, he would look at one, and remember being held down, sweet-water dripping into his mouth, and the feeling of isolation and grief was such that he returned to their rooms and huddled on their fur-draped bed until she returned to soothe him.

But this day, he saw something different. By the fountain, where silver water sprang into the sky and then fell back into alabaster bowls, there was a figure who seemed more substantial, more...familiar.

Not like Stjerne, or the others. Like him. He started toward the figure, feeling a rush of some emotion he could not name—and then halted.

The silence pressed against his brain, whispering to him, reminding him. The chain itch was a warm burn against his skin, like the prickle of thorns. "No," he said. "No." He wasn't sure if he was speaking to the emotion, or the itch, or something else entirely.

He stared at the other, hunger making him yearn even as fear kept him still. Then one of the slender creatures approached the other, taking it by the arm the way Stjerne took hold of him, leading it away.

The moment, the chance, was lost.

He turned away, turning his back on the now-abandoned fountain. "She would be upset. It would make her sad." He didn't know how he knew this, but it was true: he was not to speak to another mortal. It would make Stjerne unhappy if he did so, and he lived to make her happy. When she was pleased with him, her touch was soft and soothing. When she was angry... He shuddered. Therefore, he could not speak to another. If she was unhappy...

If she was angry, she might go away forever, next time. They would hurt him again, put him in the chair and scrape him out from the inside, and that time she would not stay with him, would not fill the emptiness inside him with herself.

He tried to imagine surviving without her and failed.

He hugged his arms around his bare chest, pressing the silver chain into his skin, bright against dark. This time, the itch against his skin was soothing, pleasure-pain, singing the promise of her return.

When he made it back to their rooms, he had forgotten seeing anyone by the fountain.

Chapter 5

Trying to set her companions up with computers had given Jan a new headache. "I still don't get it," she said in exasperation. "You drive cars. Hell, you *steal* cars, and you ride public transit, and apparently some of you buy your clothing at the mall, but none of you use the internet?" She had thought all she had to do was introduce them to the basics of social dating sites, not give them Internet 101. Hell, *Computer* 101.

"Most of us are the bucolic types," Toba said, amused, and slightly faster on the uptake than Martin, not that that was saying much. "Not so much need to be connected to the masses of humanity. And if we wish to communicate with each other…" He paused. "We don't, usually. AJ took on the leader of each group directly, to force them to listen, and even then, many refused to hear."

"We're also not much for paying for anything," Martin said, frowning at the screen and then—successfully—entering one of the fake log-ins and getting a welcome screen. "We're horrible mooches."

"So noted." Jan had already sussed that much from the way Martin had made himself at home in her kitchen. "But you have a cell phone?"

Toba chuckled. "Would you believe that I have a niece in Puerto Rico I like to keep in touch with? The younger generations are more adaptable—she likes to text." He pulled a flip-phone from the pocket of his sweater—she was amused to note that his cardigan was exactly the same soft gray color her grandfather used to wear—and held it up somewhat sheepishly.

"You can't talk to her by..." Jan floundered, not sure what she was going to say.

"We don't *do* magic, human. We *are* magic. Shifting, flying, glamourizing...no wands, no spells, no magic tricks. Just...us. The way some humans sing, and others paint, and some of you—" he shrugged, his misshapen shoulders rising under the cardigan "—do other things, according to your nature."

That made sense, she had to admit. And it explained why they all seemed so...normal. Then Toba blinked those golden eyes at her and clacked his beak in a faint laugh, and she amended that to *mostly* normal.

"It would be nice if you could at least spin straw

into gold," she said. "Although it's not like I've got straw handy. All right, Martin, are you ready to try this on your own?"

He nodded enthusiastically and then lowered his chin slightly in thought. "Yes. Yes. If yellow-eyes can handle it, so can I."

Jan had set Martin up with her old desktop for the initial demonstration. It was kludgy as hell at this point—she mainly used it as an extra monitor when she needed a larger display—but it would be enough for what they were doing. More to the point, it didn't have anything essential loaded on it that Martin might cluelessly overwrite or wipe.

Keeping the laptop for herself, Jan gave Toba a tablet her boss had sent her to test drive, thinking that it would be a better match to his smaller hands.

Toba took the tablet, and his narrow lips—she had to stop thinking of it as a beak—twisted in what she was learning to recognize as a grin. "Little computer for the little man?"

"Don't start with the sizeism," she retorted, falling into the habit of treating him the same way she did Steverino, with a mix of respect and sass. "Or Martin will start making comments about being hung like a horse."

Those too-yellow eyes widened in mock shock. "It's like you know him."

She looked sideways to where Martin was fussing with the desk chair, trying to adjust it properly.

"Yeah. But I don't, do I?" Two days wasn't enough to know anyone, and…she had proven pretty conclusively she didn't understand human men, much less non-human ones.

Toba's amused expression faded, and he cocked his head to the side. "No. You don't know any of us, not really. You never will. So long as you remember that, you'll be okay."

The knots in Jan's stomach—so familiar now she hadn't even noticed them—tightened a hitch. Every time she started to get comfortable, something happened to remind her that they weren't the sort to be comfortable around. That was, as Toba said, probably a good thing….

She might not have read a lot of fairy tales, but she didn't remember many of them ending well, for anyone.

What was that AJ had said? That mostly, they ignored humans?

"Yeah." Ignorance might have been bliss, but it wasn't possible anymore. She needed to do some real research soon, as soon as she had them up and running independently. "All right, let's get you guys motoring. Remember what I showed you; the site's set, your accounts are ready to go, and they're designed to be relatively idiot-proof. All you have to do is enter what you're looking for, and see who—or what—pops up."

"So, we look for lovers?" Martin swung around to

look at them, and his eyes got wider, like a kid told that Santa was real.

"We look for preters who are looking for lovers," Toba said, reaching out to whack him across the back of his head, hard enough that Jan winced. "Don't get distracted, kelpie."

The blue-skinned figure drifted a little closer, as though to watch what they were doing, and Jan shivered. It might be useful for protection, although she didn't see how, if they couldn't actually *do* magic, but the damn thing gave her the creeps.

Toba took the netbook over onto the sofa and settled it on his lap, hands poised as he scanned the screen. "All right. Key words, reply to potentials, skip the rest. On it."

Toba's claim to be the sole geek among the volunteered supernaturals proved accurate; he was quickly engrossed in the task, not needing any guidance beyond the occasional wording of a reply.

It didn't take Jan long to realize that Martin, however, for all his enthusiasm for any kind of flirting, was not well-suited to research—or doing any kind of long-term task, for that matter. He was too easily distracted. After the third time she found him chatting with random people who clearly weren't who they were looking for, she yelled at him; when she found him browsing over to a porn site via offered clicks, she gave up.

"You really are short-attention-span boy, aren't you?"

"He can't help it," Toba said, not looking up from the screen. "Kelpies."

They kept saying that, whatever that meant. Jan made a mental note to do some hard-core research once they took a break, and see if there was a how-to-deal-with-the-supernatural site up anywhere that had actual useful information.

"It's almost lunchtime," she said to Martin now. "We'll do this. You go pick up some pizzas, be useful."

It wasn't just make-work: There was nothing in her fridge that would feed four. Or three—she still wasn't sure what the lurking super ate, and needle-sharp tooth marks on the half-eaten melon gave her pause from even asking.

"But…"

"Be useful, Martin, or go away."

He looked mournful. "I don't have any money."

"Of course you don't." She grabbed her wallet off the desk, and handed him two twenty-dollar bills. "Don't go too crazy. Down the street and turn left, go to Gene's Pizzeria. Two pizzas should be enough. I have soda and juice in the fridge already."

"Two pizzas. Got it."

"One with meat," Toba called out. "No damned peppers."

Martin paused at the doorway, looking at Jan. "One peppers and mushrooms, one pepperoni?"

Jan nodded. So she'd been right about him being a vegetarian. And, apparently, supers ate a lot of pizza. Or enough to form preferences, anyway. It made no sense, but it wasn't like much of this did.

Roll with it, she told herself. *Getting Tyler home so you can kick his ass is the first and most important thing; you can figure out supernatural culture clashes later.*

The blue-skinned super watched him leave, then turned back to stare out through the walls.

"Bet you he comes back with 'em both vegetarian," Toba grumbled, and then went back to work, poking at the screen with two fingers.

Jan didn't go back to the site-trolling immediately. First, she entered a quick search for basic mythology sites and then—a sense of responsibility digging at her—took a look at her work email. The company she worked for maintained websites and social media for companies that didn't want to maintain their own departments. Right now, untangling someone else's coding screw-up seemed seriously unimportant, but there would still be bills to pay after, and while her job was a little more secure than Ty's—she was an actual employee, not a contract-hire, and could take time off without getting kicked to the curb—she didn't want to push it.

Somehow, heroes in fantasy adventures could always just drop things and rush off to save the world.

The backlog wasn't too bad: she answered the questions she could handle easily, and redirected larger problems to other people, then looked at her project time line. The two projects she had in the queue could wait another day or so before the deadlines started getting crunchy, without anyone yelling, and since she'd been in the end of a project when Tyler had disappeared, everyone would think she was still hip-deep in that for another day or two.

And if someone yelled for her, and she wasn't able to hold their hand right away? She'd worry about it then. Hell, maybe they'd find the connection right away, some "enter here for the elves" sign, and AJ's crew could go do their thing and…

Jan sighed. She didn't know what was going to happen, but she knew it wasn't going to be that easy.

From across the room, she could hear Toba muttering. "No, no, no…"

Just listening to the dismay in his voice made Jan remember why she'd been so damn glad to find Tyler and cancel her memberships. It didn't help that the key words they'd settled on were designed to find the most desperate, affection-hungry women, who would overlook anything that might otherwise be hinky in the hopes of meeting The One. Or at least The One For Now. The whole thing made her skin itch.

Sighing, she closed out the work browser and

looked at the top hits for mythology sites. They all seemed basic, generic as to be useless—or they were for some writer's obviously made-up world. Giving up for now, she bookmarked some of them and then opened her own faux accounts. Almost immediately, a pop-up hit her screen, inviting her to chat, and she scanned the would-be-chatter's profile before declining.

"Damn you, Tyler. If you'd been able to keep it in your pants…neither of us would be in this mess, right now."

She said it low, but Toba apparently had ears like an owl's, too.

"Moderate your anger, human. The preters are very good at what they do. That is not to excuse your leman's behavior but… Your history is filled with examples of otherwise virtuous souls who have been lured to ill fates."

"That's not making me feel better."

"No. Sorry."

For a while, there was only the sound of typing keys and faint beeps of incoming chat requests.

Finally, the silence started to wear on Jan—or not the silence exactly, but the silence with two other people in the room with her. At least Martin made noise, even if he didn't hum the way Tyler did, or…

"Hey. Toba."

"Yes?"

She hadn't really thought about what she was

going to ask; she had just needed to say something, and hear him respond. "What… I mean…who…"

"What am I?"

"Yeah." First-person research was always better than relying on Google, anyway.

"In some places, we were called *Splyushka*."

That didn't help worth a damn, but he didn't explain further. "And Martin?"

"A kelpie."

He'd said that before, as if she was supposed to know what that meant. Without turning around, she made a "go ahead" gesture at him over her shoulder.

Toba hesitated. "Kelpies are…"

"Flirts?" Wild guess, there. Not.

"Yes. Among other things." He sounded as if he was thinking things through before speaking. Jan let him. Finally he went on. "Be careful of yourself, around Martin. I don't think that he would ever deliberately harm you, but…we cannot help but be true to our nature. We, Martin and I, we understand humans the most, of the volunteers, and so were considered the best to help you. That does not make us…safe."

"Is AJ safe?"

That made Toba laugh, a sharp hacking noise. "No. AJ is not safe. But he has another job to do, one that needs his…nature."

She thought of the teeth set into that muzzle and those claw-tipped fingers. "He's out there, isn't he? Nearby." Part of the protections they kept talking about? Toba had said that AJ was the one who talked people into doing stuff....

"We have sworn to protect you, while you aid us. AJ and his kin are...best at that."

"He's a werewolf." That much at least she'd figured out.

"He is *lupin.* He is no more wolf than Martin is, in fact, a horse. Janice."

The sudden seriousness in Toba's voice, and his using her full name, distracted Jan from the screen, and she turned in her chair to look at him.

"There is a reason our people stay apart, even as we share this space. Good reasons, hard-learned. If it were not for this threat, you would have lived your life ignorant of us...and it would have been for the best." His beak clacked softly. "I meant truly what I said before: do not fall into the trap of thinking that you can understand us—or that we can understand you."

The lurker by the wall stirred, its entire body rippling as though a breeze passed right through it.

"But..." She studied his expression, trying to read it, and nodded. "All right." She thought he was wrong—there was always a way to understand someone, if you tried hard enough to listen—but they could argue about it later. "I think I have a few we should consider. You?"

Toba did a quick count. "Seven, all from women.

It would appear that our guess is correct, and they are still targeting males more than females."

Jan looked at her ratio and had to agree. "If we're right about them being preters. They may just be human females playing on desperation, too. Reply to them with the script." She had remembered some of the responses she'd gotten from men who wanted a date in the absolute worst way, and cribbed something together for them to use. If Tyler had fallen for the kind of lures they were seeing, and responded... Was it better, or worse, that as Toba said, he'd fallen for a well-honed trick? She would never know if he might have been responding to other women....

"Maybe they were right. Maybe it wasn't real at all, he was just looking to piss his family off, or I was projecting what I wanted to see, or..."

"What?" Toba turned his head at a disconcerting angle, looking at her from behind the laptop's screen.

"Nothing. Never mind. Just talking to myself." She clicked on the accounts she'd flagged as being potentials, and stared at one of the photos. Was the face a little too pointed? The eyes a little too round, the face slightly...alien?

"Here's one that might be," Toba said, looking up. "Lonely woman with everything except a reason. Spend my days working, my nights dreaming of you. Want partner to walk in moonlight, watch the sun rise, live in a perfect dream. The key words match—moonlight, perfect, dreaming...."

Jan winced. "Oh, god, that's so bad it almost has to be from a human."

"Humans actually fall for this?"

Jan stared at her computer screen, seeing not it, but that first email Tyler had sent her, after they'd connected. She remembered how it had felt, reading it, that leap of hope, that awareness that maybe, just maybe, there was someone out there who could understand, who would love her....

"Yeah. We fall for it. Every time."

Before Toba could respond, the door to the apartment opened, and Martin came in with two pizzas, a brown paper bag balanced on top. He handed the bag without a word to the silent creature, who disappeared into the bathroom. Jan presumed it went there to eat in private. After what it had done to the melon, she was just as glad.

"Put 'em on the table," she said, indicating the remaining pizza boxes.

"You two have any luck?" Martin asked, putting the two boxes on the coffee table. He lifted the lid off one box, pulling a slice out for himself and sitting on the sofa to eat it.

Jan thought about telling him to go get a plate, and then shrugged. Pizza stains were hardly the worst thing this apartment had seen. Besides, he was a neat, almost fussy eater, folding the slice and eating it carefully from the sides, so that no grease or cheese escaped. She should get him a napkin, though, just in case. The shirt he'd put on, a solid blue button-down, looked too nice to get grease stains on.

God, she sounded like a suburban housewife. These weren't her kids; they weren't even her friends. They weren't *human*. Let him deal with his own damn clothing.

"No luck at all, just a lot of hard work," Toba said. "Not that you'd know hard work if it bit you on the face."

Jan went into the kitchen to get a plate for herself, as well as napkins, listening to the tone of their exchange rather than the words. Their squabbling was undercut with more annoyance than AJ's words had carried; AJ and Martin were friends. These two weren't. But they were working together to help her— no, not to help her. To keep those other things from getting a toehold here. She was just a tool, a way for them to get what they wanted.

That was okay: they would be her tools, too. She wasn't comfortable thinking like that, but she could learn. Maybe.

And skeletal, blue-skinned thing? Jan had no idea what it was or wasn't, wanted or didn't, and she wasn't sure she wanted to find out, either. She just hoped it wasn't going to lurk over her while she slept.

"Hey, does anyone want soda, or is orange juice okay? Or milk, but it's skim, and I'm, um, not sure how old it is…."

There was a noise outside, a rough, metallic clatter cutting through the bickering in the living room, and Jan frowned. It sounded like one of the street sweeper machines cleaning the gutters, or maybe a maintenance crew taking down trees, but it was late in the day for both of those things. The sound grew, until it sounded as though someone was revving an engine just beyond the wall, and Jan went into the main room, intending to look out the window and see what was going on.

"Down!"

The moment she was through the doorway, Martin's body hit hers with a thud, knocking her against the wall rather than taking her to the floor. He dropped to his knees, reaching up to pull her down with him. Once her shoulder hit the carpet, his body arched over hers as though to protect her from nonexistent debris.

"Cover your ears and sing!" he shouted in her ear.

"What?" She had to have heard him wrong.

"Sing!"

She covered her ears with her hands, although it did nothing to shut out the metallic clamor, and sang the first thing she could think of, which happened to be some inane pop song Tyler had been singing in the shower, last time she was over there, about having sex in the subway. The totally inappropriate lyrics made her blush—until a shrill screaming noise cut through everything, and she faltered.

"Keep singing!" And Martin pressed his own

hands against hers, his low voice chanting in a language she didn't recognize, occasionally stopping to shout out something to Toba.

"Busy here!" Toba finally shouted back, or she thought that's what he said. Then there was a terrible crash and then a scream, a real scream of something in pain, and the high-pitched keening got louder, and then there was a sudden, horrible silence.

A heartbeat passed, her singing and Martin's chanting cut off all at once, as if someone covered her mouth, and then she was being hauled to her feet. Martin's hands were no longer soft and reassuring but hard, practically dragging her across the floor when she didn't move fast enough to suit him.

Something was wrong: they had to get out of the building. She'd already realized that. But when she would have gone for the elevator, Martin dragged her the other way, toward the end of the hallway.

"Where are we going?" she demanded, more angry than scared just then. She didn't like being hauled around like a sack of whatever it was people hauled around in sacks—she didn't know, but she knew she didn't like it.

"Not the stairs," Toba said behind them, his voice shrill. "Window. Faster."

Jan half turned to look at him, her elbow still in Martin's grasp. "What?"

He didn't answer, only shoved her daypack into

her hands. From the weight, she thought he'd managed to grab her laptop, too.

And then the noise wasn't outside anymore; it was inside, coming closer, and there was a shadow coming out of her door, mottled gray-blue and stretching out as though blindly feeling for something. Jan's eyes widened, the memory of similar fingers reaching through the floor of the bus....

"Oh, god," she said faintly, thinking she might throw up. Or pass out. Or—

"Go!" Toba said, and shoved her at Martin, turning to stand with his back to them. Jan started to ask what the hell he thought he was doing, when he *blurred* somehow, the same way Martin had, although she was able to keep her eyes open enough this time to see his hunched shoulders straighten, wide brown-feathered wings stretching to fill the hallway and block what was coming from her sight.

"Toba…" He was beautiful, even from the back, even with panic screaming in her veins.

"Go," Martin said, and pulled her elbow hard, moving her in front of him, and pushed her toward the window at the end of the hallway. "Go, and don't stop!"

Nobody came out into the hallway to see what was going on. Hopefully, everyone was at work, or school, or just not in the building. For once, Jan was thankful that she'd never made any real friends in her building. She ran for the window, struggling to open the sash and weeping in frustration when it refused to open, warped by too much paint and time.

She looked over her shoulder again and saw Toba go down on one knee, those wings now shredded and tattered, gray-blue fingers tearing and plucking at him. The sound of jaws munching might have been a product of her overstressed imagination, but her stomach churned nonetheless.

"Toba?" She tried to turn, to go back to him, although what the hell she could do she had no idea, even if Martin hadn't been blocking the way.

"Move," he said, pushing her away, and then his elbow hit the glass, shattering it just as something swooped outside.

Jan, her nerves finally shot, flinched away from the window, trying to shelter against his chest from this new threat. Instead, he pushed her forward, even as he was knocking the glass away with his other arm, ignoring the shards that sliced at his arm. She finally realized that he was clearing a safe space for them to escape through.

He stepped back and reached for her again, even as there was the sound of something falling with a heavy thud in the hallway behind them.

"Now!"

She got into the window frame, slinging the daypack over her shoulder and bracing her knees against the ledge, and looked down five floors to the parking lot below, wondering what the hell Martin expected her to do—there was no fire escape on this side of the building, so unless he had a rope....

The sound of something hovering made her look up, and she gasped, trying to shove back into the building: something huge fluttered outside, dark and fierce, limned in red from the afternoon's fading sun.

"Jump." Martin's voice was smooth again, intense, and his hands lingered on the nape of her neck, the sensation making her skin prickle. "Trust me."

Between that and the thing behind them, there wasn't much choice. She jumped.

Chapter 6

There was a painful sensation of free fall, her gut up somewhere around her nose and her bowels shriveling up in fear, and then something caught her, wrapping her in thick, suffocating folds of smoky gauze, a sharp, clawlike grip pinching her skin through the folds. Adrenaline filling her veins, Jan struggled, trying to escape, but was held tight, the gauze thickening and the grip tightening in response to her movement. The more she fought, the more she was trapped.

Feeling the unnerving stomach-swoop of being carried upward rather than falling, Jan finally swallowed hard and held herself very still, praying that whatever it was that had her was friendly and not prone to dropping things.

The moment she calmed down, the gauze thinned again, enough that she was able to breathe, if not move. The adrenaline ebbed, leaving her feeling sick and shaky in the aftermath. It was so quiet, the folds around her acting like insulation, that the only sound was the beat of her own blood and the sound of her breathing, harshly nasal. Time lost meaning, although the tingling numbness in her arms and legs told Jan that she had been like that for a while—it usually took half an hour for her legs to fall asleep when she was sitting too long, and this felt way worse.

She had started to doze off—impossible but inevitable, once terror turned to near-boredom, when there was another swoop, this one longer than before, then the accompanying sensation of being dashed headfirst toward the ground before being pulled up at the very last minute. Jan dry-retched, a foul taste filling her mouth, even as the folds around her unwrapped, and she was dropped to her knees on a soft, muddy surface.

Fresh air and relief made the dry-retching turn into full-on heaves, her stomach folding in on itself, trying to find something to expel in punishment for what it had been put through.

"As heroines go, you're not too glamorous," a vaguely familiar voice observed. "What happened? Where's Martin?"

Jan wiped her mouth with the back of her hand and sat back on her heels, thankful that she'd only had the single slice of pizza, before all hell had broken loose. Her gut hurt and her throat was sore, but at least she wasn't covered in vomit.

"Turncoats." Her voice was scratchy and dry. "They came...Toba..."

Vivid in her mind's eye, the sight of bloody feathers, drifting down on the old, pale green carpet of her hallway, returned, and Jan retched again, her muscles protesting the action but unable to stop.

"The *bansidhe?*" AJ asked, his voice an urgent growl, not seeming to notice her distress.

"The what?" She shook her head, trying to focus, wishing that she had a toothbrush or a piece of gum to clean her mouth and get the taste of vomit out. "Is that what the blue thing was? I don't know. Toba— he went back. Martin dragged me out of there, threw me out the window."

All right, she had jumped. Out a fifth-story window. And been caught by...

"What...what carried me here? Where is here?" She looked down and saw her daypack sitting on the muddy ground next to her. She lifted her hand— shaking, she noted absently—and pulled open the flap, looking inside. Her laptop was there, the power cord still dangling from it like a tail. It looked intact, but she didn't have the energy to check it. She had her laptop, her phone, her wallet—her inhaler.

Somehow, that made it all worse, instead of better.

"The *bansidhe,*" AJ said again. "It brought you here. Its job was to protect you against the preters."

The blue thing. Now she knew what it had been. Was, she hoped. Still was. She shuddered, thinking of how long she had spent wrapped within its…arms? Wings? It didn't matter.

"They came, the turncoats. Martin and I ran, Toba, he…."

There was a tiny golden-brown feather caught in her hair. She pulled at it, weightless in her hand. "Toba's dead, isn't he?"

"Yes. If the turncoats found you, it's likely. He would not run until you were safe." AJ crouched next to her, his once-disturbing face now almost ordinary in comparison to what she had seen. "That bothers you."

Her stomach clenched again, as if it suddenly thought of more it had to get rid off. "Of course it does! To die like that…" To die at all.

"More are going to die, if you insist on leaving safe zones. And just as badly. Come on. If Martin got away, he'll join us at the Center."

His matter-of-fact tone made Jan want to scream, to make him show something, some emotion or expression. Instead, she got to her feet, reaching for the bag that had fallen with her and slinging it over her shoulder before following the werewolf—the *lupin*—away from the muddy clearing and deeper into the woods. The city was lost behind them; she had no

idea how far the *bansidhe* had flown, or where, or
for how long.

It wasn't her fault. Was it? For insisting that she
go home, insisting…they had to go back to her apartment. Her computers were there, and she had to check
in with the office, and…

The feather was still in her hand, clinging lightly
to her palm. She closed her fingers around it. They'd
had to go back. But they shouldn't have stayed.

"Toba is dead." Her voice was flat, exhausted.
"Martin is probably dead. Because I…"

"Because of the turncoats. Because of the preters.
Because they had misinformed ideas about how to be
heroes. Don't hog all the glory for yourself, there's
more than enough to go around."

His voice was still matter-of-fact, almost cold. But
Martin had been his friend, maybe. Toba had been…
And he had sent them both with her. Jan heard the
guilt in his own growl and shut up.

The ground under her feet as they walked was
dry, unlike the muddy area where the *bansidhe* had
dropped her. The trees were huge, towering above
them, even their lowest branches over her head. The
leaves were the size of her hand, still green, and the
undergrowth was low and sparse, which she thought
maybe meant something, about wildfires, or how old
the forest was, or something, but she couldn't remember what, or where she might have learned it.

When AJ had said they were at a center, she had

assumed it was a building, some sort of gathering hall or even a community center, although what sort, she couldn't imagine when she thought about it.

Instead, he led her down a path through the trees that started wide enough for a car to pass through and then turned left and right, narrowing with each turn, the corners becoming less distinct even as the greenery grew thicker on either side, until she couldn't have said how far they'd gone, or in what direction.

And then one final spiral turn, and the path opened into a clearing too large for it to make sense, large enough that she could barely see the other edge, only that there were groups gathered around small bonfires here and there, and at the very middle, a tree different somehow from the ones they had walked through. It had to be a hundred years old or more, rising straight-trunked and green-gray, limbs reaching out far above her head, tipped with leaves that were the green of fresh spring, and the scarlet of autumn, alternating on the same branches.

"The Center…" She looked behind her, almost expecting the path they'd taken to have disappeared. But no, it was still there, about the width of a closet door, but clear and distinct. She could, if she worked at it, make out half a dozen other such openings in the woods around them. "The Center of what?"

"Everything that matters," AJ said. "Come on."

As they emerged into the clearing, there was a shout from one of the bonfires and then a glad cry of "There you are!" before she was engulfed in Martin's embrace, her face pressed against his chest so that she could feel the thump-thump of his heart, as though he'd just run far and fast and not yet had time to recover.

He was also damp and smelled of something she couldn't identify, not unpleasant but...different.

"Toba?" She didn't want to ask, she already knew, but she had to hear it. The little owl-man had been... he had been honest, and he had answered her questions, not danced around them or evaded entirely, and he had died because of her. She owed him, something. Even if just to hear the truth.

Martin didn't pull away; in fact, he held her more tightly. His voice was muffled through her hair, but she heard him clearly, anyway. "Gone. I'm sorry."

"Mourn later," AJ said. "Martin. I'm glad you made it back. Do you know where to find them yet? Do you have a preter on the hook?"

Jan backed out of Martin's embrace and turned to glare at the *lupin*. "We'd only just started when..." She bit back her flare of temper, realizing that it didn't help, and it wasn't AJ's fault. He was cold, but he was right: more would die if she didn't do her job.

Toba. She let herself think of the little man, with his beak-hard lips, his oddly gentle golden eyes and his snarky common sense. *Toba, I'm sorry.*

"Maybe," she said out loud. "We'd just started. I'd gotten a few queries, Toba had, too. But..." The passwords were all in her computer, safe, thanks to Toba's quick thinking—and unreadable, right now, out here in the middle of rural nowhere. "I'll need to log on in order to check responses, and I can't do that…here. I've got a decent battery charge, but it doesn't do much without connectivity."

It was just a guess, that they didn't have Wi-Fi, but she thought it was a pretty safe guess, at that.

From the look on AJ's face and the way his elongated jaw twitched, she'd guessed right.

Tyler had lost track of how many times it had happened: the sessions, like the days, faded into each other, everything that had been, fading away and no reason to hold on to any specific moment. A day, a month, a year? He didn't know.

The sheets underneath him were smooth, almost too soft, and his body ached from the bones on out. He opened his eyes slowly, half hoping something had changed, knowing it hadn't.

"Ah, darling, you're awake." Stjerne smiled and offered him a cup, its wooden shape smooth and dark, as though generations of hands had held it, staining it with their sweat. The liquid inside was sweet and fresh, and filled his mouth without easing his thirst. There would be other things to drink, later. But in the morning, when he woke, he had this. The cup and her smile, her hands smoothing his skin and petting his close-cropped hair while he drank as though everything were all right, when it was not. This moment, this pause, he was himself, able to think, if not clearly, able to question, even though he knew there would be no answers.

There were others like him now, in the great hall, or the gardens beyond. Not many, maybe a dozen. Quiet, trailing behind their companions, or sometimes walking hand-in-hand. They wore clothing like his, jeans or khakis with soft gray tops that tied at the hip, like a martial arts uniform. Occasionally, he would see a woman, wearing a dress like their tops, but down to her knees. Her ankles were wrapped in strands of something that gave off a delicate tinkle, like copper bells almost too small to see, and her companion always escorted her with his arm over her shoulder, his fingers sometimes playing with her pale red hair as if he was combing fire.

They all seemed content, if dazed. Occasionally there would be someone new, whose body was still jerky, who seemed not to belong, but they never lasted long. Or maybe they learned to accept and be quiet.

Being quiet was better.

Each of them had a companion, like Stjerne. They wore different clothing, and their hair was different colors, but he knew them even at a distance: the same cheekbones, the same slender builds and long legs, the same way of going very, very still when they stopped moving.

And when they put him in the chair of thorns and

did those things to him, the things that hurt so badly, they all had the same expression, the one that he could read now.

Hunger.

When they looked at him like that, when the scrabbling biting cold things touched his head and reached into his brain, he almost remembered something. A voice, laughter, and hands that were gentle, not fierce. He couldn't see a face, couldn't remember a name, but it was there, he knew it was there.

Stupid, but he *wanted* to remember, so badly— and then the pain came again, and only Stjerne could make it endurable. Only if he fell into her, she said, over and over, only if he let her fall into him, give her all his memories, all his doubts and his pains, gave himself to her, could she help him.

So, each time, he fell.

And forgot.

It was better that way.

Now, under her patient smile, he finished the last draught in the cup and faded into gray.

"Better, sweet boy." Her fingers trailed along his cheek, nails scraping his skin. He stared up at her, eyes vague, lips parted. "You're almost ready. Almost there."

Martin had taken her hand, after she'd broken their embrace, and she had allowed that. Truthfully, she had clung to it for a little while. He was alive. She could feel the strength and warmth in his skin, the way his fingers curled around her palm, his thumb occasionally, almost instinctively stroking the inside of her wrist, as though he, too, was reassuring himself that she was alive.

The *bansidhe* had flown off after it dumped her, and had not returned to the Center; she didn't ask after it, ask where it had gone. The thing had saved her life, but she remembered the high keening noise in her apartment, the feel of the pale blue flesh wrapped over her face, and she decided that she would rather not have to thank it for any of the things it had done.

Jan still had no sense of where she was or how long she'd been airborne—or how nobody had *seen* them, skimming through the air. More supernatural glamour, she supposed.

"The only time my life has ever been glamorous," she said, "and nobody there to see it."

One of the supers within earshot, vaguely catlike but walking on two legs and without a visible tail, gave her an odd look at that, but kept moving, while Martin led her and AJ to one of the campfires.

The attack on her apartment had come mid-afternoon; by the time she'd come to the Center— the Center of Everything Important, AJ had called it—the sun had started to fade behind the trees surrounding it. Night had come quickly after that, and by the time the three of them had been settled, a deep, full night had fallen.

There were no streetlights or buildings to lend illumination: Jan couldn't remember the last time she had been anywhere so dark. The only lights came from the half-dozen campfires scattered around the glade and the stars overhead.

The campfires were relatively isolated, each large enough for a group, but the other…people, she supposed, at the Center did not huddle around them, but rather moved from one to the other, sometimes dancing or capering, sometimes striding gracefully— some of them moving in ways that Jan couldn't quite name, that made her uneasy to watch. None of them came to the fire where Martin, she and AJ now sat, blankets draped against thick logs to make seats, the fire not so much for light or warmth, as comfort.

"It was the turncoats." She wasn't asking a question: she had seen the thing—the things?—that had attacked Toba, recognized the coloration but more than that she had recognized the *feeling* she got when they were nearby. "You called them gnomes?"

"Gēnomos," AJ said. "Earth-movers. Metal, rock… they manipulate it, shape it."

"How did they find me? And how did they get up five stories? They shaped the bricks of my building? And what was that noise? The thing that sounded like machinery?"

"I don't know." Martin looked distinctly worried. "I'd never heard it before; it was like a dragon, except nobody's heard or seen a dragon since...since forever."

"It sounded like a machine to me."

"No," Martin said, "definitely alive."

"What, a dragon?" She wasn't rejecting the idea—well, not entirely. "You said they were all dead."

"No, I said nobody's seen them in forever. That's not dead. But there's no reason for them to be helping gnomes."

"Someone's looking into it," AJ said, and that seemed to put an end to the discussion, at least for Martin. Jan, on the other hand, still had one horribly important question.

"How did they find me?" she asked again.

AJ tossed another stick into the fire. "We don't know."

He wouldn't look at her. She stared at the profile of his face in the firelight, the stubby lines of his muzzle, the way he'd used a headband to pull the shaggy hair off his face, and thought about what he'd said and what he hadn't said.

"You think someone told them."

"I don't know. It's a possibility. The preters love to use peoples' greed against themselves, and humans...aren't universally adored, even among the gentler races. Someone could have been turned...but I don't know who."

"But...why?" From everything she had seen, everything she had been told, the preters would make this world horrible. Then again, she reminded herself, a cold clench in her brain, she'd only been told, and shown, what AJ wanted her to see.

No. Jan reined in the paranoia. She had to pick a side, she had to believe in something. She chose to believe that…all right, not AJ, maybe, but that Martin would not lie to her. That Toba had not been lying to her.

Martin picked up a stick from the pile but, rather than adding it to the flame, instead poked at it. "None of this is new. Gnomes…it wasn't a surprise that their entire race went turncoat, not in retrospect. They're full of what-should-be, never satisfied with what is or was, always looking for the chance to better themselves, even if they have no idea what that thing might be. It's their nature to be contrary, to be unwise. Preters have always been able to use that—in humans and our kind, too. They coax and then they twist and then…. You do things you would never have thought to do, alone."

"The devil made me do it," Jan murmured.

"Yeah. Pretty much."

"So not just the gnomes who turned their coats? And not just maybe one or two among your volunteers, either?"

AJ growled, but Jan knew it wasn't directed at her, only at what she said.

"Some of the races, the ones we warned you about. The isolationists. With this incursion, they see a chance, too. They ignore history, and pretend that they can control things they cannot...."

"You never mentioned this before," Martin said.

"To what purpose? Would it change anything we're doing here? Some supers don't like the way humans treat the world, and think they can do better. They tell themselves that the preters are more like us, that they will share the world, let it go back to the mythical Way It Was."

Martin snorted, a wet and distinctly disgusted noise. "I like the world the way it is."

"That's the joke, Martin. There never was a way it was. It's always sucked."

Another time, another place, Jan would have argued with him over that. Not here, not now.

"So it was someone...here?" She managed not to look around, but the back of her neck prickled. "Or at the warehouse?"

"The Center is safe. And the warehouse...I trust everyone there implicitly. But they have friends, family. All it would take is one mistake—there was a saying you humans used when I was a pup: loose lips sink ships. Or kill humans. Either way, we need to get you away—cut any possible connection, any link that might be used against us, to betray you, even unknowingly."

"But I thought you said it was safer where you already had protections?" Not that the ones they had set up around her apartment had done any good. She remembered the noise, the sight of Toba being taken down by those things, the gnomes, and blanched.

"We're supernaturals, not superheroes. A glamour can only distract the eye, cozen it into believing something more palatable. Once someone is convinced they know where you are, and want to get at you—it fades like mist. The turncoats went to your home, the places where you were known. Glamour cannot stand against knowledge."

The guilt came back, a sticky, bitter coating on her tongue, but AJ was still talking, still making plans.

"We need time, time for you to catch us a preter. Time to unravel how they're controlling the portals. So we need to put you somewhere they do not know, and then create the illusion that you are somewhere else, to draw them away. And then the *bansidhe*—and others—will be waiting for them, when you find out *their* weak spot"

It was sneaky. It was supernaturally sneaky, and Jan wasn't sure if she should be impressed or terrified. So instead she asked the question she didn't want to ask, because she had to know.

"Did the gnomes…do you think they bothered any of my neighbors?" And by bothered, she meant "ate."

"No," Martin said, beating the *lupin* to the punch. "Not unless anyone came out to see what was going on."

"They wouldn't." It was a nice building, well-maintained and safe, but not the kind of place where people investigated, not unless it knocked on their own doors.

"Then they probably slunk away, once we were gone. Same as they did on the bus. They have no interest in others—and no interest in getting human attention. The desire to be left alone is a survival instinct."

"But—" Jan started to say, when AJ interrupted her. No, he didn't interrupt: he overrode her, as though she hadn't been speaking at all.

"You can't worry about them now. Martin, you need to take her away. Disappear. You're the only one I can trust to make sure that she does what she needs to do."

"Me?" His dark eyes went wide, and he shook his head, a shank of hair falling into his face before he roughly shoved the offending lock away. "You want me to take her? Alone?" The stick he'd been using to poke at the fire was still in his hand, the ember-lit end pointing at the ground, and it rose now, sweeping up to point at Jan. "Alone?"

The tone in his voice she'd thought was surprise, wasn't. It was fear.

"There's nobody else. We didn't get that many volunteers to begin with, and…. You know what the preters are, what they'll do, given a chance. That's motivation enough for you to protect her, until she's done. After that…." AJ looked away from the fire, his face shadowed, the muzzle made more prominent. "After that, it's up to you what you need to do."

Martin looked at AJ, then let the point of the stick drop again, and went back to staring into the crackling yellow flames of the fire. "All right."

Something had gone on just then that Jan didn't understand. But in the past—twenty-four, thirty-six hours?—there had been so much she hadn't understood, it was too much to question. Easier to just let it go—for now. Her brain hurt, her head hurt, and dear god, her body hurt.

"I need something to eat, and I need to sleep," she said, instead of asking them what the hell was going on and getting more answers that would explain nothing. "Anything else—everything else—is going to have to wait until morning."

AJ disappeared for a while, then came back with her meal: a small round piece of tender meat she rather thought was rabbit, but ate, anyway, and a makeshift, dry salad of field greens. It did not replace the abandoned pizza, but she ate it greedily, wiping her fingers clean on the grass when she was done. The plate was a dull gray metal, like pewter, she thought, but when she flicked her finger against it, a sweet, singing tone rang out, like crystal. She wondered if it was dishwasher safe and where she could put hands on a full set. Did fairy-made goods last longer, or change into, what, straw, in the morning?

That would solve the problem about the dishwasher, but what would she do with the straw afterward?

Martin had gone somewhere else while she ate, muttering about the need to stretch his legs, and she had appropriated the blanket he had been sitting on, wrapping it over her shoulders as the night got chillier. He didn't come back, even as the other bonfires quieted down, their residents settling in for the night. AJ banked the fire, hemming it in until it seemed as safe and steady as a candle.

"Do you really think we can find them, catch a preter, make them give up? Do you think we can really stop them?" Her voice carried all her doubt, her exhaustion, until she didn't recognize herself in it.

"No." The *lupin* face didn't really lend itself to being read, at least not by her, and his voice was flat. "But the only other option is to just sit here and let it happen." In the darkness, his eyes reflected a more vivid red from the remaining fire. "I'm not the kind to lie down and let someone else determine my fate. Are you?"

Jan thought about all the things she'd put up with her entire life, the things she'd accepted as the-way-it-is, because she couldn't imagine her voice would change anything. Small things and large. Important, and petty.

"Yeah," she said. "I guess I am."

He looked at her, those eyes glittering in the firelight. "Then why are you here?"

"Because…" Because they hadn't given her a choice. Had kept her so off-balance and confused, she hadn't had a chance to stop and be scared. "Because Tyler needs me. Because…" Jan sighed, annoyed at herself for not being able to come up with some noble, heroic response. "Because I can't exactly go home now, can I?"

AJ let out a barking sort of laugh. "Good enough." He stood up, his legs unfolding in a weirdly backward, graceful way that reminded her, again, that he wasn't human. "You'll do. Now go to bed."

It hadn't been a suggestion. Jan, following long-ago memories of Girl Scout camping, made sure that her socks and shoes were off the ground so nothing could crawl into them overnight, and then lay on the fire-warmed ground with her blanket underneath and Martin's blanket around her, her arm crooked under her head for a pillow. She didn't think she could sleep, so she stared up at the sky and tried to count the stars.

She fell asleep before she realized that she couldn't recognize any of the constellations.

Chapter 7

"Jan. Janny." There was a soft, featherlight touch on her cheek, warm breath on her neck. "Janny, wake up." The touch deepened, stroking down to her collarbone, over her shoulder, a seductive shiver, and Jan stretched into it, luxuriating in the feel of skin-to-skin. It had been too long, almost a week since she and Tyler had last—

Tyler never called her Janny. Ever.

She sat up so fast, her head clunked against Martin's, sending him back on his ass in the grass.

"Ow," he said, glaring at her. "You don't wake up pretty, do you?"

Her skin still tingled from his touch, the feelings it had brought up making her angrier than she would have been normally in the situation. "Do you always wake people up like that?"

"Yes."

His response was so matter-of-fact, almost surprised that she was asking, that all the air left her, as if it had been a physical punch.

"Of course you do," she said. She'd been warned, hadn't she? Toba and AJ both had told her, if not in so many words. She'd let down her guard, thinking of them as allies, people to be trusted. But they weren't. Allies, yes, but not people. And not to be trusted.

"Don't touch me," she said. "Especially not like that."

His eyes, chocolate-brown and seemingly guileless, reflected surprise, and then he nodded, as though it didn't matter to him one way or the other. "All right."

Awake now, she rubbed her eyes and looked around. The clearing was empty; all the others camping there overnight had gone before she'd woken up, not even a trace of the campfires left behind. Just an expanse of grassy meadow hedged in by trees, and a pale blue sky overhead.

AJ was nowhere to be seen, either. Just her and Martin. Great. Their fire had died down to coals overnight, and she shivered, even though the air was relatively mild. She'd thought to grab her bag when they'd escaped the apartment, but not a jacket, and the clothing she'd put on the day before, thinking they'd be hanging around her place, didn't do much against morning chills.

"Next time, I'm going to have a go-bag ready. Change of clothes, extra meds, passport…and a toothbrush. God, I'd kill for a toothbrush." Her mouth was dry, and she ran her tongue over her teeth and grimaced, rubbing the back of her hand against her face and wondering if she looked as grimy as she felt.

"There's a shower over there," Martin said, pointing across the clearing. "If you want."

She wanted, badly.

The walk across the clearing in her bare feet was surprisingly pleasant—none of the rocks or twigs she'd expected—as though someone—or something—groomed the area regularly. The grass tickled the soles of her feet, and dew left them damp.

"Forget about carjacking; they should hire out as gardeners."

Maybe they did. For all that she'd learned in the past few days, she didn't know bug-all. There could be thousands of them; there could be millions. Or, there might only be a few more than she had already seen. And they could make their livings a hundred different ways.

"When this is over…"

She stopped, both verbally and physically, standing at the edge of the tree line, the words echoing in the silence. The comment about the go-bag, and then this…when this was over…what? She would hang out with Martin over pizza once a week? She would do an in-depth study of the supernatural aspects of the natural world? Or she'd pretend that none of it had ever happened, that the entire episode had been some kind of weird bad mental breakdown and she was all better now?

"Worry about it when it *is* over," she said finally. She carefully did not consider option four—that she wouldn't make it to the end.

They were protecting her now, because she was useful. But she didn't know how far that went, or for how long.

The shower turned out to be a large bag suspended from a tree limb about ten feet off the ground, with a simple rope pull next to it. On a stump next to the shower-tree, there was a stack of coarse towels, folded neatly, and a clay pot of some white substance that felt and smelt like soap.

"Great." Jan wasn't the outdoorsy type—she'd hoped for at least some kind of shelter. But the grimy feeling of her skin and scalp didn't leave much room for debate.

Taking off her clothes, she folded them neatly and placed them on a flat rock that, from its shape and distance from the water-bag, had probably been put there for exactly that purpose. She hesitated, then slipped off the silver bracelet, too, and reached up for her earrings, only to discover that, at some point between yesterday morning and now, they had disappeared.

"Damn it, I liked those. They were expensive."

She didn't have the urge to stand around and mourn, though: The air was a lot colder, without her jeans and sweater, and her skin pimpled with goose bumps.

Standing naked underneath the bag, Jan scooped some of the soap up with her fingers and lathered her skin with it. It spread easily, clearly meant to be used on dry skin, and the smell was pleasant, like bright flowers and sunshine. She scrubbed it into her hair, too.

"Two days without conditioner, and my hair is going to look like hay," she muttered, but short of a CVS appearing in the clearing, there wasn't much she could do about that.

Lathered up and shivering, goose bumps running along her arms and legs, Jan took a deep breath to brace herself, reached out, and pulled the cord.

The water that rushed over her, contrary to expectation, wasn't cold. It wasn't hot, either, but warm enough that she wanted it to go on and on forever.

It didn't. She waited a minute, in case the bag needed time to refill, then pulled the cord again. Another gush of water rushed over her, and this time she remembered to rinse out her hair before the waterfall ended.

"Here."

She took the towel being offered and then yelped. "Damn it, Martin!"

He stepped back, looking down at his boots. "Sorry. I just…" He looked up again, and the bastard was smiling. "You're good to look at."

Just that. No apology, no stuttering excuses, just that statement.

She swallowed down her outrage, aware that it was just the two of them there—unless there were others, hiding? Invisible? The thought gave Jan the skeeves even more than being alone, and she shoved it away, wrapping the towel around herself as a protection.

"It's generally polite to wait for an invite before you look," she said, tartly.

"All right."

He stood there, waiting, and Jan—despite herself, despite everything—laughed. He had no shame at all, none. "Go *away,* Martin."

He heaved a sigh, and ostentatiously turned his back and walked away. Jan didn't trust him not to change his mind, though, and so made quick work of drying off and getting back into her clothing. She considered going commando rather than putting her underwear back on, then wrinkled her face and wore them, anyway. The jeans had dirt on them, and the shirt was sweat-grubby, but they were decent enough for now. Her apartment was out of reach—she didn't want to think about her apartment, or the damage that must have happened during the attack—and god alone knew when she'd see another department store…. She could rinse them out when they got to wherever they were going.

Where the hell *were* they going?

"Don't," she told herself, feeling the sense of being punched threatening to strike again, the past few days jumbling together into one massive panic attack that she couldn't afford without her asthma meds. "Don't… Just keep moving. Think about what it all means after you survive. Otherwise you're going to curl up and not move again, and that's not going to solve anything, and it sure as hell isn't going to bring Tyler home."

As pep talks went, it sucked, but her breathing evened out again, and she could walk back to the Center without feeling the sky falling in on her or her insides spilling out. Right then, she'd take that as a win.

When Jan reached the remains of their campfire, the blankets she'd slept on were rolled up, the fire pit itself cooled, and the grass already starting to regrow in the charred soil.

"No magic. Right." No wonder the other campfires had disappeared by morning. The National Parks department would love to learn how to do that. And they'd save a fortune reseeding the baseball fields every year….

She realized then that Martin was nowhere to be seen. Jan scanned the clearing, frowning, and then saw him. Or she assumed it was him, anyway, since there hadn't been any horses in the Center when she'd woken up. He turned and trotted toward her, a smooth gait that was eerily reminiscent of the way he walked. At a distance, less stunned than she had been the first time he'd transformed, she could see where he was different from a real horse: his neck was longer, his body more compact, and his legs looked as though they were hinged differently. But the main difference was in the eyes: as he came up to her, she could see that they were still Martin's eyes.

It was creepy as hell, a reminder that she was alone with something not-human. That she was up to her ears with things not-human.

As though sensing her discomfort, he stopped a pace or two away, and lowered his head to crop at the grass, casual-like.

"Toba died to save you," she whispered, reminding herself. "The *bansidhe* carried you to safety. AJ rescued you, fed you. Martin's here to help you. You can't trust him…but he won't hurt you."

It wasn't enough, but it gave her the strength to walk up to Martin, who was still nibbling at the grass, and cough slightly to get his attention. He lifted his head and looked at her, then dipped his head at the piece of black fabric on the ground near the folded-up blankets.

"If you're so magic, how come you have to use soap and campsite showers?" she wondered, not ex-

pecting an answer. If he could talk in this form…
that would be too freaky, she decided. There had to
be limits.

Martin snorted, an impatient sound, and indicated
the fabric on the ground again. She bent down and
picked it up, letting the narrow strip run through her
fingers. It was soft, some kind of cotton, maybe, a
hand span wide and about the length of her arm.
"What is it?"

He snorted again.

"That's not much help." She looked at it more carefully and sighed. "A blindfold?"

Apparently, yes. She was supposed to blindfold
herself before they did anything else.

"What, because there's something that's going to
freak me out, now? Seriously?"

Martin just waited.

"I am so very much not liking this. I just want that
said." But she tied the fabric around her eyes, anyway, and waited.

A warm body brushed against her, and she reached
out instinctively, her hand coming to rest on what had
to be Martin's shoulder. Haunch. Whatever it was
called in this form. Once her hand landed, he pushed
against her again, not quite knocking her off her feet.

Clearly, even without words, she understood: he
wanted her to get on his back.

Jan hesitated, remembering the warning from AJ.
She wasn't supposed to do that, not get on his back.

That was the one thing that had been made clear: it was dangerous. Dangerous enough, out of all this, to get specific mention.

Martin made a noise that rang out, a descending nicker of impatience, and gave her another push.

"All right. Fine. But if you throw me, or anything, I swear, I'll make a coat out of your hide."

Another push, this one gentler, and her fingers were clenching in his short, coarse mane, his body somehow encouraging her up, even as her arms pulled and her legs swung. And then—like magic—she was on his back, legs dangling to either side.

She'd never had more experience on horseback than the occasional pony ride as a kid, but she didn't think it was supposed to feel like this, as though the inside of her knees had melded with his sides. As though someone else was posing her, her body canted forward, her arms angled and her hands buried themselves in his mane, the longer strands wrapping around her wrists.

Unlike those pony rides, there was a sense that she wouldn't fall, that she *couldn't* fall. Martin would hold on to her.

And then he moved forward, not a walk or a trot but a jolting run, and Jan leaned forward against his neck and tried not to think about how fast they might be going—or where. Riding blind—literally— was not an experience she had ever wanted, and she wasn't enjoying it now.

Where were they going? Into the trees? Jan flinched in anticipation of branches hitting her or running into a tree, or...

Martin's body flexed underneath her, his hide rough and warm under her cheek, the muscles in her legs and arms aching with the unfamiliar exertion. He took another stride, and she took a breath, the stride lasting the length of a heartbeat, then another, and another, until she wasn't sure if it was her heart or his hooves making the beat. Blind, she had no option but to trust him.

And then he leaped, her heart leaping with him, a sense of weightlessness unlike anything else, even the moment of takeoff in a plane, even being carried by the *bansidhe.* But before Jan could decide if she enjoyed it or not, they were coming down again, landing with a hard splash.

Jan had barely enough time to realize they were underwater—where the hell had there been water that deep?—before water filled her nose and ears, forced its way into her lungs, and she blacked out.

She came to again with a start, coughing even though her lungs were clear of liquid. Jan drew in a cautious breath, half expecting an asthma attack to hit her, but everything was working properly, no coughing or wheezing. Slowly, without moving again, she tried to take stock. Alive, check. She was on her back, staring at a popcorn-textured ceiling that had seen better years. Her fingers ached, and when she lifted them to look, the knuckles were red-swollen with coarse strands of black hair caught under her nails and still wrapped around her fingers.

Martin's mane.

"Ow." She flexed her fingers carefully, wincing, and the strands fell onto the sheet covering her, dark against the over-washed cotton.

She sat up gingerly, feeling her back and shoulders protest, too, and looked around. She was alone in the room. Naked. Naked, damp-haired, and alone in a small room that held only the narrow bed, a single straight-back chair and her.

Getting off the bed was an effort; nothing seemed broken or torn, but she was wobbly-legged, and her stomach told her it had been a while since she'd eaten. It took a moment to remember her last meal: the plate of probably-rabbit and salad, by the campfire.

Her clothing was draped over the back of the chair. She reached for them and then stopped. They were clean. Laundry-clean, smelling not of the soap she'd used in the forest-shower, but of ordinary detergent.

Someone had washed them while she slept.

It was hard to put a sinister interpretation on that—what was she supposed to do, demand her sweaty, muddy clothes back?

Standing naked in the middle of the room, Jan reached overhead and stretched, then tried to touch her toes. Her lower back hurt more than her shoulders, she determined. Flexing slightly, Jan decided that her thighs were achy, but there was no actual pain.

Wherever Martin had taken her, she hadn't been on his back for very long.

"Or, magic," she said out loud, trying to be reasonable about it. "You were under water, after all."

Underwater and not dead. The sensation of not being able to leave his back, legs and butt like they'd been glued there, Martin refusing to let her go. Magic, she thought. Yay. Now to figure out where they were and what the plan was.

"Which you're not going to find standing around here," she told herself, reaching for the clothing again. The clothes were not only clean, they still had the lingering warmth that said they'd been in a dryer not so long ago. So they hadn't been here long?

Dressed, she found her silver bracelet resting under the clothing—the metal had been polished, so bright it looked brand-new. So that answered the question about silver and supernaturals, anyway. She slipped it onto her wrist, considered her still-muddy sneakers, then shook her head and left them there.

Her bladder was insisting—loudly—that she find a bathroom before anything else, even worry.

Thankfully, the door farthest down the narrow hallway was open, revealing familiar ceramic shapes. So far, it was all ordinary, in a way that should have been reassuring, but wasn't. She used the toilet with relief and then borrowed the single toothbrush without guilt, scrubbing her teeth and tongue until her sinuses tingled from the spearmint in the toothpaste. The reflection that greeted her in the mirror looked bedraggled and slightly frantic, but clean. She touched her hair, running fingers through it without hitting any tangles.

Her hair always tangled when she washed it. Always. And the wind that had whipped through the damp strands when Martin started running…

"Magic," she said again, finding that somewhat easier to deal with than the idea that someone had carefully brushed out her hair while she'd been unconscious. Clean clothes were okay, but that was… creepy.

"Still. Nothing broken, nothing too bent." She looked at herself in the mirror again. "If there's coffee and Wi-Fi somewhere, I might make it." Tyler used to say that, when he woke up at her place. Every time. Her throat tightened, and she bit down on her tongue to stop the tears.

"No. None of that. Find Martin, figure out what you're going to do, then do it. No crying. No stopping."

AJ didn't think they had a chance. Maybe supers could do that, keep going even when they knew they were doomed. She had to believe they had a chance. Otherwise, she'd give up now, curl up and not move again.

She looked for mouthwash in the medicine cabinet but found only a half-empty box of adhesive bandages, some off-label aspirin and a sticky, half-full bottle of cherry-red cough syrup. The cabinet below the sink had a plunger, a six-pack of toilet paper and a bottle of cheap gin. Or at least, she assumed it was cheap; it was in a plastic bottle, and the name on the label was one she didn't recognize.

"Nice place you brought us to, Martin," she muttered, and went in search of her companion. The hallway led to two other bedrooms, as bare of furniture as the one she'd woken up in, with small windows that looked out onto another house, with its shades drawn, and then to a large living room, which at least had the basics of a sofa, a wooden rocking chair and a television.

The TV was on but muted, and Martin was nowhere to be seen. There were larger windows here, but before she could examine the view, she was interrupted.

"You're awake. Good. I made breakfast."

Apparently, he had been in the kitchen. She crossed the living room, trying not to notice the pale blue—*bansidhe*-colored—carpeting underfoot, and followed him into the kitchen. Like the rest of the house, it was bare-bones and distinctly un-lived-in. Unlike the others, it smelled good. Bacon and eggs and coffee.

She sat down at the small kitchen table, careful

with her weight until she was certain the rickety wooden chair would hold her. "Where are we?"

"Shannsburgh," he said. "Little town in the middle of nowhere you want to be. A friend of mine owns this place, lets me use it when I need to. Between tenants right now, so we don't have to worry about anyone showing up."

"You have human friends?" The question slipped out before she could think about how it sounded.

Martin served up the bacon and eggs on a plate and put it in front of her. "Some. Not many." He didn't seem to have taken offense.

Jan picked up the bacon, looking at it curiously, surprised that a vegetarian would cook meat. Not that she was complaining, at all. She took a bite before he could change his mind, and the morning got better immediately. The savory crispness overwhelmed the freshness from the toothpaste, but she didn't mind.

She was pretty sure it was fake bacon, though.

He sat down opposite her, a mug of coffee in his hands. "It's difficult. I like people. I really do. And not just in that way, despite what everyone thinks. And people like me. But..." He shrugged, sipped his coffee. "I'm a kelpie."

That word again. A water-dwelling, horse-shaped supernatural; she'd gotten that much from observing, even without the unhelpful and now aborted internet search. "And that means what, exactly? AJ warned me about getting on your back—" she thought ad-

mitting that was safe enough "—but I did okay.…
I mean, other than passing out." She thought about
asking now how long they'd been in the water, how
long she'd been *under* water, but suspected it would
just make her hyperventilate.

"I'm a kelpie," he repeated, as though that should
be enough explanation.

It wasn't. She picked up her fork and started eating while she waited.

"It's… I like people," he repeated, then his entire
face lit in a faint smile. "Some people, anyway. I want
to keep them with me." The smile faded. "That…
doesn't end well."

"Because…?" AJ's warning and the feeling she'd
had when Martin had first shifted, being drawn to get
on his back, and the smell of water, and the memory
of water filling her lungs, it all stirred and swirled
and she put down her fork and stared at him. "Because you go underwater. And they can't get off your
back. And you drown them."

"It's a thing."

"A *thing?*" Her voice rose in disbelief.

"A thing. Yeah." He shifted, clearly uncomfortable
with the direction the conversation had taken. "Look,
I don't pick on you for your habits, do I?"

Picking up women and killing them was only a
habit if you were a sociopath. "I…" Jan decided that
if she followed this particular discussion any fur-

ther, she'd definitely start to hyperventilate, and since she'd left her spare inhaler in her bag, that—

"Oh, god, my bag." It was easier to focus on that than what Martin had just admitted to. "My computer. Where's my laptop?"

"The water ruined it. I'm sorry. I have someone bringing another laptop. You can work on another laptop, right?"

"Yeah. It should be fine." She'd used the same password on all of the accounts, since she didn't care if someone hacked them. "Someone?" She took another bite of her breakfast, and her stomach rumbled, urging her to eat more, faster, now.

"I said I have friends. Human ones."

Friends who knew better than to get on his back. Maybe the friends could get her a new inhaler. Or go to her apartment and get her meds. Shit. Oh, shit. She forced herself to calm down. If she stayed calm and stayed still, she'd be okay. The last attack had been set off by the dust in the warehouse; this place was empty but clean. She'd be okay. She'd get his friends to refill her prescription, and she'd be fine.

She'd been on his back. And not drowned. Had that been why the blindfold…? Or was that just so she wouldn't panic when they went into the water?

"Your friends…they know what you are?"

He shook his head and reached out to touch her hand, the one holding the fork, and stilled while she talked. "No. Only you."

Jan felt a shift of something inside her, weirdly warming. She'd never had anyone's secret before. Not like this. Never mind that he'd told her under duress, that she was here only to save Tyler; she had a secret of his, something his other friends didn't know.

Yeah, that he was a murderer. A serial murderer, probably, if…

She started eating again, focusing on the food rather than what she was feeling.

"When Craig gets here with the new computer, we can get started again," he said, all businesslike. "See if anyone replied to the accounts, and follow up on them. Um." His voice flattened. "How do we follow up?"

She finished the eggs and picked up the second slice of bacon, crunching it with satisfaction.

"Some people like to go back and forth in email first, or phone calls. But you can cut to the chase and meet them right off. You suggest somewhere local, and public, not in your own neighborhood, just in case they're skeevy…" She stopped. "But they're going to be skeevy, aren't they? That's the point? But they're also going to want to meet up fast, too. Oh. What if they're not local? How—"

"They're coming from another plane," he said, his voice still smooth, not showing any exasperation at what was a particularly dumb question. "However they're opening portals, they're able to go to specific areas, directly to the person they're seducing.

We didn't understand why or how, but you just explained that: they get the person to choose a place to meet specifically." Martin shook his head, a clump of hair falling over his forehead, exactly the way it did in his other form. "Oh, that must have made them gleeful, to know that their prey would be sitting there waiting for them...."

"But how? I mean, okay, they're using the internet, I get that, and, yeah, it would make it damn easy for them to focus on targets, the same way scammers do; whoever's dumb enough to bite." Like Tyler. She shut that thought off and focused on the puzzle part of it. "But if they're in another...world? A parallel universe? Whatever. The question is, then how are they connecting? I mean, some kind of spell, hooking them up..." They'd said they didn't work spells, but maybe preters were different. "How did they even find out about the internet, much less dating sites?"

Martin looked at her, and his face went utterly blank. "That's part of what we need to know now, how they're doing it and how to shut it down."

"Oh. Right." Kelpies, at least, didn't seem to have much use for theoretical tech discussions. She felt congestion build, either from the thought of what they were doing, or some dust they'd disturbed in the house, and took a sip of the coffee, letting the hot liquid settle her lungs back down again. Maybe her bag was around here somewhere, maybe her inhaler hadn't been too badly damaged, maybe it would dry out and she'd be able to use it, after all.

Too many maybes.

Then she asked the question that had been hiding behind her thoughts all the time. "And if nobody bites on our bait?"

He sighed, leaned back in his chair, which creaked alarmingly, making her brace for its inevitable crash, and stared at the ceiling. "Then we try again. And again."

"Uh-huh." She decided that his chair was more sturdy than it sounded, and leaned forward, waving her fork at him. "Look, Martin, I have a life, you know. A job. People are going to notice if I disappear, too." Unlike Tyler, she wasn't the sort to suddenly give notice, or disappear. Her friends would worry…wouldn't they? Or would they think she'd run off to join him?

He looked at her, those dark eyes and long face mournful. "We thought you wanted to help your leman?"

"I do. Of course I do. I…"

She shoved the rest of the bacon in her mouth, no longer enjoying the taste. That wasn't fair.

And it didn't matter. The truth was, even if she wanted to leave, she didn't know where Shannsburgh was, and if her laptop was ruined, then so was her phone, and god knows if her credit card or ATM would work, so how would she get home? She could go into a police station and announce she'd been kidnapped, she supposed. But something inside her flinched from that. She'd have to tell them about Martin and AJ then, or risk giving a description of someone who might be innocent, and both options made her feel as if she'd swallowed a lead weight.

She knew she wasn't crazy. She was pretty sure that she wasn't crazy. But trying to explain this to anyone else... She had a lot of friends, casual and otherwise, but none of them would believe any of this. They'd just think that her worry about Tyler had led to a terminal crack-up.

"Huh. You said, AJ said, this has been going on for months, or maybe longer, but months since you've been paying attention."

Martin nodded.

"Is there anyone else doing this, like me, the trying to catch a preter thing? Or...just us?"

He didn't want to tell her, she could read him that well at least.

"Martin."

"You're the third human I know about, who poked around when someone went missing, who was willing to do something. There might've been others. I didn't know them."

He was using the past tense. "The turncoats got them." They had told her that. Got them...ate them. That was why Martin had taken her here, to be safe.

She almost laughed. Be safe, so she could be used as bait.

"The turncoats, they were told where to find those humans, right? Someone betrayed them, the same way we were betrayed, only earlier, before you could even get there. That's what AJ thinks. Right? One of your people."

"Maybe. I don't know. I didn't want to believe it, but…" Martin pushed his coffee away from him in a rough gesture. "We may not have much use for humanity, but we like our independence. We're clannish, breedish. The preters…they think everything should fall under them, like vassal states to their magnificence.

"The gnomes, all right, I sort of get it; they're little pricks always out for themselves, they never got along with the other races, not even in the back when. So I can see where a preter could make them an offer they'd accept, and everyone else go hang. But one of us? Selling out to those bastards? Once, yeah, it could have been an accidental slip, but three times makes it a conspiracy, right?"

And a fourth time almost meant her death.

"The only other explanation is that the preters know, and if they do, we're screwed. They already have all the other advantages; the only one we have is that they can't predict what we're going to do."

"Mainly because we don't know, ourselves," she offered.

Martin missed the humor in that, nodding his head seriously in agreement. "AJ has a plan. But he doesn't tell us, only the bits we need now."

Jan was less certain AJ had a plan, or at least, a thought-out big picture kind of thing. But that kind of big picture thing wasn't her strength, either, so…they knew what they needed to do. She'd focus on that.

"You want more coffee?" he asked, getting up with his own mug in hand. She shook her head and covered her own mug with her hand; coffee was good for keeping the asthma controlled, but the last thing she needed was a caffeine hyper on top of her nerves.

"We're all kind of…disorganized. We don't talk to each other much, either, not just humans, and we're territorial and AJ says hidebound. *Lupin* are different, they run in a pack, so they're used to taking orders and stuff like that. And thinking about groups, not selfishly. He's one of the ones who figured it all out," Martin added. "Saw something wrong, dug into it, got us organized despite ourselves."

That didn't surprise her at all. And he was probably right about there being a traitor, someone else who thought the world might be better off with preters in it. But unless Martin was the one spilling secrets—and if he was, she was dead, anyway—they were safe. Right?

As safe as she could be, working with someone who thought drowning humans was a "thing." She could feel the hysteria start to burble up again and changed the topic.

"How many others do you think there've been? I mean, all the people who might have been worried about their family, their friends disappearing, since this all started?" She thought about her conversation with the cop, god, only yesterday? Tyler hadn't even been missing a week, but it felt like a month. "How many are we talking about, do you think—ten? A dozen? A hundred?"

"Don't know." His blithe unconcern surprised her; he had seemed so impassioned before.

"Do you think that the turncoats got them, too?"

"Don't know," Martin said again. "Maybe. I don't know. I didn't know them."

He didn't know them, so he didn't care. It was because they were human. They weren't real to him, didn't matter. Supernaturals might not be soulless, but...Toba hadn't been like this, or AJ, or even Elsa.

She was starting to understand why the others had warned her about Martin. If he'd been human, she might have thought him charming but sort of cold...yeah, exactly like the description of a lot of serial killers. But they also set him to protect her, so he must be trustworthy. Right? Jan's thoughts fluttered like a bird in a trap, then settled. He knew her: that was the key. Sociopath or just supernatural, she mattered to him now.

"Lucky me," she muttered. "So we're dealing with

preters who want to enslave us, turncoats who'd be happy to eat us, some unknown spy or spies, and an impossible task that, let's face it, even if I somehow manage to nab us a preter, you still have to get the information out of it, somehow. What makes you think I'm going to do any better than the last humans who agreed to help you?"

"Because you have something they didn't," Martin said, suddenly cheerful again.

"Yeah? What's that?" But she had a feeling she already knew what he was going to say.

"Me." His tone was smooth, reassuring, and filled with absolute confidence in his own wonderfulness.

"Oh. Lucky me," she said again, and ate the last piece of bacon.

He had run. There had been no plan, no thought in his head, no inkling of rebellion in the scraped-dry hollow of his soul. They had been walking through the garden in the misty afternoon, speaking nonsense he barely registered, his mind still scraped and sore from the most recent session in the briar-chair, his fingers laced with hers. One moment he had been content at her side, obedient as a dog, and the next— like a dog—he had scented something, some passing breeze, something familiar and haunting, a tune he had nearly forgotten.

His body had moved without volition, bolting off the soft trail, downhill across the soft grass and into the woods. Two steps in, they were so thickly planted that he couldn't see where he was going, the undergrowth blocking his sight and pulling at his limbs as though to stop him. And yet his feet were unerring, following his nose downhill as though drawn to something, the lure of some stream waiting at the base, clear cool water summoning him to lap at its shores.

He did not know, he did not think, he only knew that he needed to be there, he needed to follow that scent, find the source....

Something hit him, hard, in the left side, and he went down into wet mulch and mud, hard enough to stun him for a second. That second was all it took. His brain screamed at him to get up, but the weight of something heavy and rank on his back, heavy breath dripping onto his neck, kept him facedown and motionless.

If he moved, something at the base of his brain told him, he would die.

"Yours, Stjerne?" A male voice, light but unmistakable. It came from above him, not the weight holding him down.

"Mine."

Her voice, slightly breathless and tight with anger. He had displeased her. Why had he done that? Why had he run?

His captor hauled him over, dropping him hard on his back. One of them, from the shape of the face, but more slightly built than Stjerne and the others, and wearing clothing better suited for hunting than the cold palace. The thought—that there were more of them beyond the silver walls and quiet gardens—shook him for a second, a sense of wonder and fear too great to handle. No. Quiet. Hollow. The flicker of rebellion gone, emotions washed back to gray, and he rested his cheek on the dirt. Dimly, he saw the thing that had held him down slink off to one side. A beast—hound-shaped, but with a human head and hands: hairless, with mottled gray-green skin that seemed to shift even as he looked at it. So he looked away again, holding to the hollow quiet as though that would save him.

"Where did you think you were going, pet?" Stjerne stepped closer, towering over him, demanding that he roll over to look at her. He opened his mouth to explain, that he'd had no choice, he had to follow the scent—

The first blow took him by surprise: he had not seen her move. She made sure that he saw the next, and the third, her nails raking him across the face so hard he felt the blood rising through the cuts before he tasted it dripping into his mouth.

He lifted his head, and the tease of that half-known scent drifted under his nostrils again, fading, then lost in the taste of bittersweet iron, and then even that was gone.

The soft-spoken male hauled him to his feet, even

though he was an easy foot taller and bulkier, and held him there, the blood running freely from the cuts, splattering onto his pants.

"Do you want to keep it, or should I feed it to the dogs?"

Stjerne considered him, her lovely face composed again. She lifted one finger to her mouth and licked the blood off of it delicately.

"We're almost done with the cleansing," she said. "It seems a shame to waste all that work. And he is…occasionally diverting." Her eyes narrowed, and she looked directly at him, the finger coming forward to lift his chin. "But if you ever try that again, human, if you ever defy me? I will shred the skin from your flesh, and the flesh from your bones, and gnaw on what remains, while you yet live. Do you understand me?"

She was terrifying and beautiful, and when she drew him forward for a kiss, he fell into it entirely and let it consume him.

At their feet, the hound-shaped beast whined, as though it knew it had been deprived of a meal.

Chapter 8

First dates were hell. It didn't seem to matter if they were "real" or the setup to a sting, there was still that utter agony of awkwardness and fear, with a dollop of stomach-churning anticipation.

Jan stood in front of the restaurant door and steeled her nerves, then walked inside with as much breezy confidence as she could fake. "Hi. I'm Janelle." Close enough to her own name that she'd remember to respond to it, but not so close that a preter could use it to hold on to her. That was part of their glamour, Martin had told her: a "true name" thing. Jan didn't understand it, but at this point, there was a lot she was just taking on faith and hope and a heaping dose of WTF.

The man, who matched his photo reasonably well,

offered her his hand to shake, "Hi, Janelle. I'm David. Obviously." He laughed, embarrassed. It was a nice laugh, and as much as Jan wanted him to be a preter, for him to lead her to where they were keeping Tyler, she also didn't want a guy who seemed so nice to be some inhuman evil creature.

But then, the preters would seem nice, wouldn't they? Or, no, not nice: Sexy, maybe sweet, maybe a little dangerous, but appealing. The only way she could tell if someone wasn't a preter, would be if they were jerks.

Jan wanted to apologize, to turn around and leave, but that wasn't an option. The fact that she had felt like that on dates with—as far as she knew—totally human guys made it a little easier to go on. But only a little.

Knowing Martin was nearby helped, too.

Martin. Her focus drifted, although she was able to maintain her share of small talk about the weather and how nice the restaurant seemed, as they waited for their table to be ready. What was she going to do about Martin?

The first night in the rental house, still shaking and confused, Jan had gone to bed, and tears had overtaken her, hard, hot tears. She had tried to stifle them against the pillow, letting the shudders take her, silently, until she'd fallen asleep. She had thought she'd been successful, until she'd awakened to find Martin sharing the bed, her hands held in his, her head resting against his shoulder. At some point, while she'd been crying, he had come in and held her.

It had been oddly intimate, disturbingly so, but she had rolled off the bed and gone to take her shower, and when she had come back, he'd been gone, making ostentatious noises in the kitchen.

They'd not spoken of it, not when his friend—an older guy in a suit, not what she had been expecting at all—had come by with two secondhand laptops, not when they'd spent hours surfing from site to site, sending out lures and evaluating the bites. Not when she'd tried to explain to him what she did for a living, putting out fires and trying to convince her co-workers that she was at home, safe and busy, with him hanging over her shoulder, being way too in her personal space.

Not even when he'd lain down beside her that night, uninvited. He'd slid under the covers and gathered her in his arms, her face resting against his chest. He hadn't spoken, hadn't tried anything, just held her until her breathing eased, and she'd fallen asleep.

Sociopath, maybe. Killer, self-admitted. Not human, obviously. Not to be trusted…but she did.

The house they'd ended up in wasn't as bad as Martin had said, but it wasn't all that great, either. Jan had ventured outside the second day, just to not be in the house for a little while, and been quickly bored by the quiet roads and run-down, too-quiet houses. But it was less than an hour into the city by bus, so they could continue the search without having to relocate.

And nobody would think to look for them there. Nobody—not even AJ, Martin had said—knew that he knew the owner.

Three of the females who had responded to their fake overtures had seemed like reasonable possibilities, but a basic web search had turned up too much of a digital footprint for them to not be human. There was a fourth, but she was being coy about setting up a time and place to meet, which also weighed against her: Martin didn't think a preter would waste time playing hard to get.

Meanwhile, this was the first male they had thought a likely target.

The hostess gestured to them, and David indicated that she should go first, following the woman to their table, where a waitress appeared before they'd even had a chance to open the menus.

"Getcha folks anything to drink?"

Jan desperately wanted a beer. But the last thing she could do right now was let down her defenses at all. Just like a real date, she thought—don't drink until you know what's going on. Except usually all she'd had to worry about was that the guy was a sleaze or that she'd be bored.

She'd welcome a little boredom right now.

"Iced coffee for me, please." It had warmed up

a little outside, and she was sweating slightly. Or maybe that was just nerves, in which case the caffeine wasn't going to help.

"Same here."

That was one of the warning signs, Martin had said. If he tried to mirror what she did, make her feel an immediate connection.

"That's what you do on a real date, too," she had told the kelpie, annoyed. "Something more helpful, please?"

"Mirroring," he had repeated. "That's exactly what they do, AJ says. And asking about your family, how close you were to them. They want someone who has no ties here, no one to miss them if they disappear."

That had hurt. A lot. Tyler had someone. He'd had *her*.

Clearly, it hadn't been enough.

"Also, look in their eyes."

"Their eyes."

"They're like us, in some ways—different forms—and some of them are more human than others. But the eyes give them away."

Like Toba's. The owl-man had seemed mostly normal, until you saw his golden-rimmed eyes. And AJ's eyes were the cunning, careful eyes of a wolf. But Martin's were normal enough. Or maybe she had just gotten used to them? Maybe that was how he lured his victims....

Now, leaning across the table, she tilted her head up and looked into David's eyes.

Normal. Brown and round and black-pupiled and black-lashed, and quite nice-looking, actually, but human.

If she looked into Martin's eyes for too long, she felt dizzy.

"So. Tell me about yourself," David said. "You do websites, right?"

David was an orthodontist. She should have known from the start: no preter would ever claim to be an orthodontist.

"I design and support websites, yes. I work for a company that does that, rather. It's not as exciting as it sounds." It didn't sound very exciting at all, actually. She just happened to be very good at it.

Her shoulder muscles twitched, and she was aware of the fact that this was wasted time: he wasn't a preter, and she didn't care about David the Orthodontist, no matter how nice a human he seemed to be, or how pretty his eyes were. Or how nice his hands were. She seemed to be noticing hands—Martin's hands, for one. How something that transferred into hooves could be so smooth and gentle, she didn't know, but they were. Like a sculptor's hands, she imagined. Although she'd never met a sculptor, to check.

Their drinks came, they ordered food, and she turned the question back on him, asking about his job and faking a reasonable amount of interest while she tried to figure out how soon she could bail.

Halfway through their sandwiches, she excused herself to go to the ladies' room, hoping that Martin, who was allegedly lurking nearby, would be around, and she could improvise a sudden emergency or something. But the kelpie had either decided that David wasn't useful on his own and left, or he utterly failed to pick up her "come rescue me" vibes.

His failure to show up stung more than she'd expected. First Tyler leaving her, then Martin…Jan twitched away that thought. It wasn't the same thing. At all. Martin was there.

The kelpie was dangerous. She knew he was dangerous. Not human. But he had stayed, and he had held himself back, not killing her, and he'd held her when she'd cried, and, god, this was fucked up, but no more than anything else that had happened, so, okay?

So she'd trust him.

Jan washed her hands and splashed water on her face, and stared at herself in the mirror, wondering if she should bother reapplying lipstick, or touching up her foundation, a cheap shade she'd bought at the local drugstore the day before, when she'd gotten her asthma meds replaced.

She swiped on more color, as though reapplying armor, and left the relative sanctuary of the ladies' room.

On the way back to the table, some floating bit of conversation caught her ear.

"So, Nathan, you're an only child? That must be lonely."

Jan changed her direction, circling around as though she needed to go outside, and looked over her shoulder. A man and a woman, sitting at a table. The woman was leaning in, her hand on her companion's. She was attractive, honey-blond hair cut short to her ears and slightly spiky, a heart-shaped face, and long neck leading to a rather low-cut black blouse. But it was her intensity that caught Jan's attention. Intensity was one of the hallmarks, too, Martin had said.

Jan stared, shamelessly, and the woman must have sensed it. She raised her head, looking away from the man and around the restaurant, like a cat sniffing out a mouse.

Then she turned her head, looking toward Jan, and Jan's breath caught. Too far away to be sure, but there was a glitter in those eyes that wasn't human. Not if you knew what you were looking for.

Martin's eyes had that glitter, too, sometimes.

She looked away, hoping that the woman would think she'd been rude, rather than hunting. When she looked back again, cautiously, the blonde had gone back to her companion.

Her prey.

Jan's heartbeat sped up, and she made her way back to her table in a blur. Apparently, she'd been gone too long, because David had finished his sand-wich and was working on a second coffee, and looked a little annoyed. Her inability to focus on the con-versation didn't help, either, and when they finally parted, there was no "we should get together again, I'll call you," just a pleasant enough, "this was nice."

Not that it mattered, since she'd given him a fake name and email address.

Once Jan left the restaurant, she should have met up with Martin and gone back to square one. But there was a preter in the restaurant, right there, with a human male who looked to be buying her line, without any clue what was going to happen to him.

Jan wasn't impulsive. She thought things through and planned, and once decided, she stayed the course. But the past week had been such a chaos of improb-able and impossible—she had flown, and seen mon-sters, and met people only to have them die, and her only help was a kelpie who had disappeared on her.

And there was a preter not ten feet away from her, about to lead a human to his fate…maybe. Or maybe she was hallucinating. Everything that was happen-ing…without Martin around, without the weirdly re-assuring presence of AJ or even Elsa, Jan started to doubt herself. Had any of this even happened?

She found herself walking back into the restau-rant, avoiding the hostess, and heading for the table where the blonde preter and her prey were sitting.

"Nate?"

The man looked up. He wasn't particularly good-looking, with an oversize chin and a nose that had been broken at least once, but his eyes were deep blue and totally human.

"Nate, it is you! I'm so glad, I've been trying to find you since forever, but it's like you disappeared! I'm sorry, I don't mean to intrude, but it's so good to see you. It's been, what, five years? Six?" She was babbling, the words falling out of her as though someone else were talking. "Here, give me your number, and I'll call you! We can catch up. The entire family will be so thrilled." She thought about mentioning something more about family but didn't want to push it. Enough that the preter knew that someone would miss him, if he were taken. She risked a glance at the woman—the preter—and thought she saw a look of annoyance or disgust cross her face, quickly hidden behind a polite facade.

Good, Jan thought, and then smiled brightly at Nate, who—not wanting to admit that he had no idea who she was—had written a number on his napkin and handed it to her.

"Great! So lovely to run into you! You two have fun, we'll catch up tomorrow, Nate!"

Jan tucked the napkin into her pocket and fled the restaurant, praying that nothing triggered an asthma attack until she was away from the preter. She was halfway down the street before she realized she was being flanked—and not by Martin, either.

"AJ." She breathed a sigh of relief. "And…I don't know you?"

"Stop talking. You talk too much. What the hell were you doing?"

AJ sounded furious, his snout twitching under the partial disguise of his hoodie.

"What was I doing? What were you doing? Where the hell have you been? And where's Martin?"

"You alerted the preter."

"I did not. As far as she knows, I'm just some dippy-headed human who interfered with her guy-nabbing."

"You really think you dissuaded her from her target?"

The other super hadn't spoken yet, and Jan wondered if he even could: his face was even less human-appearing than AJ's, with fangs that curled out of his mouth at an uncomfortable-looking angle. They didn't seem as though they could let him chew much, so…

A thought occurred to her that maybe it wasn't flesh this super ingested, and she inched a bit closer to AJ. Meat-eaters were somehow more acceptable than blood-suckers. Which, on the face of it, was insane, but somehow, the *lupin* made her feel safer. Even when he was bitching her out.

"All you did was make her more cautious—now it's going to be even harder for us to get to her. What were you thinking?"

"Of saving her victim!"

They'd reached the end of a street, where a large black limo waited, the passenger-side doors open.

"Get in," the other super said, not so much a suggestion as an order.

She got in.

Martin was already there, sitting in the backseat, and he reached out for her, his hand taking her own. It should have been creepy, the way his actions echoed the preter's in the restaurant, and it was creepy, a little, but Jan still held on like a lifeline.

"You should have come out here and gotten us, and we could have made a plan. Instead, you went gung ho, and she ran. The moment you left the restaurant, she up and disappeared." AJ had gotten in behind her, sitting on the seat opposite them. The other super had gotten in front, she assumed, or been left behind to guard their flank, as the car pulled away from the curb and slid into the afternoon traffic.

Jan had only ever been in a limo once before, for her prom. She'd felt nervous and needed to throw up then, too.

"I'm sorry."

AJ growled. "No, you're not. But you won't do it again, will you?"

He was right, on both accounts. "No."

The *lupin* sighed and leaned back, understanding her negative for agreement. "This car costs a fortune, you know that? But it keeps us moving, and it's harder to track than a bus. I take it the date was a bust?"

Jan nodded her head, still shaking a little from the adrenaline, not even wondering how AJ knew what they'd been doing. Martin must have told him, when he'd disappeared. "He was human. And for all our planning, I just stumbled across one today, about to munch on her own prey."

Martin shifted, and she shot him a glare. AJ or not, she still hadn't forgiven him for disappearing on her back at the restaurant. "How many are there, and why can't we hunt them down directly?" She had assumed that preters were rare, elusive, and needed drawing out. That had been the only damn reason she'd agreed to be bait.

Well, that and they hadn't given her any time to refuse. "Look, you asked me because I knew tech and could figure out what they're doing, lay a trail for them to follow like some kind of rat trap. But the truth is that technology doesn't always speed things up—especially if you're waiting for someone else on the other end. This bait-and-hook scheme isn't going to work. It takes too long—there were three others I've got lunches set up for, but that's four days and they could all be busts—and you said Tyler doesn't have much time, not if we're going to get him back."

Back in useful condition. They had said if the preters held him too long… No. The thought of Tyler looking at her, empty-eyed, nobody home anymore, was not acceptable. Even though she was furious at him, she wanted him to be aware when she bitched him out for being such a skanky two-timer.

"You're suggesting that we should canvass every coffee shop and café in the city, on the off chance a preter shows up? And hope that she or he doesn't scent us and spook?" AJ's scorn was immediate. "Even assuming that they come here on a regular basis, without knowing where they are going to meet their prey, and when… We can't scent each other out of an entire city, but in close proximity, the moment we know they're around—they know we're there, too. That's why we need humans to do this, Jan. Otherwise we wouldn't have involved you at all."

The car swerved, just as she was going to respond to that, and Martin's hand on hers squeezed tightly. It might have been a reaction to the car's movement… or it might have been a warning. Jan, still smarting from AJ's earlier words, took it as a warning, and bit back what she was going to say.

"We need one alive. We need it bound and within our grasp, to get the truth from it."

"Any preter?"

"One of the hunters," AJ amended. "One of those who know how to cross over—and can tell us how to shut down their connection, to expose them for what they are."

"And rescue Tyler."

"And rescue Tyler, yes."

Jan felt a flicker of unease at how her boyfriend was becoming an afterthought, but forced it down. This was the only chance she had. They might have their agenda, but getting Ty home was hers.

"All right. Fine. Bait and snatch. But if it's mainly women doing the hunting, which it seems like from the responses we were getting, what then? I can't go in wearing drag—" well, she could, but she didn't think that would be effective "—and if they can tell you're there—" which explained why Martin hadn't been in the restaurant with her, and it would have been nice if he'd thought to tell her that! "—then how are we going to approach them?"

"Set up the date, and then scope them out from a distance. They might scent us, but they're on our territory, they have to assume it could be an innocent walk-by." AJ was talking as if she was a slightly dim ten-year-old for not figuring that out.

"Uh-huh." If she were trying to kidnap humans in order to invade, she wouldn't assume anything, and she suspected the preters wouldn't, either. AJ sounded and acted tough, but she suddenly wondered if he really was hard enough. So far, everything they'd done had been defensive, not offensive. Even the attempts to lure them were bait-and-wait, passive, not attacking the problem at its source.

The car turned another corner, and Jan wondered, for the first time, if her supernatural allies actually knew what the hell they were doing.

"How close do you have to be, before they smell you?"

"Smell?"

"You know what I mean." She was tired and as annoyed as he was—maybe even more so because it hadn't been his apartment that had been broken in to and god-knows-what and all her stuff lost and she might not even have a job anymore. And it wasn't his boyfriend who was being held captive by evil mind-sucking elves. If she had to pick up the slack and figure out what needed to be done... Well, it wouldn't be the first time, but he got her into this, damn it. He and Martin, and Tyler, who couldn't keep it in his pants.

"We're not sure," AJ said. "It's been a while since...well. It's better to stay out of line-of-sight. A lot probably depends on if they're looking for us, same as if we're looking for them. And thanks to you, they're paranoid now. They'll be more careful."

"Fine. I get it." This wasn't the best plan, but it was the only plan they had. Right now. "Give me a damn laptop and somewhere with connectivity, and I'll get you some more chances."

She had to. Tyler was depending on her.

Chapter 9

He had woken in the starlight, restless and alone. The air was still and quiet; no insects sang here at night, no birds at dawn. Drawing on his robe, he wandered down the hallway, the rose-colored tile floor cool under his feet, until he came to the archway that led into the garden.

She was there, sitting on a stone bench that looked out, away from the sleeping garden and out into the misty fields beyond. He had no idea what lay beyond those fields, if there was a city filled with life and lights, or farmlands, or nothing at all, the world fading out into mist until there was only the void.

"You're restless." Her voice was a rope that drew him to her, and he did not even think to resist.

"Something bothers you."

"And that drew you from slumber, and to my side."
She sounded more thoughtful than usual, less amused
at his expense. He knew that about her now, that she
took amusement from his confusion and pain, and
did not resent it. How could he? Her whim was his
reason.

"I have been here too long, and I grow weary of
these walls," she said. "Weary and fretful, and I do
not like either sensation. I know the logic, I approve
of the reason, I agreed to the limits, agreed to this
experiment, and what I must sacrifice. But we are not
meant to be caged, penned like beasts, told whither
and when we might go. Not this long, without respite.
Not once we have tasted the airs of freedom."

He had no idea what she was talking about. She
wasn't speaking to him, for all that he was her only
company.

"He orders us to his bidding as though it were his
right to do so, and yet I may not go out into the world,
not with my work undone. He is fretful, worried, bitter, and I have no desire to listen to the others bleat-
ing at my failures while they sit and do nothing. And
all the while it sits there, taunting us. *She* taunts us."

He sat, quiet and empty, letting her words fill him,
direct him. He must have done it well, because she
turned to look at him, considering. Something inside
him quailed, some least remnant of fear, and then was
silenced by her presence.

"But, yes, I have options they do not; options that could give me an advantage." Her beautiful eyes were now clouded, as though she were looking somewhere that he could not see. "Yes. If it could be done, it would put me ahead, perhaps be the chance I need. I could claim it as a test, and none might gainsay me. All I need do is manage it."

Her voice softened, and he could see that she was aware of him again. Her entire demeanor changed, from distant to coaxing, enticing. "Would you accompany me, sweet man? Would you walk beyond these gardens, your hand in mine?"

There was a moment of doubt, something like cold sweat in his mind: leave? Go beyond the silvery walls and the pale-misted gardens? No. Oh, no. He could not leave. He could not leave; there was nowhere else for him to go. Leaving was… But…the frantic skittering of his thoughts halted, running against the wall of her words. She was leaving? If she left and asked him to go with her, if he were to accompany her—that would be all right, surely. He would not be punished for that, not if she commanded. But she had not commanded; she had asked. Was this a trick? A test? What was the right answer?

Fear and love were too intermingled to unbind. "I would not be parted from you." She was cold and cruel in her love, but she had claimed him, protected him. Without her, he would be at the mercy of the others, the ones with the hard hands and fierce tools, and mercy was not a thing they knew.

"You will walk with me through the veil? Take my hand and carry me through?"

He had no understanding of what she asked, but he knew what she wanted him to say. "Yes."

Her smile was clear and bright, the sun finally broken through the ever-present fog. "Excellent. Come."

She was standing, without his sensing her move, but he was used to that by now. Something moved in his memory, sluggish and deep; they had done this before? No. He would have remembered that, surely. There was nothing save the cold palace, the gardens and the thorn chair. And her.

He placed his hand in hers, the cool, smooth fingers closing around his, pulling him to his feet and into—not an embrace, but an enclosure, her arms going around him, sliding into place like… He could almost remember the thing it reminded him of now, almost, but the memory was hidden behind mist and thorn-sharp pain. He had learned his lesson well: the only way out was to forget. He let the memory go.

There was only now, only her holding him, her breath cool on his neck, and then they were walking off the path, into the mist, the dampness wrapping around them.

"Lead the way," she said to him, urging him forward, and he didn't understand, didn't know how he could lead rather than follow, but once commanded, his feet found the path underneath them, step by step.

"Yes." Her voice curled around inside him, her very self carried within him, the prickling feeling in his flesh as though the thorns were within him, pushing out.

There was a shout, distant and muffled, as though someone had taken note of their leaving and objected, and then the mist thinned into nothingness, his skin burned, his lungs cramped for air, his eyes and nose dried out, and they were…

Elsewhere.

The noise took him by surprise—like a blow he'd felt before, his body cringing in reflex until it recognized it as sound. It washed around him, did not hurt him. Her hand was still in his, the skin oddly warm and wet against his skin as the screeching, shuddering noise was replaced by someone yelling at them, furious and scared.

"You morons!"

He wore pants, and a shirt, and shoes upon his feet; he did not remember changing, from that moment in the starlight garden to this moment under too-bright sunlight, but he did not have time to question it, or the feeling of familiarity the clothing gave him, as he pulled her out of the roadway, away from the traffic and onto the relative safety of the sidewalk.

The cars—yes, cars—moved past them, and other than a few odd looks from people passing by, no one paid them any heed. He knew this, but he couldn't recognize it, once the moment of danger was past, couldn't remember how to act.

"Walk," she told him, and he did, some instinct setting his feet upon a certain route. Down this street, past that storefront, the display of bicycles and mannequins that were different from the last time he had seen them.

When was that time? How did he know this place? His brain turned, but nothing more fell out. This place was both familiar and alien, and he did not know what to do.

Stjerne raised her face to the sunlight, her pale features flushed as though she had a fever, and her smile sent shivers through him. As though he had drawn her attention back to himself, she tilted her face and directed that smile at him. "Take me somewhere I can get a cup of coffee."

For an instant, he wanted only to run, to flee: she was a beast, baring too-sharp teeth and intending him harm. The instinct passed; she trusted him to lead, to keep her from harm. He focused on that and let the odd sense of having been here before fade into background noise in his head, just enough of a hum to lead him and not enough to interfere. Her hand on his arm was the only thing that was real, even as other people moved past and around them, cars and bicycles passing them on the street, the smells in the air harder, stronger than the misted air he had been breathing....

"Here."

A small café with tables outside, people sitting with dogs that looked up and studied them warily as they walked by, through the door with a gently tingling bell overhead, and then they were surrounded by the thick smell of coffee and pastries.

Something at the base of his spine twitched, a deep, instinctive longing for something lost. Her hand moved, as though she sensed it, to cover that spot.

The longing stilled, filled by her presence, and she led him to a table at the front of the café, where a couple was just getting up.

"Wait here," she said, drawing out a chair for him.

He sat, obedient, and waited.

If first dates were hell, blown dates were purgatory. The café was bustling, people waiting for tables. Jan sat in the wrought-iron chairs that were prettier than they were comfortable, and tried not to fidget. She hated waiting even on good days, and now, with the time ticking off constantly in the back of her head, a monotone of "Tyler's in danger, Tyler's in danger," she begrudged every minute wasted.

He'd been missing for fifteen days. She'd asked Elsa once if time ran the same for preters, in their sphere or whatever, as it did for humans. Elsa's discomfort with the question had made her not ask again.

Maybe, maybe, time was slower there, like legends said. If so, maybe Tyler thought he'd only been gone for fifteen hours.

This was her third "bait-date" in two days, and she suspected that this one was going to blow her off. Had she sounded too needy? Had she rushed too hard, trying to follow AJ's instructions? Whatever the reason, the guy was twenty minutes late and hadn't called or texted.

"This isn't going to work." The couple at the table next to her gave her a pitying look, her coffee cup untouched, the chair opposite her unused. It seemed as though the café was filled with couples, old and young, and she was the only one seated alone. Waiting. Unwanted.

Tick. Tick. *Tyler's in danger. Tyler's in danger.* And she sat here, and waited for her quarry to come to her.

"Damn it, AJ, I told you this wasn't going to work." But when challenged, she hadn't been able to come up with anything better: short of sending the supers out into the streets to find another preter, and that, she had been told, was not possible. They had only so many volunteers, and more than half of them were not the sort you let out in the general human public. And once they got too close, they'd spook them off, anyway.

No, it had to be her. Even when a woman responded, they sent Jan in, to check her out.

"If you can't convince more of your own people to help, why not bring in more humans?" she had asked, at her wit's end. "I'm only one person—you could cover three or four times as much ground, just by bringing in more people. And a guy would be able to go right up to them, be proper bait."

AJ had stared at her, then stalked off; she could almost see the sway of a tail, stiff with annoyance, as he walked away. Martin, who had been sitting beside her as she worked on the laptop, only shook his head.

"You're right. Of course you're right. And how are we to convince them? If you were to approach even your closest friend and say 'we need to rescue my leman from these creatures who have taken him captive…' How would she respond?"

He was right, of course. Most would have her tanked to the eyelids ten minutes after she'd finished her story, convinced that she had lost her mind. And yet, Jan had almost called Glory, anyway; Glory of all her friends might be hardheaded and clear-eyed enough to see that Jan was not crazy, had not had a nervous breakdown or psychotic episode. Or she might play the concerned friend, and have Jan committed, saying she had always known that Tyler would be bad news, in the end.

She couldn't risk it, couldn't take the chance. Not with the clock ticking and Tyler still in preter hands.

All she had to do was hook one preter, and he would tell them how to find Tyler. And she could bring him home again. That was how it would go. Jan frowned, her forehead creasing. Yes. AJ had said that only someone who cared, who really loved, could defeat a preter. The way Martin didn't care about anyone, not really…she had to be part of the rescue effort. All she had to do was nab them a preter.

Jan took a sip of her coffee, which had gone from lukewarm to cold, and looked down at the cell phone again. It wasn't hers, but one that Martin's friend had given her, along with the laptop: a prepaid phone, and no one to talk to, no one to call. She was alone, dressed up as bait and sent into the shark tank.

No, not alone. Martin and AJ had gone nose-to-nose—muzzle to snout?—about that, and AJ had been the one to blink. She was assured that there were supers all around her, watching and waiting, but staying far enough away to—hopefully—not spook any preters she might meet. The thought wasn't comforting at all.

On impulse, she shifted the phone in her hands and started typing, the quick thumb-moves of an experienced texter.

Hey there. No time, kinda busy but wanted to give you a wave. Life crazy. Let you know the deets asap. <3.

She hit Send and watched the flicker that meant the message was en route. It was late in the U.K., but Glory would still be awake. If she was by her phone—

The phone gave a faint beep, and she looked down, surprised at how fast the response had come.

u ok?

Not Glory. Martin. After she had bitched at him about abandoning her in the first restaurant, he had become almost overly protective. He'd even told AJ to go away, that they were doing fine on their own, like they'd been told. And AJ had gone, muttering.

Given a cell phone that matched hers, Martin had also taken to texting every three minutes, it seemed, letting her know where he was (down the street), what his coffee tasted like (bad), how many times he didn't hit on the waitress (three, and the third time she gave him her phone number. Probably a fake one, just to shut him up, Jan had thought but hadn't texted back).

Bored, she texted back now. Think this is bust.

idiot. i'd meet you for coffee any time.

Jan almost smiled. You say that to all the girls.

true.

No matter what Toba had warned, after a week living with him, she was starting to get the hang of

Martin. It helped that she'd been able to surf the Net
a little while waiting for responses, do some more
research. The sites she all found were fiction—she
thought—but the details were pretty clear. Kelpies
were water-horses, yeah. Handsome ponies who lured
children onto their backs, and then drowned them
without remorse.

Martin, to a T.

Their other form was human, and they were given
the same theme of seduce-and-kill AJ had ascribed
to the preters.

And that raised unsettling questions. Martin was
set to protect her, and he had—but for how long? If
a kelpie killed…how long could he hold his nature at
bay? That had been what AJ had meant, when he'd
said that Martin would have to decide…after.

Jan didn't want to believe that he could kill her,
but she knew one thing for sure, deep in her gut:
they were all dangerous. The preters, Martin, the
bansidhe, even Toba with his beak and claws, and
the gnomes, with their grabbing fingers and gnaw-
ing teeth. Maybe even Elsa, who looked too slow
and solid to harm anyone…she had looked Elsa up,
as well. A *jötunndotter* was another name for troll,
and troll had unsavory reputations, too.

Kelpies lured victims onto their backs, and killed
them. All the stories were clear about that; if you got
on, it was game over.

Jan shifted in her seat, her thoughts taking her

places she didn't want to go. Nothing of the fairy world was to be trusted, all the websites she had visited—except the seriously new-age touchy-woo-woo ones—had been clear on that. It was Martin's nature to kill, same as it was his nature to flirt. He would, eventually, inevitably, lure her onto his back and take her into the river, and she would drown. For all that he was her ally, her partner in this, she could not trust him. Even he had admitted that.

But she had been on his back and been underwater, and not drowned. He didn't seem particularly homicidal to her. He held her when she cried, and sent her funny texts to cheer her up, and...

AJ, on the other hand... Now him, she could easily see him taking someone's throat out. And yet, even when he was yelling at her, she felt safer around him than she did any of the other supers, even Martin. It made no sense. Maybe because his teeth were front and center, and he made no pretense....

It didn't matter. The supers might be more dangerous than the preters, in terms of history—after all, the only thing she could find about elves was that they took humans as pets and lovers, and didn't always return them. No eating, no drowning... But they had taken Tyler.

She took another look at the time and sighed. Half an hour after the man on the other end of the site-connection had agreed to meet her.

he's not going to show up, she started to text,

when the door's chime sounded, and she looked up, not even hopeful at this point.

A woman came in, slim and elegant in jeans and a bright red blouse that looked vaguely Russian, and then a dark-skinned man, wide in the shoulders, with a stubborn set to his jaw.

Jan's breath caught, a painful hitch halfway between lungs and throat.

Tyler.

Chapter 10

"Don't."

Martin's hand on her shoulder sank her back into her seat before she'd been aware that she was halfway to standing. She didn't even wonder where he'd come from or how he'd gotten there so fast—or had she been caught in some kind of time warp, staring in disbelief?

"But that's—that's Tyler," she said, her voice a harsh whisper, as though afraid to spook him, or herself, or the entire coffee shop. "It's Tyler!"

"Look twice, Janny. He's not alone."

Jan felt Martin's hand fall away—he was leaving? She felt oddly abandoned, and then his words sank in. Not alone? She slid another glance toward the so familiar, so beloved figure sitting at the table across the room. Tyler—it *was* Tyler—looked tired, and his hair was shorn too close, the thick black curls she had loved now a bare fuzz against his scalp, his dark skin carrying gray shadows under his eyes, visible even at this distance, under the harsh lights overhead. Never bulky, he seemed even thinner now, as though he had been ill for a month and poorly fed. Jan was amazed now that she had recognized him; but it was him. She had no doubt.

He's not alone.

Martin had left. She could get up and go to Tyler, hug him, rage at him, ask him what the hell he had been up to, make such a scene that he'd have no choice but to tell her.

He's not alone.

She looked again, and this time she saw the way his gaze kept going to the front counter, as though something there held all his attention. She let her own gaze follow, tracking through the crowd.

There. Jan felt as if she'd been punched in the stomach. The tall, slender woman who had come in just before him. The woman turned just then, looking over her shoulder as though scanning the room, and Jan swallowed hard, her mouth suddenly dry. The woman was golden-pale, with thick black hair around a pointed face, cheekbones that a supermodel would kill for, and eyes too large to be natural. Even without looking into those eyes, Jan knew.

Preternatural.

How did no one else sense it? How could no one else be aware? Jan's stomach twisted in on itself, her skin crawling, and she took a sip of her coffee to try and cover the shudder that went though her. The one in the café had not set off such a strong reaction, but she hadn't had time to observe it carefully. Or maybe she just hadn't been sensitized enough yet. AJ and Martin, Toba, and even Elsa, all of the things she had seen—even the turncoats and the *bansidhe,* they had been odd and frightening and fierce…but they had *belonged* here. They were part of this world.

This…creature, did not. AJ had been right. It was an abomination.

Preternatural. Outside of this world.

And it held her Tyler in its delicate hands. Jan understood that, as the preter approached the table bearing two coffees, and Tyler rose to his feet in a way he'd never done for her, his gaze never leaving her face, as though he was terrified that she might disappear, might turn out not to be real.

Jan had hated a lot of people and a lot of things in her life. But it all faded behind the rage she felt toward the preter—to all preters, right then. All the beauty in the world—in two worlds—couldn't hide what it was, a vile *thing,* as hideous as its turncoat tools. She wanted to stomp on it the way you would a cockroach, erase any sign it had ever existed.

We need one alive, AJ had said after the disaster

in the restaurant, leaning across the sedan's backseat toward her, his wide-set brown eyes glimmering with a feral red light deep within. *We need it bound and within our grasp, to get the truth from it.*

They needed to know how the portals were being opened, and how to shut them from this side. That was their only protection. Jan had promised to follow AJ's plan. Had promised not to confront a preter directly, but to follow it, trap it…. But this was the bitch who had taken Tyler from her. This was that bitch Stjerne, Jan was certain of it. And Martin had gone off and abandoned her….

No. Jan's rage subsided a little, her practical nature reasserting itself. Martin hadn't abandoned her. He wouldn't: she knew that now, as well as she had known it was Tyler, the moment he'd stepped through the door. Martin had come in to warn her, to stop her from doing anything stupid, but preters could scent him; if he had stayed, the bitch would have been alerted. Whatever reason they had for being here, she would flee—and take Tyler with her.

Or would she? If threatened, might not the preter abandon the human, cast him aside as a decoy, to distract her enemies? The thought, the possibility, filled Jan with determination. AJ had said that she was Tyler's only chance to escape, that only her love could free him. Tyler's showing up here was a gift, however it happened, and she would be a fool to ignore it.

Never mind what she had promised AJ. She would not let that bitch take her boyfriend away again.

Everything around him was noisy, so noisy and too bright, and almost-familiar without being familiar at all. Still shaky from the portal-crossing, still uncertain where they were, or how they had gotten there, he waited the way Stjerne had told him to, holding the table against others who might try to take it, glaring away those who tried to abscond with the empty chair. If he could do that properly, obey perfectly, the uncertainty and discomfort inside him should disappear.

Finally, Stjerne returned to the table, bearing two cups and a look of peaceful satisfaction on her face, a look he had never seen before, and one that made him shiver with fear, not pleasure, as though it somehow boded ill for him. But how? Had he done something wrong, after all?

He thought to hold his tongue, and not risk angering her, but the fear and uncertainty overran him. Once he opened his mouth, though, the words that came out were not the words he had thought to say.

"I know this place," he said, even as he was accepting the coffee from her hands as though it were a precious gift. "I brought you here…but I don't know how. Or why."

She sat with grace, her long legs stretched out before her, seemingly unconcerned by either his worry or how they'd arrived there. "I desired coffee. You knew where there was coffee to be had. You performed your duties perfectly: think no more of it, my pet." Her words matched her expression, a satisfied purr that not even his best efforts had been able to evoke. It reminded him, uncomfortably, of the looks on the faces of the ones who held him down, who did things to him, after he gave in. Hunger...sated.

He didn't think it was the coffee that had made her feel that way.

Still. She said he had done well. A quiet burn of pride kindled within his chest, warming away his unease.

"Drink your refreshment, and we will be on our way. I have things I need to do here. So long as the portal holds, it would be foolish to abuse this opportunity, before we must return."

"Return?" He wasn't comfortable here, but the thought of going back was not pleasant, either.

"It is not yet time for us to stay," she said, and her voice thinned a little in annoyance. "Not yet. He wants at least thrice-ten portals in our hold, before we show our hand. But soon we will be able to come back, and stay. And then we will see who holds the power...."

He didn't understand anything she said, but there was something fierce in her, like the sound of wings beating against a cage or the roar of a lion over its kill. He felt himself harden at the sound, like a dog hearing a bell ring. Unlike when such a thing happened back in the structure of stone and mist, he felt a flush of embarrassment that she could play him so easily.

He stared down into the coffee, and in that flush of emotion something poked at his thoughts, the faded ragged edges of his memory, prying its way in. The music playing in the background of the café reminded him of another tune, something too-distant to grasp, but tantalizingly familiar.

"Black coffee." He looked up, a fact clear in his memory, and compared the shades of his to hers. "You take yours plain."

"Yes." The fierceness in her remained, but muted, as though she had turned down the sound. "It is not a thing we have, and I have developed a fondness for it." She was speaking to him, but he was hearing something else. Another voice, a woman's voice, ordering coffee with just the slightest touch of cream.

"I want it to be the exact same color of your skin. Oh." Her eyes, her sweet green eyes, had gone wide, and she'd looked horrified. *"Was that racist?"*

He had laughed, and cuddled her, and reassured her that it hadn't been, that she was purely incapable of being that mean. And then he had put aside both their mugs and kissed her....

"Oh, pet." Stjerne's voice was steel and fire. "Look at me."

Tyler raised his head, unable to deny her. The eyes

that met his were not green but golden, and filled with something that unmanned him.

"Too soon," she said. "He was right, the overbearing pretender, he was right. Too soon; you are not yet ready, and I was too eager. But no damage has been done, only a small setback. Give me your hand."

He placed his hand in hers, and the gaze and the touch pulled him forward, soothed and anchored him, and the memory faded, the music faded, until all that was left of him was her.

"There. Better." She smiled at him and leaned back, sipping at her coffee, still holding that fingers-to-palm contact. "I was not wrong; the bond held. The others worry far too much. So, a postponement, for now. A small delay, until you are ready. Soon enough we will claim what should be ours, put an end to this endless foolishness, and then no one—nothing—will keep me constrained, limited to what has been."

He nodded agreement, although he had no idea what he was agreeing to, and drank his coffee, her presence and her pleasure enough to banish the last uncertainty and confusion.

It was unbearable. Or, like bears tearing at her insides. Or something, she didn't know what, and she couldn't calm her thoughts long enough to be rational. Jan waited at her table, her body practically quivering, trying hard not to stare, as though the hatred in her gut would somehow alert them...and it might.

It was a vivid, tail-lashing thing, like a cat about to strike, and she was afraid that it could easily give her away, if she let it.

But she didn't dare move; as much as she might want to make a scene here, drag Tyler away, scream at both of them, she hadn't gone that far over the edge. No. She needed to get Tyler back, but she also needed to trap the preter, the way AJ wanted. Somehow.

So she waited until her mug was empty, and she had no more excuse to linger, and yet they sat there. They did not talk after that first exchange; every time she glanced their way, the preter sipped her coffee, that narrow mouth curved in a smile, and Tyler...

Jan's stomach hurt, and the cat-anger lashed its tail again. Tyler stared at the preter as though he were unable to look away, trapped in her web.

"He's been taken. Trapped. It's not his fault." She murmured that to herself over and over again, willing it to be true.

But she hadn't forced him to hook up online—there were plenty of men who had gotten the lure and walked away. Just not him. Anger spat again, deep inside, and while most of it was directed at the preter—and Tyler—some of it curled around and burned her, too.

"Let it go," she told herself. "He needs you. They all need you, all the ones who had been taken." Because there had been others—at least three others, people whose lovers had tried, and failed, to rescue them. "You have to be strong."

Besides, Glory would kick her ass if she knew Jan was beating herself up over a guy's screw-up. And she'd be right to do so. Jan knew that—intellectually.

Glory. God, what she wouldn't do to be able to talk to the other woman. Tell her what was going on…. Get some *human* perspective on all this. But Jan didn't even know where to begin, how to explain any of this without sounding like she was two fries short of a Happy Meal.

Her phone let out a gentle, insistent beep. She looked down to see a new text from Martin. Come outside

The text was a relief—an excuse to do something rather than sit and watch the love of her life moon over something not-human, and wonder about her own sanity.

Jan got up, carefully, nonchalantly, not drawing any attention to herself, and walked toward the door. There was no way to avoid it; the path took her right past their table. She walked past, close enough to reach out and touch his arm…and neither one of them looked up.

Then she was at the door, through the door, a step away from the door, and Martin's arms were around her, pulling her close. To the outside it might have looked like a playful hug, the kind old friends or siblings might give, but the intensity in his hold was unmistakable. It was the same sensation she'd had when riding his other form, that she couldn't have slipped away, couldn't fall, even if she'd tried.

"Oh, God." She gasped, feeling the coffee she'd had rise up as if she was going to vomit, and gulped it back down again, despite the horrible taste. She would not show weakness. She would not let that bitch cause her to lose it.

"I have you," his voice promised against her hair, even as he was moving her away from the door. "I've got you, I'm here. Hang on and I won't let you drown, I swear it."

She clung, until the shaking in her legs eased, and her stomach settled. Tyler was alive. He was here, within reach. She should go back in there and demand answers, beg him to come back, throw something at him—maybe throw something at that bitch, too.

Instead, she stayed within Martin's embrace, letting him guide her away from the coffee shop. His body was solid, reassuring, even without the magic of his other form.

Tyler was leaner, his chest narrow, his arms looser around her shoulders, somehow less comforting. That was unfair, she thought, but the comparison remained.

Magic. Martin used magic, glamour, something, to make her want to come with him, to keep her on his back. It wasn't real. But it *felt* real.

Her Happy Meal was probably missing six fries and a soda at this point.

"Not too far away," she said, her legs suddenly unwilling to move.

"No," Martin agreed. "Just out of direct sight."

So the preter couldn't sense him. Right. She followed meekly, until they came to a bench in front of a storefront, currently empty except for a few pigeons fighting over the remains of someone's sandwich. He sat down, tugging her gently until she joined him, their hands still joined.

Tyler was here. She grabbed at that thought, tried to make sense of it, then shook her head. Away from the sight of him, it seemed impossible. You didn't just get captured by elves and then walk back into a coffee shop like nothing had happened…did you?

"Why are they here? Why…how?"

"I don't know. You're sure—of course you are." He answered his own question before she could get pissed off at him. "We never thought they brought humans back, once taken. You said that you knew this café?"

Jan nodded and then shook her head. "We came here a few times, but not often. It wasn't our place, or anything like that."

They had come here a few times, early on, when the relationship had still been new and uncertain, and they hadn't been quite comfortable just hang-

ing around on the sofa. Did he take all his new girl-
friends there?

The anger sparked again, but it was weaker now,
as though Martin's presence, his glamour, dampened
it, kept her calm.

"There's a theory," Martin said, hesitant. "About
portals."

"What?"

"It's just a theory."

"Martin!" She tried to pull her hand away, but
not seriously.

"All right. We've been trying to figure out why
they're taking humans, so many of them, I mean.
And how it's connected, if it's connected at all, to
how they're getting here."

"And?"

"And Elsa—you remember Elsa? She's got a theory that the preters are binding humans to them somehow, and then using that connection to cross over. So
it would make sense, when they pass through the
portal, they return to somewhere the human knows.
So, if she's riding him back…he might bring her to
somewhere familiar."

"You mean…he deliberately brought her here?
They… He's not a captive?" She didn't want to accept it, but it explained everything; how he had sat
there and looked at her, that intense gaze that didn't
acknowledge anything else in the world. The same

look that he used to give her, when he thought she wasn't looking...

Martin freed one hand and stroked her hair, bending forward to rest his lips against the crown of her head, when she wouldn't look at him. "Things change, when preters get their claws in. We're not immune, but humans are always so vulnerable.... We warned you about this. I'm sorry, Janny. It's not something I understand, but I'm sorry you're hurting."

Her jaw clenched, her teeth grinding against each other. She forced the muscles to relax, resting her forehead against his chest, breathing in the odd but not unpleasant scent that was distinctly Martin. Humans were vulnerable. But she could break that connection, AJ had said that she could.

"I need to get him away from her."

He sighed and pulled away, leaving her feeling oddly chilled, despite her jacket. "I was watching them. Watching him. She's had him for too long; he won't crack."

"But—"

"I know we said we'd rescue him, but if he can't be convinced to betray them, Janny, we need to find someone else. We can't risk her alerting them, that we're hunting...."

He was right. She knew it, but seeing Tyler there, and then being told that he was impossible to reach, was the last straw. Anger, unable to hit one target, found another. "Screw that. This is what I came here for. This is the whole and only reason I'm in this. You help me, damn it, Martin. Help me get him back. Tell me how to do it. Or, so help me, call in all your weird friends for backup, because that's the only way you're going to stop me—and you're going to have to find someone else to be bait because I'm done. I swear it."

They stared at each other, her green eyes meeting his brown ones steadily, without any give whatsoever. And, just like that time with AJ, Martin blinked and looked away first.

Humans could stare down supernaturals. That was interesting, and possibly useful. Jan tucked that info away for later.

"You love him that much." He wasn't asking a question, so Jan didn't bother to answer it. She just wrapped her arms around her body, suddenly feeling a chill, and waited.

Martin didn't fidget or make faces when he thought; he went very still and quiet, and the only way you could tell anything was going on was the way his jaw clenched and then released, over and over again, as though he were literally chewing something. "If I tell you, if I help you… You have to promise me something in return. A debt. A debt to be collected when I ask it, with no hesitation or denial."

Supernaturals weren't to be trusted. They lied, they seduced, they were coldhearted and had their own agendas. AJ was using her as bait, had sent her out here with Martin—Martin who admitted that he was a killer, that it was in his nature to lure and drown innocents…innocent humans.

Jan stared at him, then said, "Agreed."

Martin sighed and closed his eyes. "You need to lay hands on him, and hold him. That's the only way you can save him. She has her hooks into him—yours have to be stronger, like thorns, like a briar patch that won't let go. Grab him, hold him—no matter what happens, don't let go. She will try to shake you—scare you. Don't give her power."

Jan nodded. "She'll fight. I got that. You'll help me?"

"I can't." Martin got up, and stepped away from the bench. She thought for a moment that he was going to keep walking, washing his hands of her entirely. Then he stopped, still facing away from her, but his voice carried clearly. "If she senses me, she'll panic, same as the other one did. And… I don't care about your Tyler, Janny. I can't help you hold him. If anything, I'd…be a distraction."

There was a level of pain in Martin's voice that made her want to put her arms around him, to comfort him the way he had comforted her. But she had to focus on Tyler: Ty was the one who needed her. "So. How do I do this? Just grab him? He'll come with me, and then he's free?" It sounded too simple: nothing had been simple for days; she didn't buy it.

"He won't want to come. You have to remember that. She's had him for two weeks now; her claws are into him but good. He won't recognize you, remember you."

Jan shook her head, denying the words even as he spoke them. "That's impossible."

"Did he see you in the café?"

"I wasn't trying to get his attention."

"You saw him the moment he walked in. You sat there, not ten feet from him, and he never looked up. Never felt your gaze." Martin turned now and faced her.

"Janny, listen to me. You think you know us, what we're capable of, but you don't. The fairy tales had some of it right: we're not nice. And preters are worse, far worse than us. For whatever reason she took him, in his mind, his *soul,* he's hers, now. He will resist you, fight you. You can't let him go. Not even for an instant."

"I won't," she promised, filled with a trembling excitement. All she could think about was that she could soon have Tyler back with her.

Martin just sighed.

The Center was more than a place; it was a neutral meeting ground. No matter what else was happening in the world, no matter who was feuding with whom, what group was having a hissy fit, who was declaiming their superiority, when you came to the Center, all that stayed outside. You would share your fire with anyone who came to it, if not as friends, then not as enemies, either.

Jan had not been the first human to come to the Center, either. Some found their own way, others were brought. Very few ever returned. But very few did not mean none.

"I am here to voice a protest," the old man said.

"Your protest is noted."

The human sat down on the log next to the fire pit and stretched his legs out, placing the wooden cane alongside him, within reach if needed—the force of old habit, more than any indication of distrust. They had a long history, the old man and AJ. "Noted, and ignored. As usual. You should not treat her so."

"What would you have me do, old man?" AJ didn't bother to ask how the old man knew. It was the sort of thing the human kept track of. He scraped his fingers along the leg of his jeans, watching the fabric whiten slightly under the pressure. The moon was almost full: a *lupin* was not bound by the phases, no matter what legend claimed, but he felt them, deep in his flesh. That was what he told himself, anyway, feeling the tension ripple inside. "We needed her—and we have kept her alive. The turncoats would not have been so kind."

"Kind." The human let out a scornful noise. "Your sort are many things, but kind is rarely one of them. You've lied to her, used her, binding her to you. I know how well that ends."

"You seem to have survived well enough." But the response was flat; they both knew the human would not have chosen his life, although he now could not imagine changing it.

"She came into this of her own free will." AJ paused. "Mostly. Technically."

"Don't you try word games with me, old wolf." The human glared at AJ, and AJ glared back, wolfen eyes meeting faded blue without flinching.

They both relented at the same moment, the way they always did.

"She's not a child. I didn't know what else to do," AJ said, not admitting wrongdoing, but no longer denying it, either. "We need humans to do this. Only you have the passion that can change worlds."

"And well I know it." The human had been young once, and handsome, before age had stooped his back and sagged his face. He had chased a dryad through a forest once and been caught in her grasp, and if he did not regret never escaping, he did not wish that fate for anyone else. "Still, this is beyond need. You left her in the care of a kelpie!"

"Luck of the draw." Luck, where luck was damned bad fate. "Martin…" Martin was impulsive, headstrong and occasionally an idiot. "Martin cares for her."

"Oh, that reassures me immensely." The human's dryad had cared for him, too. The affection of a supernatural was not something to be wished for lightly, or at all.

"Blast it, Huntsman, I've done the best I could. But we need her, and she will serve, and it's done."

The two were silent for a while. Around the clearing, others were setting up their campfires, preparing meals, meeting, and taking their leave in an endless cycle of social and political reinforcement. They avoided the central fire pit, out of caution as much as courtesy; the human and the *lupin* were old, and known to be cranky even on good days.

"And after? If she survives, if she fulfills your requirements, what then? Do you leave her for the kelpie's mercy?"

"No one is ever forced onto a kelpie's back," AJ said, exasperated and defensive. "Humans have free will."

"That's not an answer, old wolf."

No. It wasn't. Mainly because AJ didn't have one to give. There were so many things that could go wrong, and so few likely to go *right*.

The sun shifted, a cloud passing, and the air chilled, reminding the *lupin* that time was passing. "I have to get back."

The human raised one gray, bushy eyebrow. "Not me keeping you here, is it?"

No. He had come to soak in the peace of the Center, but peace was not his to be had, not now, not yet. "Will you come with me? This is your battle, too."

"It was my battle decades ago," the Huntsman said. "When I could raise my axe and scare the bejasus out of a young, dumb wolf."

"We're both too old for this shit," AJ said, almost smiling. "Give my best to Red."

Chapter 11

The sun moved overhead, the people kept passing by, and Jan grew increasingly agitated when Tyler didn't emerge from the coffee shop. He had never been the kind of guy who just lounged around; one cup and he'd be ready to move on, do the next thing. She had been the one who was lazy, who would curl up for hours at a time.

"Calm," Martin said.

"This is calm," she said, trying not to grit her teeth. The kelpie looked like someone had given him a Quaalude or something, his body loose and relaxed, legs sprawled in front of him, his arm draped around her shoulder, his right hand clasping hers, resting on his thigh, to all observation a young couple enjoying the crisp autumn air.

The truth was, he held her hand as much to remind her to stay put as to give comfort.

Eventually, exhausted, Jan closed her eyes and rested her head on his shoulder, breathing in the scent she now identified as his, something musty that should have been unpleasant, but wasn't. She wondered, briefly, what she smelled like to him.

Finally, Martin tapped her hand with his thumb, indicating that their prey was leaving the café. Jan opened her eyes but didn't otherwise react. She breathed in, then out, letting her gaze rest on their hands, the iridescent black of his nails against the dun of his skin.

"Are you sure you're ready for this?"

Jan just glared at him, which was no answer at all, and they both knew it.

He nodded. "All right. Come on. And remember what I said!"

He pulled her up from the bench and then dropped her hand, letting her walk half a step in front of him. They followed the other couple for a while, keeping a safe distance back. Jan was acutely aware of the distance and the people around them, afraid that they'd lose track of Tyler, or that something would happen to alert the couple.

She tried not to stare, but her gaze kept returning to the pair as they walked along the sidewalk. It

seemed as though half the city was out, heading home
from work or out to dinner. The preter was holding
Tyler's hand, leading him along through the crowds.
Jan's blood sang with rage, looking at that slender,
too-pale hand circled around his. But the rage was
coated with a tissue of doubt, a niggling of honesty
that made her remember, just then, Martin's hand
holding her own.

Her hand, clinging to Martin's.

He—they—had trapped her, as much as Tyler was
trapped. Different reasons, different intents, but...she
had slept in a bed with Martin's arms around her, his
breath in her ear, and had been comforted. Had felt
safe, protected...cared for.

"Not the same. Not the same at all," she whispered, not sure what she was denying, even to herself. She moved faster, as much pulling away from
Martin—and her own thoughts—as trying to catch
up with her prey.

Then the preter and Tyler turned a corner, heading on to a smaller side street with far fewer people,
heading into the more run-down part of town. Jan
followed, anyway, Martin two steps behind, their
pace slowing slightly to avoid being obvious without
other pedestrians to mask them. If the preter sensed
Martin... Could he pass for a random supernatural,
innocently crossing paths, or was it always a con-
frontation?

There were, Jan realized, way too many things she

hadn't thought about, hadn't known to wonder about. And it was too late to stop and ask now.

The street was lined with boutique-looking storefronts, rising above into brick-faced buildings that looked like apartments, their windows closed and curtained. Most of the stores were closed now, and the few people on the street seemed intent on their own business.

The preter and Tyler had disappeared. Jan bit back a gulp of disappointment, even as Martin grabbed her hand, tugging her forward. There was an alley she had missed, across the street, barely wide enough to drive a car down without scraping the sides. Their prey had gone down there.

"Is that…" Jan asked in a hushed breath, pointing toward the end of the alley. A faint haze hung over it, as though fog had rolled in from somewhere else. It made her skin prickle, the same way the preter had.

"Wait here," Martin said, and pushed Jan against the wall of the building, the brick cold and damp through her sweater. Then he stepped into the street, narrowly avoiding being hit by a car. The driver honked and swore, but Martin kept moving, heading into the alley as though drawn by a line directly to the couple, his head down and his shoulders squared, as if he was intent on getting into a fight.

There was no way she was staying put. Jan followed, dodging another car, praying to a god she didn't believe in that her asthma wouldn't kick up now, not now of all times please god.

Martin had just passed the mouth of the alley when he must have made some noise, or gotten close enough that they could sense each other, because the woman stopped and turned, swinging Tyler with her.

Jan paused, pressed against the wall, and held her breath, hoping not to be noticed. Please, god, she thought again, aware that she didn't actually believe in god but she hadn't believed in elves or kelpies before, either, and look how well that had turned out.

The preter drew back her teeth, less a smile than a snarl, and stared at the kelpie, intensity—and malice—radiating from her. Tyler, confused, looked first at her, and then at Martin, then took a step away—not too far, but enough that he was out of range if fighting broke out.

Now, something, some instinct told Jan. She darted forward, slipping along the wall past Martin, swinging up and grabbing hold of Tyler from behind, the way she used to when sneaking up to kiss him while he was making dinner.

"Hey!"

It wasn't Tyler's voice, not the voice of the man she knew and loved. It was flat and cold, and he twisted and fought her grip.

There was a flash of uncertainty: was she wrong? Had they grabbed the wrong person? No. She kept her arms wrapped around him, under his arms, around his rib cage. "Ty, it's me, it's Jan."

"Let go of me." Cold, his voice and his skin, cold as though he'd been sitting in snow. Tyler, who loved to sit in the sun and soak up warmth like a lizard, whose body always seemed to run hot; again, Jan thought she might have grabbed the wrong person, and was about to let go and apologize when Martin's words came back to her.

"Don't let go. Whatever you do, don't let go."

"Tyler, I love you. It's me, Jan. I love you." She kept repeating those words over and over again, hanging on to him, her fingers locked together over his stomach, her body snug up against his, as though that familiar pressure would reach into his memory, recall her to him.

Like a thorn, she thought. Like briars. Get under his skin and hang there.

"Let him go!" a woman's voice cried, commanding her. Jan dug her face into his back, refusing to look up, refusing to let that creature see her face, catch her eye. Would the preter attack? Martin hadn't said anything about that, just that she had to hold on, no matter what.

"I love you," she said against the fabric of his shirt, rougher than his usual cotton T-shirts, rougher and smelling not of his detergent but something else. "I love you and I won't let you go."

And then that cold body chilled further, chilled and changed, and Jan had to adjust her grip as his body seemed to grow narrower, harder, even as she held on. She pulled back enough to see what was happening, and almost screamed when, instead of a human body, she saw the massive form of a serpent, its scales green and gold, a wedge-shaped head turning to stare at her, a long forked tongue flickering out, hissing at her in warning.

"Don't let go. No matter what happens."

"I love you," she said, and tightened her grip, sliding her arms tighter around that thickly muscled snake-body, not letting it slither away. She had seen Martin change form, she had seen Toba grow wings, she knew that magic could do things, and never mind that it was Tyler and he wasn't magic, she had to believe. She had to hold on.

The body twitched and shuddered, changing again under her hands. No matter how much she tried to keep her eyes open, she couldn't, feeling the change rather than seeing it, the dry scales turning to something warmer, softer, furred.

Then a snarling scream nearly broke her eardrums, and she jerked back even as the giant tiger's jaw snapped shut where her head had just been tucked against the snake's body.

Unlike the snake, which had been limited by its bulk, the massive tiger was lithe and far stronger than she, and one paw came free, slashing at her arm. Sharp pain hit her, and dark red blood dripped from the shreds of her sleeve, making her feel woozy and faint.

Tyler was trying to kill her.

"Jan!" Martin's voice: too far away, and useless. He couldn't help. He'd refused to help. Jan bit her tongue against the pain, let the tears run down her face but did not acknowledge them. She held on, her fingers now tangled in the thick ruff of the Tyler-tiger's fur, even as hot breath raked across her face and it tried to paw and bite at her again.

"I love you," she said, and then cried out as his paw caught at her shoulder, tearing the flesh again. "I won't let go. Not even if you tear me apart."

The body shivered under her fingers, and she tried to tighten her grip, preparing for another change. How long could this go on? How many changes could that bitch put him through, before she got tired, ran out of energy, gave up?

The fur shifted into something else; Jan's fingers slipped, unable to maintain their grip. She shifted, trying to get a better hold, and felt herself shoved off balance as the form under her reshaped into wings that spread out, beating wildly in a desperate attempt to get away.

She opened her eyes and found herself face-to-beak with a giant crow…no, not a crow, as much a crow as the tiger had been a house cat, a massive beast with glossy black feathers and an evil-looking beak designed to tear flesh from prey, and talons that were wickedly sharp and raised to strike at her face.

Jan cried out, her fingers slipping against the

feathers, their pinions cutting into her flesh. The wings beat again, and her arms were knocked away, almost breaking her hold. Desperate, she lurched forward, ducking under talons and beak, so that it could not strike at her without harming itself, and throwing herself at the exposed breast.

"I love you," she said, her words muffled against the feathers that still, somehow, smelled of Tyler, not the cheap aftershave he refused to give up, or the faint trace of his dandruff shampoo, not anymore, but still, somehow, the smell of him. But there was another smell there, too. Cold, and dry, and with the definite tang of sex.

Her. He had been sleeping with the preter, that bitch. Not just sleeping. Fucking her.

Bile rose in Jan's throat, and a pain worse than the claw marks on her arm and shoulder wracked her, making her fingers numb with agony, her body falling backward in denial even as she called out, her voice hoarse and faint, "I love you."

The wings beat again, that beak came down like a scalpel against her neck.

She had let go, she had no choice but to let go or die, and he was gone.

"Janny!"

"I have to find him. I have to go after him." She was blinded by tears, her body screaming in agony, but all she could think about was that she'd lost him, that she'd let go. She'd failed him. "I have to…I have to…" She choked on the words, her breathing tight. A cough caught in her throat, and she flailed, chest squeezed tight, unable to breathe.

The hands holding her shifted, her body turned until she was resting against something warm, and then the familiar shape of her inhaler was pressed into her hand and instinct raised it to her mouth, sucking the medication into her throat, her lungs.

The panic subsided, then flared again. "Tyler!"

Martin's scent wrapped itself around her, his voice warm in her ear, his hands holding her upright, cradling her gently. "He's gone. They went through the portal."

"I can't… I let him go." Guilt bludgeoned her, replaying those last seconds over and over again. "Why did I let him go? I suck so hard, I let him go—"

"Janny!" Martin's normally gentle voice rang out so harshly that she had no choice but to stop babbling and look at him. Everything was blurred. She wiped her eyes with the back of her arm, then swore when the blood got into her eyes.

"No, let me do that." He wiped her eyes clear; his touch was firm, but not gentle, and she winced a little, feeling the anger in him. At her? Why was he angry at her?

She wanted to crawl back to her apartment, hide underneath the covers, and she couldn't even do that, didn't even know if her apartment was still intact, if the landlord had evicted her for damages.... "I can't do this. I can't, I'm not strong enough. I suck."

"You have to be. Jan, you promised."

"What?" She shook her head, not understanding.

"The portal's closing, Jan. The mist is fading. We can't open it, once it closes. We have to go, now. Just the two of us."

"I can't. We can't. You saw..."

His gentleness turned fierce, almost bruising her. "Janny, you promised me. When I asked, you said you would do it."

Her nose was running, the snot mixed with blood. "That's not fair."

"I'm not fair. I'm a kelpie." His words had an odd echo to them, the anger, worry, and...sorrow?

"You let him go because you had to. You wanted to live, more. There's no shame in that. But you can have another chance," he said, and his voice was urgent, almost panicked. But Martin didn't panic, not ever. "If we go now, we can find them again. But the portal's only open now, Jan. We have a chance to stop it, find a way to end their incursions from that side, rather than waiting for them here. But the mist is thinning: we have to go now."

There was something wrong with his logic, something that didn't fit with what AJ had said, what Elsa had said, but Jan hurt too much to argue. The thought of moving, of doing anything—she had failed. What more could they expect of her, when she couldn't even hold on to the man she loved?

"Janny."

She had promised Martin she would do what he asked. Martin didn't lie to her. Martin didn't cheat on her. He wasn't human, she couldn't trust him— but he had held to his part of the bargain. Now it was time for her to do the same.

"All right." She let him help her up, felt him wrapping something around her arm, then draping his jacket over her shoulders. Martin smelled of green water and moss, she thought, finally nailing it; stagnant water and a smoky tang that she couldn't quite identify. He smelled...safe.

"Hold on," he said, and her eyes closed, telling her what he was doing, so when she opened them again she was not surprised to find his horse-form next to her, waiting.

Don't get on my back. Don't trust me. I kill.

She reached up with her uninjured arm, gripped his mane—solid, unlike Tyler's ever-shifting form— and hauled herself onto his warm, broad back.

"Let's do this."

Martin should have reported in by now. AJ scratched at the back of his neck irritably, aware that his nerves were dangerously close to cracking: events were making him twitchy, and he needed to get out and run for a while.

"Not much chance of that," he said out loud, knowing that even if anyone in the warehouse was close enough to hear him talking to himself, they would prudently ignore it. He would be bitter, or angry, if there was any point. There wasn't. His body could stretch and go for miles on end without tiring, especially if it were a full moon, but his brain was needed here.

His brain, and his physical presence. AJ didn't kid himself that anyone else could hold this group together and keep them focused. His deputies dealt with the details, but he had his eye on the big picture.

A year ago, when he'd first scented something wrong, he'd started trying to roust the others. He knew the stench of their kind, even if the rest of his pack had somehow forgotten; old enough to remember the last time those arrogant bastards had come sniffing around and the chaos they had caused, and he hadn't been able to rest until he confirmed it.

Too many preters, showing up at times and places that broke with tradition. Here, and in Europe, Africa, South America... He hadn't known about the humans disappearing then, hadn't gotten that far, but he knew enough to worry.

Something was up. Something bad.

It wasn't disbelief he faced, trying to get others worried, so much as indifference. The preters came, the preters left, they made incursions and messed with the humans, but for the most part they'd always left the supernaturals alone. Either because they had nothing the preters wanted, or they simply didn't have enough time here, and humans were easier…

But this time was different. Something had changed, and that meant that everything might change. And they would be caught unaware.

Three-hundred-and-seven supers, from eight different species including his own, had responded to his call. Three hundred and seven, out of seven million. He'd lost eleven of them since then: nine to the turncoats, while two had simply disappeared.

No, twelve lost now. Toba was dead. And Martin was six hours past check-in.

AJ was painfully aware of the weight of the motley crew behind him, someone using a low-humming power tool on one of the chop cars that had come in overnight—reselling parts paid for the warehouse, and food, and supplies—others rustling about, waiting for orders.

AJ had never even wanted to lead his pack, much less save the world. He resented the fact that he was here, he resented the fact that so few had listened to him, and he resented even more the humans who— blithely ignorant, insanely oblivious—were somehow making this intrusion possible.

It had been nearly a hundred-and-twenty years since the last time a preter had been scented here. He'd been younger, living in the here-and-now of the pack and the hunt. The idea of hunting down preters was a game, a challenge to be leaped at.

And they had hunted the intruders down, driven them back, thought they'd won.

Then AJ had seen the humans the preters abandoned in their retreat, tossed aside like unwanted dolls. Shell-shocked, uncomprehending, unable to ever return to what their lives had been, their families unable to understand, and him unable to explain. The game had ended for him then.

Preters made incursions, every chance they got. Humans made up prettier stories, made movies about dwarves and bluebirds and princes riding to the rescue. Supernaturals, for all that they skirted the truth, had no such escape from reality. Preters damaged everything they touched.

And now Martin, a kelpie, a creature that acknowledged no pack, no clan, no bonds other than its own whim, who had chosen to answer the call for reasons AJ had never dared ask, was off with one of those too-delicate humans, a human they needed, sent off by AJ himself, and they were missing.

And he was stuck here, in this damned warehouse, *supervising.*

"Meredith!" he shouted, and the sound of scurrying feet on cement floor answered him.

"Boss?" The only other *lupin* on his team sounded breathless, anticipating the chance to *do* something. He envied her.

"Go find Martin and his human."

Her muzzle twitched, and she sketched out a fast salute. "Gone."

It was all he could do. One super and one human couldn't matter, not with so many other lives at risk.

Chapter 12

They hit the portal without warning, Stjerne yanking him through; but the sensation of air leaving his lungs, the moisture sucked from his body, was almost an afterthought this time. Everything hurt. Things he didn't even know he had hurt. Too much sensation to catalog, overloaded beyond his ability to manage, he curled in on himself emotionally and retreated, even as his body was shoved forward—

—and then a cool, gray emptiness enveloped him, soothing the burns and easing his fevered not-thinking.

"Wake up, love. Get up."

Feathers. Scales. Teeth. A woman's voice, holding him, her hands soft even as he thrashed. Had she been the feathered, toothed, scaled one? Or had he? He couldn't tell, he couldn't remember, and not even Stjerne's voice was enough to bring him back.

"What happened?" A voice, crackled like old paint and just as thin, came from somewhere in front of them. Too close, too strange, too cold, and those soft hands were gone, leaving only cold mist and confusion. He froze, not wanting that voice's attention on him.

"Get out of my way." Stjerne, fierce as a storm, and he shrank into himself a little more. As bad as the unknown voice felt, she was worse. If he did not move, if he did not breathe, they would not notice him. Maybe.

"What happened? You took him over." The voice crackled some more, and the slip-slide of a serpent's hiss entered the words. One of the guards who patrolled the walls. "Stjerne, you fool. This was not approved. Your impatience has cost you before…when will you learn?"

"I am the vanguard. You do not command me, watchdog."

"No, I do not. But there are those who do. And they will hear of this."

There was a slithering noise, then the clank of metal and a heavy thud. He managed to open his eyes, coming back to his body enough to discover he was on his hands and knees in a grassy hollow, cool gray stone at his back and a small creek in front

of him. The taint of marsh water came to him, and
he wrinkled his nose: it was familiar but off-putting
somehow.

"Get up." Stjerne's voice was still cold and angry,
but he could not resist her, even now. He got up,
heated pins in his knees, a rippling mass of flame
between his shoulder blades, every inch of skin between feeling as though it had been scalded, and his
insides…like the worst case of runs he'd ever experienced, cramping his gut and nearly sending him
back to the dirt again.

"Up!"

She commanded, and he managed. There was
something in front of him, thick and motionless, and
he was not able to step over it, falling hands out-
stretched. Soft, muscled, and scaled, and he jerked
back in shock. It did not move, despite his weight.

The owner of the crackling, disapproving voice.
Dead? Had Stjerne killed it? Killed it, but not him.
He was still alive.

Sensations of scales and wings, muscles tearing
and bones cracking, overwhelmed him again, and he
tried to retreat, emotionally and physically.

"Up!"

Her voice cracked like a whip, and he rose, drawn
by ice-cold strings.

"I will not let you fail. You are mine." The strings
dug deeper into his abused body, pulling him back to
her, allowing no hiding space, and he was too drained

to protest, even if he dared. "They will not allow me another, not after this, and I will not be left behind, lessened in status...."

"What did you do to me?"

That was his voice: thin as a wisp, shaky and soft.

She didn't ask what he meant. "I protected what was mine. You came to me; she has no further claim on you. Now get up!"

She? The one with the soft hands and the whispering voice. He had...hurt her. His body spasmed again, and he almost fell, but the strings kept him upright.

"Come with me."

The memory of those hands and voice were overlaid by the agony of his body, combining until he could not tell one from another.

Sticky-sharp pain, scraping him out from the inside. He could not bear the thought of being placed in the chair again. Stjerne made the pain go away. All he had to do was let her in. Do what she asked. Not resist. He made his body move, followed her.

Behind him, there was a whisper of noise in the trees above, the echo of a disapproving whisper, and the skin that did not burn with pain crackled with uneasy anticipation.

But nothing came after them, to stop their leaving.

Jan stared at the staticky oval in front of them, seeing where Martin was right; it was already starting to fade. Martin had called it a portal. A portal was a door. Okay, it was a door between worlds, but even so, how hard could it be? Tyler had done it—three times now, maybe more. So could she.

Her previous experiences didn't help: the last time she had climbed onto the kelpie's back she had been blindfolded and had passed out soon after, and the *bansidhe*-driven flight had faded into a merciful blur. Even the warnings in her head, the ones that should have been screaming, were muted to where she could ignore them. Shock, maybe. Or more magic.

"Hold tight," she heard Martin say, although she knew that his horse-form could not shape words. Warned, and remembering how fast he could run, she twined her fingers tightly into the coarse mane, leaning forward until her cheek rested against his arching neck, and her legs tightened against his flanks. He would not let her fall, she knew that...but there might be things that would try to tear her away. Turncoats, certainly, and...

Her imagination failed her; she could not conceive of what might wait for them. *Are you insane?* The voice in her head finally managed to scream. *Seriously, are you insane?*

Before she could change her mind, refuse, try to climb down, her muscles froze, kelpie magic keeping her still. She felt a wave of betrayal sweep her, then Martin's body tensed, bunched and leaped forward, and her body instinctively stretched and moved with his.

In half a heartbeat, no time left to second-guess, they entered the narrowing haze.

In the second half of that heartbeat, the air was sucked from her throat, her lungs nearly collapsing, worse than any asthma attack she'd ever had, and Jan tried to cry out in pain, but the void took that, too. Things pulled at her, tiny barbs setting into her skin, trying to yank her off the kelpie's back, but she held on despite the pain, clinging to his mane. She turned her cheek, seeking comfort from his physical presence, and discovered that if she let her mouth and nose rest against him, she could breathe. Not well, not easily, but there was enough air to survive.

To calm herself, Jan tried to count his strides, but although she could feel his body moving under her, there was no sensation of forward movement, the only sound her own raspy breathing, and even that seemed muffled, as though the void despised even the hint of life. His muscles bunched and released, again and again, but she had a sudden horrid thought that they were trapped in amber, forever held like some Victorian-era toy, moving without motion for some massive child's entertainment.

And then the tempo changed, and Jan was rocked forward as Martin came to an actual stop, her face hitting his neck hard enough to make her teeth rattle and her nose feel as though it had been thrown out of alignment.

"If you broke my nose I'm going to kill you," she

said, and then realized that she had enough air to speak. Rising slightly from her crouch against his neck, she drew in a cautious breath, then another, deeper. The air tasted strange, but she was so thankful to feel her chest ease, she didn't question it.

A shudder ran along the kelpie's back, and Jan took that as her cue to slide off, her fingers once again sore and cramped from holding on so tightly. When her feet touched ground, her knees buckled, even as she felt the familiar eyes-shutting sensation that meant he was changing form again. Sharp static zinged off him, burning her skin, making her jerk away, half turning and half falling. Humans and magic didn't mix well apparently.

Turning away didn't help; she was still caught in that odd blindness until he was finished. Her eyes opened, and she looked out.

"Oh. Um, wow?"

The city was gone. She had expected that—you didn't go through a rabbit hole and expect to end up where you started—but it was still…startling. She blinked and stood up slowly, taking in her new surroundings.

They were standing on grass the color of emeralds, almost too bright to be real, and when she bent to touch it, it was plush as a puppy's fur. The grass filled a narrow patch of clearing, with a small brook a few paces below, and trees all around. But these were no trees that Jan had ever seen before, tall and smooth-trunked, the bark a pale green, with leaves of dark red triangles, restless even though there was no breeze. Jan let her gaze move up and noted, almost casually, that the sky above was…not blue or gray, but something in-between, shot through with an occasional iridescent rainbow. Like an oil slick on water, she decided, staring at the hazy movements. It was hypnotic, really, like—

"Get down." And Martin's hand grabbed her shoulder and pulled her down, gentler but no less urgent than his movement back in her apartment, even as she noticed that something other than the rainbows was moving in the sky.

"Oh. Holy…"

"Shhhh."

She shushed, watching the serpent wind its way down through the trees. It sparkled like a diamond under the odd light, twining around the trunk of a tree in a smooth, sinuous movement, its great flat head occasionally lifting to survey the territory. She had the sudden awareness of how a rabbit felt, hiding from a hawk, and had a sudden and intense wish for her inhaler, to ease the tightness in her chest. But she didn't dare reach in her pocket for it.

Oh, god. Had she put it back in her pocket? Or was it lying, abandoned, on the pavement in some alley, for an asthmatic homeless person to find? She managed to slide her hand forward enough to feel her right pocket. The familiar, comforting shape was not there.

Above her, Martin lay still as the grass, except for the occasional shudder that went through him, and into her. "Shhhh," he murmured again, his hands on her shoulder, his torso crossing hers, as though to hold her down. She wasn't going, anyway; not so long as that serpent was making its way down the tree, like a king surveying his domain. The air smelled of smoke and seawater, and she stifled the urge to sneeze, fighting off mild panic.

Finally the last of the serpent's massive body slithered onto the ground and then disappeared. She had a moment of panic that it was racing toward them, hidden in the grass. But then Martin let out an exhale and released her, sitting back on his haunches with the air of an all-clear.

She sat up more slowly, her hand patting her left pocket, just in case. Nothing. "What was that?"

"Snake."

"That was just a snake?" Her voice broke on the last word, squeaking slightly.

"No, that was Snake. The Snake."

"As in archetypal, Garden of Eden, source of all evil, Snake?"

He looked at her curiously and shook his head. "No, just the Granddaddy Snake. The one that holds the sky together."

"Oh." All the breath left her again. "*That* Snake. Would it have…hurt us?"

"Oh, definitely." He reached for her hand, and she let him take it. "Jan, listen. Everything here, anything here…assume it will hurt you. Because odds are, it will. We don't belong here any more than they belong in our world."

She nodded, then shook her head. "You've never been here before, either. How do you know any of this?"

"How do you know fire burns?"

"Usually, you touch it once and learn."

He gave her a wide-eyed look that she couldn't tell was real or not. "We're born knowing. Safer that way."

"I lost my inhaler," she blurted, as though that was the most important thing in the world just then.

He stared at her, and then that too-long face and too-dark eyes eased into a smile that was classic Martin: a little shy, a little sly, and unexpectedly hot. His hand reached out and unfolded, and there, in his palm, was her inhaler.

"I know you need it," was all he said.

She took it from him, her fingertips brushing his palm, and he shuddered, a full-body quiver, as if he was cold—or trying to restrain himself from reacting.

He wasn't used to being touched, for all that he was constantly touching her. That…was sad, even though it made sense.

She had no sooner shoved the inhaler safely back into her jeans pocket when he got to his feet, not offering her a hand up this time. "Come on. They're already ahead of us. We have to— Oh."

She turned quickly, staying low to the ground, to see what had caught his attention and warranted that tone of voice, half worried and half disgusted.

"Oh. Oh, god…" A vaguely human head stared up at her from the grass, its face covered in delicate scales like a lizard's, its eyes round and open to the sky, staring in a way that left no doubt that it was dead—even if the body hadn't been a few feet away, still leaking a deep black blood from what had once been its neck.

"That just happened. She must have been interrupted, or blocked, and lost her temper."

"The… It did that?" The body was a chunk of muscle, scaled or not, and the preter hadn't looked as if she could crush a beer can, much less take off a creature's head.

"Don't think of them as human, Jan. They're not."

"Yeah." She got to her feet, feeling parts of her body protest. Sitting in front of a computer was crap training for this. "So. What're we waiting for?"

Her bravado was utterly forced, but her voice didn't shake, and Martin took it at face value—or was willing to allow her the illusion of courage, at least. "See if it had a weapon."

"What?"

"A weapon. A knife, or…"

She gave him an "are you kidding" look, but stepped forward carefully, as though the body might suddenly jump up and say boo. It lay still, quite dead.

"A knife?" She knelt down by the body, swallowing her distaste at having to actually touch it. The body was still warm, the blood down to a slow seep, and to distract herself she tried to estimate the time of death based on the evidence. "Recently" was about all she could come up with. Although who knew how hot this…whatever it had been, got, and—

"Knife. Got it." She unhooked the knife from the creature's thigh, where it was tied with leather cords. The pants were rough cloth, the same as the shirt that was now stained with that black blood, and she wondered only faintly what the creature might look like underneath.

"Come on. Don't touch it any more than you have to."

"Why?" She moved her hands away and stared at the body, trying to find anything else that might possibly be a weapon.

"The skin might be toxic. Maybe. I don't know. I don't know what that is."

"Not much comfort," she said, sitting back on her heels and scooting backward. "In fact, no comfort. Here. Have a knife."

"It's not for me, it's for you."

She looked at the knife, a horn-handled butt of metal about the length of her hand, then nodded, sliding it back into the leather sheath. Martin, if he had time to change, had hooves and bulk on his side. She had nothing.

"I don't know how to use it," she said.

"Stick it into anyone who threatens you," Martin said. "Come on. We need to go."

Jan looked at the knife in her hands again, then shoved it, sheath first, into the pocket of her jeans. It would be awkward to sit down, but it didn't seem as though they were going to be lounging around any time soon.

"They've got a head start," she said, shaking her head, "and this is her world. How are we going to find them? Can you scent them from here?"

"No," Martin said. "And not we. You."

Jan felt her eyes go so wide, she probably looked like an anime character. "Me?"

Martin nodded, his face as serious as she'd ever seen him, the long lines of his jaw even more horse-like, somehow. "Don't search for her, search for him. He's your leman. You are connected, you can find him."

"Connected?" She didn't feel very connected, not after the coffeehouse, not after she'd failed to hold on to him in the alley.

"Connected. The thing that AJ talked about, the

reason love can pull a human back from a preter's grasp. Human to human, lover to lover. It may even be why he came to that café, of all the places they could have walked into, because you were there." Martin shrugged, his hands spreading to indicate he didn't know for certain. "That's the legend, anyway. A preter can obscure that connection, but not sever it. Not so long as you hold true. And here, with so few distractions, so few other human ties…"

Jan tried to parse that and shook her head. "I couldn't hold on to him, before. When—"

"Not physically. Emotionally. With your heart."

Jan turned away, staring at the rows of smooth-trunked trees, as though they might explain it all to her. Her heart. Tyler.

He had cheated on her. He'd abandoned her willingly, at least the first time. Had gone off to meet another woman, been dragged into her snare; but he wouldn't have, if he'd stayed home where he was supposed to be.

Jan held the thought, examined it. She loved him. No matter how angry she was, no matter how *pissed* she was, she still loved him. She cared about him. Wanted him home, safe.

"So. Okay. How…"

"Listen. Feel." He stepped away from her, and she shivered. "Tell me where he is."

She tried to listen, but all she could hear was the

odd sound of the wind in those unnerving leaves and the utter silence, as though there were no birds here…or at least, none after the Snake slithered down. And that thought made her listen more intently for the sound of something moving in the grass, coming toward them…

"I will protect you," Martin said, his voice sounding as though it came from farther away than the few feet between them. "Just feel."

She tried. She tried to remember the way Tyler's skin felt under hers, the way he would smile just before he fell asleep, sheepish and sweet. Instead, she felt the twist of feather-scale-fur under her hands, the snap of the giant jaws as they closed too close to her face, the way the shapes had struggled to get away from her, while she repeated her love, over and over again.

She tried to remember the sound of his voice. It had only been a couple of weeks; surely she could remember the sound of his voice early in the morning, crackling before that first sip of coffee, the way he'd laughed, like a low rumble in his throat?

The smooth echoes of Martin's voice intruded in her memory, but she pushed them back, concentrating.

Another echo sounded, and she turned, as though drawn by a lodestone.

"That way."

Into the tree line. There was no path through the

trees, not even anything she could guess was a deer track—if they even had deer in this place—but that was where their quarry had gone—Jan was certain of it.

Chapter 13

They walked in silence, Martin caught in his own thoughts, Jan too afraid of losing the faint thread of Tyler's presence to risk conversation. But she kept looking around as they walked, stealing glimpses while also trying to keep an eye on her footing.

The area of the world where they'd landed was entirely rural—no cities, no villages, not even any roads, just empty stretches of emerald-green grasslands, broken by dark patches of woods. The sky was fogged in; she knew the sun was there only by the indirect light that filled the air. It reminded Jan of summer on the Maine coast, when she'd been a teenager, before the morning haze burned off. But this wasn't morning; the world seemed perpetually overcast.

Jan didn't have the luxury of studying fairyland in depth, though. Following the trace of that echo was difficult work, even concentrating, and the worry that they were falling too far behind kept clawing at her, adding to the stress.

They didn't see anything else moving as they walked, not a bird or beast or anything on two legs. Martin paced beside her, his head held up, his entire body alert to any physical danger. That hyper-awareness made Jan doubly aware of the knife, stuck sheath first in her pocket, balanced on the other side by her inhaler.

Not seeing any threat didn't mean there wasn't one lurking somewhere.

"Where are they going?" she wondered, near to exhaustion and wanting only to stop and curl up and sleep for a little while. They had been walking—she didn't know how long, she couldn't tell where the sun was in the sky, and she'd been tired when they'd begun. Did night even fall here? Or was it perpetually gray?

"I don't know," Martin said, which she knew already. If he'd known, he would have told her. Probably. Maybe. She wanted to reach out and touch his hand, let him drape an arm around her again, help support her weight, but she did none of that. It didn't seem right, somehow. Not when she was here to rescue Tyler.

They walked a while longer, moving from the

grasslands into one of the wooded areas. Jan expected to hear sounds once they were directly under the trees, but there was still nothing, not a bird, not a squirrel, not the crashing noise of a deer racing away from these intruders. It was still and silent, and that made it all worse, even worse than when they were out on the plains.

The light dimmed as they went farther in, the ground became uneven, and they had to keep stepping over tiny creeks that cut through the woods. Her sense of time disappeared entirely: they could have been walking for days, or ten minutes. Fairyland-time, she thought. It was all surreal, pressing against her like too-warm air in a sauna. Martin kept looking around, that intense awareness mixed now with uncertainty.

He didn't like being in the woods, either.

Jan was so tired, so tightly focused on that narrow thread of connection, that when the first soft whisper came, barely a breath of air in the curve of her ear, she thought she had imagined it at first.

"Who?"

She didn't stop, but frowned, tilting her head slightly. "What?"

"Who?"

She wasn't imagining things, that was a definite whisper, coming from somewhere in the trees. An unfamiliar voice: not Tyler. But not that bitch, either. She'd never forget that voice.

"Who are?"

Now Jan did stop, unable to listen, to hold the faint, thread-thin connection and walk all at the same time.

"Who are you?" the whisperer asked, barely audible but perfectly clear.

"Did you hear that?" Jan said.

Martin had stopped just behind her. "No."

"Liar." She tilted her head to the right as though that would let her hear better. The trees still rose above them, dark red leaves still now, the smooth-barked trunks soaring into the misty sky and disappearing.

"Don't answer," Martin said, trying to nudge her forward without actually touching her.

"You do hear it!"

"Jan, this isn't our place. Listening to things that whisper out of the mist is not a smart life choice."

It was hard to argue with that logic. And yet…

"Who are you?"

The voices were soft but growing louder, as though the speaker was coming closer, until the whisper was almost in her ear.

"Jan, don't listen!" Martin's hand was now hard on her shoulder, squeezing until the bone ached in protest.

"You're hurting me," she said, a little petulant.

"You can't listen. Don't let them coax you into saying anything to them, not even your name. You need to remember what happens if you listen to preters."

"What, they'll lure me off somewhere and drown me?" She didn't know why those words came out of her mouth, so ugly compared to the whispers, but she didn't apologize, even when she saw him flinch.

"Who are you?"

This time, the whisper was right behind her ear, close enough that she could almost feel the weight of breath against her neck, hot and fetid.

Martin was right beside her, but his voice felt farther away. "Jan. Janny."

This time, she leaned back against him, resting against his solid build, with its reassuring scent of water and moss, and the whispers retreated.

They stood there, two heartbeats the only sound, under the mist-shrouded trees.

"Keep moving." And his hand on her shoulder pushed her forward, getting her to start walking again, following that faint, familiar tug.

The ground under their feet was still that same odd-green grass, and Jan stared at it, wondering how it got enough sunlight under these trees, in this dim light, to be so brightly colored.

Nothing here made sense. Snakes the size of school buses, voices that whispered out of the air, beautiful, soulless creatures who used internet dating sites to steal humans....

And werewolves and *bansidhes* and kelpies and trolls, on her side, while she tracked her errant lover by sense of…something. Not a hell of a lot made sense any more, period.

"Sure as hell not Kansas anymore. Not that I know anyone who's ever been to Kansas."

"I have," Martin said, his voice still quiet. "Definitely not Kansas."

Even that exchange seemed too loud, and they walked on in silence, Jan stopping every now and again to try and take bearings. The thread was exactly that, a narrow, glimmering thread in her mind that pointed her in the right direction, but never very far. If she wavered too much, or got distracted, it shortened and then faded entirely.

Jan tried to focus her mind only on what she was doing, not anything else, until the thread firmed a little more, extending far enough out that she knew where to go.

"What was it?" she asked after a while, when Martin's grip on her shoulder eased, indicating that he thought they were safe, or at least safer. "The thing whispering, I mean."

"Wil-'o-the-wisps, I think." He didn't sound confident. "I don't know. There are things that feel wrong, like I should be able to recognize them and I can't, or they're not the way my instincts tell me they should be. I can't trust what I know, because what I know isn't what it is."

"You mean you don't have the most recent up-grade? Again, so not comforting."

They were keeping their voices low, their bodies barely inches apart, and Jan reached up to touch his hand, still clasped on her shoulder.

"Would we be able to go faster, if you...changed?" Four legs, her riding; it seemed to make sense. Un-like a real horse, he could understand her—and his hooves would be useful, if they ran into anything else.

"No. Maybe. But it wouldn't be safe."

"Safe?" She thought she had misunderstood him. "From them? Or because things changed?"

"From me."

She tried to stop, to turn around and look at him, but his hand tightened again, moving her forward.

"We've warned you, over and over. Don't trust us. Especially not here, not even me. You know what I am."

Jan knew. She kept reminding herself of that. "More danger than just being here? More danger than... Do you believe that you could hurt me? That you would hurt me?"

He had slept beside her, night after night. Held her hand, pulled her from danger, let her cry against his shoulder. Did none of that mean anything to him?

"I'm sworn to keep you safe. AJ made me swear. I won't break that...I think."

"You think?" Jan didn't know where her lighthearted tone came from; it certainly wasn't how she felt. "Third time, not comforting."

His hand relaxed, as though he'd suddenly realized how tightly he was gripping her shoulder. "Jan, believe me. It's safer, if I keep in this form. If we're both…not-comforted. This shape…reminds me what's at stake. If I change…there's too much magic here. It could influence me."

Jan tried to find something to say to that and couldn't. So she shut up.

He woke suddenly, not remembering having gone to sleep, hearing voices. Instinctively he stayed still, a mouse surrounded by cats that might or might not be hungry. He had slept, but before that there were vague memories of a fight, someone trying to take him away from her, pull him away. Then it had all gone blank for a while. Then he had come to, and they'd been away from that place; she'd been striding in front of him, expecting him to follow, her black hair spitting sparks with anger.

He had been fascinated by those sparks, clear and sparkling as crystals, but when he'd tried to touch one, it had burned him.

"Where are we going?" he had dared to ask.

"Where I can think," she had replied tartly. He had fallen back a step and, chastised, been silent.

His eyes still closed, he remembered walking swiftly through the woods, coming out the other side to a narrow creek. He would have stopped, but she did not allow it, skirting the sloping, muddy bank until they came to a narrow bridge made of stone.

Something had rumbled and growled underneath, but she had not paused or looked down, and so neither had he.

On the other side of the creek, there were no trees, only a rolling plain that led, in the distance, to foothills, and beyond the foothills, a jagged mound that reached through the sky's ceiling and disappeared into the mist.

It had reminded him of something, some other mountain: he had been sitting up high, in a chair that rumbled beneath him, watching it from this same distance. Then he had been able to see the peak— no, not the peak, there had been a haze, as well, but higher up. He had felt a pang in his heart, comparing the view to memory, as though someone had dipped a needle and thread into that organ and tugged.

"Come," she had commanded, and he had let go of the memory, and followed.

Then they had made camp, he recalled, and he had lain down at her command, and now he was awake, and a voice, a male voice, was speaking.

"You should not have killed him."

Stjerne was cold, shiver-cold in her response. "You are judging me?"

The male voice was airy, mocking. "I? Never I. I am lowly, unworthy, and know my place in the wheel of things. You Court-folk will do as you will, as you always will. I am merely observing, from my place."

There was silence after that. Would she kill this mocker, the way she had killed the whisperer before? He tried not to move or do anything that would let her—or the stranger—know that he was awake. The ground was soft and warm underneath him, as comfortable as any bed, but his head rubbed up against the root of the trees they sheltered under, and he could feel the need to pee building in his bladder.

Stjerne did not strike this speaker down or otherwise show her wrath, but merely said, "It is done."

"True, it is done. And there will be those who judge. Those who have the right to judge. You are not above the Court, such as it remains."

She did not respond to her companion but said, "Human, I know that you're awake. There's hot water and a towel for you."

Caught, he opened his eyes and then widened them, seeing the figure speaking with her. Short, squat, it looked less like a living creature than a mobile stump, knee-high and covered with rough skin that looked like bark. Then it twisted to look at him, and he had to work not to flinch in reaction: stuck midway in the trunk-body was a face, bark-rough but identifiable, with lidless blue eyes staring back at him.

"All over this." The lips were almost invisible,

bark-covered and thin, set over a faint impression of a chin that sloped down into the trunk.

"Over my right to do as I please," she said, tartly.

"Of course, of course." The eyes closed once, slowly, and then it turned back, as though Tyler had been judged and deemed insignificant for further study.

He sat up, waiting for soreness or pain to make itself known, but nothing did. He reached for the memories that had been there on waking, desperate for something to hold on to, to resist the smooth gray fog already seeping into his brain, smoothing it all into a dull acceptance.

But it was gone, leaving behind the spiky, sharp prickling of thorns. There was only Stjerne, and she was expecting him to get ready.

He went to where she had indicated, and found a pot of water and a scrap of cloth. The pot was made of the same cloth as the towel, only stiffened somehow and given a glossy sheen. The water was just warm enough to make his skin turn red when he dipped his hands in, and there was just enough for him to wash his face and upper body, then dry off, and replace his shirt.

He craved a full shower but knew better than to ask.

By the time he returned, the stump-creature was gone, and she had made the blanket he had slept on disappear the same way she had made it appear, standing with her back to him, looking out at the mountain.

"What do you feel?"

"Feel?" She had never asked such a thing before.

"Feel." She was impatient with him, and he shivered. "What do you feel?"

"I…" *Fine* was his first, instinctive response. He did feel fine, but he didn't think that was what she had meant. "Physically, I am well."

"And emotionally? How does your…heart, feel?"

The question perplexed him. She was his heart, and she was here, how could he be anything other than well? She had asked, and so he must answer honestly.

He thought about the question, tried to listen to his heart. Only this moment felt real; he had only fragments and blurs of anything else, anything before her, and when he tried to look at them more closely, the thorns pricked and scraped him until he let go. He had become accustomed to it; it no longer made his heart ache.

"I am well," he said finally, not knowing how else to describe it.

"You feel nothing?" She seemed pleased by that, and so he decided—an illicit thrill that terrified him—to say nothing of the tug he had felt earlier.

Stjerne turned to look at him, then back toward the mountain. "Gathen is right, damn his twigs. Gossip outpaced us, and I need to present my case, not allow others to present it for their own means. No matter the urgency of our work, the Court plays its own games, and to be away too long, for any reason, is to be weak, unheard."

She looked at him, but her gaze was far away. "You have been isolated, pet, for your own safety, and to ensure the bond took. The Court will confuse you, distract you. But I cannot leave you behind, and so you must come with me."

He felt a splash of relief. He had not allowed himself to contemplate being left behind, brought back to the palace and abandoned like a misbehaved dog, or worse, abandoned where they were.

"Do not speak without my permission, do not approach any, save I command; keep your eyes down and stay at my side unless I tell you otherwise."

He nodded, then raised his chin and lifted a hand slightly, as though asking her permission to ask a question.

"What?"

"This is because…we went elsewhere? Or…" He had to force the words out. "Or because of what happened there?"

He didn't clarify what he meant by there. He had still little memory of that happening; only confusion and a surge of annoyance, of repulsion, the need to get away, to not be separated from Stjerne.

"Let me worry about it," she said, reaching out to take his hand in hers. It was the first time she had touched him gently since they'd returned, and he was briefly disturbed at how much it meant to him. Then he smiled back at her. If she was not upset with him, everything would be fine.

For the first time in years, Jan wished that she wore a wristwatch. Her cell phone was still in her bag, abandoned on the street corner back in her own world, probably gone through and dumped, her phone jacked and her credit cards run through. The thought made her grimace, but there wasn't anything she could do about it. Next time, she'd remember to make sure she had her pack with her when she went through a transdimensional portal on the back of a shape-shifting mass-murdering pony.

The thought almost made her laugh, but she thought that if a noise escaped, she would end up in hysterics.

The thread of Tyler's presence still led her on, and what felt like a long while after they left the whisperers behind, it brought them to an end of the woods. Martin touched her arm gently and made them pause a long moment, waiting, before they stepped from the cover of the trees.

Only then did she realize that, while they'd walked, night had fallen. When they were clear of the branches, Jan got her first glimpse of the sky, black and clear overhead, the stars a scatter of blue-white glitter, the moon a faint yellow crescent low on the horizon. "How long were we in there?" she asked.

"I think it's best if we don't think in terms of units of time." Martin was staring up at the stars with a look less of wonder than distaste. "The moon was waxing three-quarter when we left."

Jan swallowed hard. She didn't know anything about astronomy, but even she knew that meant something was wrong.

"Seven days like seven years?" The question she had asked Elsa and gotten no real answer on.

"Maybe. Maybe not. AJ said time between the halves isn't aligned. We're out of phase. That's why the portals have always been so tricky."

She rolled that around in her head, trying to think of it like code, getting two systems to communicate. "They don't sync. So, when we go back…"

"It should be fine," he said. "Tyler came back within a few weeks, remember?"

"You're saying that just to make me feel better."

"Yeah." Martin managed a grin, shaky and endearing. "Did it work?"

"No." But she wanted to hug him, anyway.

He turned away before she could act on the impulse, his body language a pointed rebuke that made her face tighten in reaction, feeling as if her only refuge had rejected her. "We should get some rest," he said.

"I'm not tired." Actually, she was exhausted. But

there was no way she could stop now, especially if that meant more distance between her and Tyler. "The pull…I'm afraid of what might happen, if he gets too far away. And if they stop to sleep, then we can make up some time, maybe?"

"All right." She could tell that he didn't think it was a good idea but couldn't argue with her points. Despite his earlier turning away, when they started walking again he took her hand in his. His skin was rough and warm against her own. It was as though he couldn't help himself, taking comfort as much as giving it, as they started down the hill away from the woods.

The thread was strong enough now that she didn't have to focus all of her attention on it. Maybe they were getting closer? But the lack of focus let her wonder about other things, like time. Time was changeable, not running equally on either side of the portal? Tyler had come back quickly enough—as they had been counting it. But if the two planes didn't sync properly, how long had it been to him here? How long, in his mind, had he been with the preters?

Her eyes itched with tears, and she had to wipe her nose with the back of her sleeve. Martin either didn't notice or pretended not to.

It didn't matter. However long he'd been here, in his mind, he'd recover. They just had to get him home. Jan focused on that, and the thread seemed to fade, then brighten again.

Or maybe she was just hallucinating that. Maybe she was hallucinating the entire thing and leading them in circles, and Tyler was somewhere else, never to be found.

The thread faded, enough that she had to stop, calling out in dismay.

"What's wrong?"

Jan held her hand up, closing her eyes and concentrating. She tried to remember Tyler's face, the sound of his voice, and failed. Refusing to panic, she concentrated again, this time not on him, but on herself. How she felt, waking up with his arm over her shoulder, his leg tangled in hers. The feeling of satisfaction she got when he laughed at her jokes or when his eyes got all soft, and he smiled at her.

The thread reappeared, not as bright as before, but steady.

Understanding hit: the strand that tied them together was as much her as him. If he couldn't remember, she would. She just had to hold on. Whatever she did, she had to hold on to him.

Time faded again, and Jan felt exhaustion hit her, muscles aching and joints creaking, but she had said they should go on, so she wouldn't call quits first. The stars were bright, but the ground was uneven, rising and falling, with occasional holes, as if an animal might have dug them. She couldn't tell if the grass was the same intense green as before; in the starlight it seemed faded. The shhhh-shhhh of the leaves rustling overhead faded the farther from the woods they went, and another sound caught her attention.

Not a whisper. Something more familiar.

"Water," Martin said, hearing the same thing. "There's a creek ahead."

"You don't sound happy. I thought you liked water?"

She couldn't understand the look he shot her, the night shadows long on his face.

"There's water, and then there's water. Especially here."

All things considered, she couldn't argue with that. "They went that way," she said, pointing to their left, following the tug of the connection.

"So, we go that way," he agreed, and started walking again. The grass was slippery under their feet now, and she was glad for his hand in hers.

The ground continued to slope downward, and the sound—and smell—of water grew stronger, until they could see it, a dark ribbon cutting across the bottom of a shallow valley. This was a proper creek, unlike the little rivulets in the forest.

"There's a bridge down there," she pointed again.

"Where?" He turned to follow her finger. "Your eyes are better than mine, I don't see anything."

"Down there. Come on."

She had been right; there was a bridge of sorts. Narrow, barely wide enough for one person to cross at a time, and made of stone that glowed palely in the starlight. On the other side, the ground sloped back up, and Jan could swear that she could see the impression of footprints in the grass, as though limned in fluorescent paint. Then she blinked, and the impression disappeared. But Tyler had gone that way; she *knew* it.

Martin pulled on her hand, enough to make her pause.

"I don't like it," he said.

"The water?"

"The bridge." He studied it and then shrugged. "But I like the idea of wading through the creek less. You go first, let me follow."

The logic to that escaped Jan, but his hand was shaking slightly in hers, and she thought maybe it was best to just get it over with, whatever was upsetting him.

The grass near the start of the bridge had been trampled down and torn up, and the stone where the water lapped against it had an odd green tint that seemed almost to shimmer. Jan closed her eyes, rubbed them with her free hand and then opened them again.

No, it still shimmered, like a pearlescent frog.

"Hurry," Martin said, as though she'd been standing there dithering for an hour. Then again, maybe she had. Time, she thought, aware that she was well beyond hysterical, was fleeting.

"It's just a step to the left…."

Martin didn't laugh. Either he didn't get the time-warp reference, or—he probably didn't get it.

There was no railing, so she had to step slowly, making sure to maintain her balance in the center. The stones were smooth but not slick, and so long as she held her arms out slightly on either side, she could move easily, like walking on a curved balance beam.

Jan had always hated gymnastics. Before asthma had sidelined her when she was in college, soccer and Frisbee had been more her thing, where quick movements were more important than grace.

She could hear Martin behind her, his breathing even and slow, and she tried to mimic him. In and out. Step, and step, until she was halfway across, at the high point of the arch, and he was a step or two behind her. The temptation to look behind her was like an itch between her shoulder blades, and an equal desire to look to the side slid into her brain, making her wonder how deep the water was, and if the plunkety-noise she just heard was a fish or a frog or…

"Shit."

Or something else entirely.

"Run!" Martin's voice was high and sharp, and she froze, terrified of falling off the narrow bridge even as she was terrified of staying there and facing whatever had made that noise, and then the bridge *moved.*

"Oh, shit," she echoed, and started to run, even as the far end of the bridge lifted itself from the banks and turned to glare at her.

The head was square, and its snout was covered in mud where it had been dug into the dirt, but even in the dark there was no mistaking the way the jaw dropped open to display rows of sharp stone teeth, or the voice that rolled out of that jaw, deep and horrible.

"Fee Fie Fo Fum...."

Somewhere deep inside, Jan started to laugh, hysterically, even as she felt the compulsion to close her eyes that told her Martin was changing form. Then there was a high-pitched scream of challenge, and she was knocked off the bridge by something warm and hard hitting her on the shoulder.

The water was deep enough to cushion her fall, but she still hit the bottom with a hard smack, sharp pebbles scratching at her face and cold water getting in her nose and ears. She gasped, and the water shoved itself into her throat. Pushing her hands down against the creek bed, she surfaced, coughing, her lungs desperate for air.

The bridge had undocked itself, squat legs on one end, that square head at the other, twisting and snapping at the kelpie on its back. Water seemed to rise out of the creek and splash over them, giving the entire scene a surreal, darkly prismatic look.

"Go!"

There was no voice, only another shrill scream, a challenge rising from the kelpie's throat, but Jan heard the order clearly and scrambled to her knees, then to her feet, trying to regain her balance. There was the sharp tang of blood in her mouth, and then something grabbed at her ankles.

"Oh, the *hell* with this," she muttered, and slogged forward, refusing to look down or acknowledge whatever it was that wanted to play. It tugged again but let go, and she managed to reach the other bank, still coughing, her hair streaming water into her eyes. She reached for her inhaler, still safe, if wet, in her pocket and took a long hit off of it, enough to quell the coughing. Only then did she turn to see what was happening.

The bridge was twisted, a Möbius strip of stone, and she couldn't see the kelpie anywhere.

"Martin!"

Another fierce challenge cry split the night air, and then there was a heavy thud as he leaped from the other side of the monster-bridge and landed beside her. Her eyes flickered shut even as she was trying to get to her feet, and she cursed whatever side effect of his magic didn't want her seeing it.

"Come on," he said, and his hand was in hers again, and they were running uphill, away from the creek, leaving the bridge bellowing in impotent rage and hunger.

At the top of the hill, they paused to catch their breath, and Jan dared to look back behind them.

The bridge was a bridge again, motionless in the clear night air, the waters streaming innocently along, and if not for the fact that she was soaking wet, covered in mud, and—she looked down to discover—the bottoms of her jeans were ripped, as though a dozen sharp claws had torn at them, Jan would have thought that she'd hallucinated the entire thing.

"What was that?"

"I…have no idea." His voice was ragged, and she swiped the slop of hair out of her face and turned to look at him.

"Oh, my god." Where her jeans had protected her, his hide hadn't: there were bright red cuts on his arms and face, raking from cheekbone to chin, the flesh ragged and raw. His face hadn't been handsome, particularly, but the sight of it damaged like that sent an unhappy quiver through her. "You need to, we need to do something about that, about your cuts, and—"

"With what supplies?" He looked around the top of the hill, bare except for grass and the occasional thrust of rock through the dirt, and shrugged. "Do you see anything? Want to go back down there and get some water to wash it out?"

"No." She was quite certain about that.

"So, we go on." He touched one of the cuts and winced, then shrugged it off. "Which way?"

Listening to anything other than her nerves was difficult. She reached out and took both of his hands in hers, the black nails no longer even but ripped and ragged along the edges. Unlike the rest of this world, he did not shimmer in the starlight, but rather seemed a pool of stillness, an anti-shimmer.

The tug was fainter than before, and Jan couldn't say for certain anymore if what she felt was really a sense of Tyler or her own wishful thinking.

"That way. I think." She loosed one hand and pointed to her left, then swung slightly forward. "That way." Under the night sky, the distance stretched, grasslands rising again into foothills, and in the distance, a jagged peak.

"There. God, that's a long way away."

"Distances are deceiving," he said.

"You're trying to make me feel better again. It's still not working."

He pulled her into a sudden hug, and she went willingly, resting against his chest, his warmth reaching through her water-soaked clothing and soothing the chill in her bones.

"I'm tired," she said, an admission of so much more than she was able to say, than she knew how to say. They'd almost died. She had thought they *were* going to die. Everything hurt. Skin, hair, lungs... heart.

"I know. I know." He held her, not too tight, not too loose, but just enough. She wished he would hold her tighter; that way she would be able to protest. It would be too easy to just let him hold her up, to stay there, and not move any farther.

"If I could ride..."

"No." His voice was sharp, and she felt it like a slap.

He felt her reaction; there was no way he couldn't.

"Jan…" Her name on his tongue was an apology, an entreaty.

She pulled away and started walking in the direction of the mountain, not willing—able—to forgive, not this time.

"Jan, even if I could control myself, they can sense me, too. Here, out here? I'd be like a beacon. The magic in this land…it would find me, work on me. And…you wouldn't be safe, then."

"Would you have pulled me into the water, Martin? Would you have drowned me, if I was on your back, when we crossed that bridge?" She needed to know.

There was a silence, as he walked beside her.

"I don't know."

Most of the windows of the warehouse had been boarded up or covered over with paint and paper. The only one that still had clear glass in it was high up along the narrow walkway that ran the length of the front. AJ stared out that window, his mind ticking over possibilities and probabilities. None of the options or outcomes made him feel any better.

Elsa shuffled up to stand behind him, looking, he assumed, over his shoulder and out the window. "It's getting worse."

"I know." Elsa meant well, but she had a way of stating the obvious that raked at every last one of his nerves.

"We can't just sit here forever. It's been three days. Martin hasn't checked in."

"I know." Martin was still missing, and Meredith hadn't returned, which meant either she was on his tail, or she was dead. More possibilities and probabilities for him to juggle.

Elsa shuffled, the sound of her body grinding against itself making his ears want to twitch. "Do you think he killed her?"

"No." Not because he had any particular faith in Martin's ability to control himself, especially over such an extended time, but because if he had, he would have come back to tell AJ.

It was a thing. It happened. None of them could be held against their nature—humans might try, but the supernaturals knew better. It would not be pleasant to deal with, though. The longer Martin was with her, the harder he would take it.

"Do you think—"

"El, I don't think at all. Not without any information. Right now, I'm going to assume that they're still chasing after leads. And we need to be focusing on these damned gnomes."

The damned gnomes in question had formed a ring around the warehouse, creeping in silently the night before, slaughtering the sentries with more stealth than he'd expected from their kind. There were nearly a hundred of them, maybe more.

They weren't threatening or making a nuisance of

themselves. On the contrary, they had settled down, sitting cross-legged on the parking lot gravel, each of them holding hands with the other, their elongated arms crossing their chests so that their left hand held the hand of the one on their right, and the right held the hand on their left.

AJ couldn't shake the image of naked Tibetan monks sitting in protest, if Tibetan monks had gray-green skin and teeth designed to rend flesh from bone. He was just waiting for them to start pouring gasoline on each other.

If Elsa was thinking the same thing, he had no idea. He doubted it; trolls weren't noted for much imagination. It was why he'd asked her to administer the site, rather than taking part in any actual planning. "You think they're going to attack?" she asked now.

"It would be suicide if they did."

Gnomes were nasty creatures, able to stretch their bodies in ways that even shape-shifters found disturbing, and their teeth and claws carried diseases that would leave you wishing you were dead, but they preferred a swarming attack to one-on-one battle, and there were at least a hundred supers in the warehouse, most of whom could be just as deadly in a fight.

Only the ones who could fight, be useful in battle, had come to the warehouse. Those who'd answered the call but were of a gentler nature he set to quieter tasks, watching and reporting, things better suited to their abilities. If those here in the warehouse fell, those others might be able to carry on. Might. More likely it would all fall over, and the humans would never know what hit them. And then the supernatural communities would fall, one by one.

"They come, we fight them off…and humans tell stories about it, never knowing why. What stories will they tell, if we fail?"

No stories, save those slaves told.

Depressed, he stared out the window and counted knobby green heads again. He had said it would be suicide; he hadn't said he didn't think they would attack. They were here; that meant they had traced the human to this place, or someone with more brainpower had sent them here.

"We can't get out, so long as they're sitting there," Elsa said.

His second-in-command had a grasp of the obvious. But she was missing something just as important.

"We can't get out, and supplies can't get in."

She still didn't understand. Sometimes, not having an imagination was a blessing, he supposed.

He had called in the ones who could fight. Which meant they had over a dozen different species here, all working under the oldest of treaties, that of survival…but it was a tenuous hold. And if they started to get hungry…

"Something must have told them to come here,"

he said, speaking more to himself than her. "Something that thinks they're close to endgame."

Not something. Preters. Or something even worse, something he hadn't been able to imagine?

Elsa was silent, waiting for him to say something more, then he heard her shuffle off again, as though her body was too tired for her to lift. He stared out the window and resisted the urge to howl a challenge at the turncoats. There would be time enough if it came to that.

"We will go down fighting," he told the silent forms ringing his headquarters. "We will go down fighting, and it will cost you."

The defiance didn't make him feel better.

Chapter 14

After a while, the echo of connection that Jan had been following faded to near nothing, and then it snapped, a worn-out thread finally admitting defeat. It didn't matter by then: they had a destination.

"They've gone Under the Hill," Martin said. "That's why you can't feel him anymore."

The closer they got to the mountain, the more uneasy Jan became, and not just because it was standing between her and Tyler. There was something about it that made her react the way she might to a growling dog: caution and an odd desire to reach out to it, at the same time. The sun rose behind them—or she assumed it did, because the stars faded, and a bright mist filled the sky—but they had covered more ground by the time the sky started to clear again than should have been possible in a day without falling over dead from exhaustion and hunger.

Either time was seriously warped here, or distances were. Or both. "Probably both," Martin had said, when she'd asked him. Physics would say that was impossible, except every day it seemed as if the newspapers were filled with new discoveries in physics, all the sciences, and people kept arguing over what was and wasn't possible or probable or doable.

So. Jan kept her mouth shut and her eyes and brain open, and watched, and thought. Anything to keep her mind off what might wait for them at that mountain.

Her clothing had dried as they walked, and her hair was a tangle of knots and curls, but the scratches on her legs were minor. The cuts on his cheek and arms had scabbed over, but some of them looked swollen. He needed antibiotics, or at least warm water and soap, and stitches. They didn't have any of that.

She wondered if he changed, if the magic would take care of any infection. She wondered if he'd listen to her if she told him to change, and decided that, no, he wouldn't. So she didn't say anything.

They kept moving, the hills having sloped down into a flat, featureless plain. There were clouds of dust in the distance that could have been a herd of something, but it never came close enough to make out any details. There were no birds in the sky, at least none that flew below the cloud level.

"This world's so empty," she said finally.

"Yeah." Martin's gaze kept sweeping from left to right. "I don't know if that's normal or not." He let out a noise, like a pfuhh of air, only harsher. "Preters come to our world and take things. Maybe because they don't have enough here? Just as glad if we don't have to worry about packs of anything slavering at our hooves. Heels."

"I guess. Yeah." They were walking side by side now; he had his hands shoved into the pockets of his jacket, but his elbow would occasionally brush against hers. She missed having her hand in his, but she refused to ask. He might have his reasons for rejection; they might even be good reasons, but it still hurt.

She was pretty sure that she dozed off once or twice as they walked, her feet still moving, trusting him to keep them safe. Martin must have been exhausted, too. How much sleep did kelpies need? she wondered. Had he slept at all at the safe house, those nights he had held her?

In her exhaustion now she imagined him curled up around her in the barren bedroom, his arms around her, his breath warm against her skin, and then the imagination turned from what had been to what had not: his hands, sliding down her arms, coaxing her to shift closer. Legs, limbs suddenly bare, tangling, the feel of a not-unexpected erection pressing against her backside as his hands roamed down her belly, sliding smoothly into the vee of her legs. Would his hands have been gentle, or urgent, sliding inside her? Would he have—

She broke off the thought, flushed and confused. Had she just been…?

Yes, she had. And her body was annoyed that she'd stopped before finishing the scene, too. That was not a supernatural attempting to seduce her; that had been her own mind and body conspiring. Jan pressed her open palm against her heart and felt sick. Blame it on the knowledge that Tyler hadn't been faithful. Blame it on the close quarters and emotional drainage. Blame it on exhaustion and the impossibility of this world around them. Blame it on anything, but don't think of it again!

But once in her mind, the sensations were impossible to revoke. The smell of his skin was on hers, the feel of his arms around her…she knew it too well to forget now.

The things you can't forget, you deal with. You move on, and you…deal with it. That was all. She tried to summon her practical side, but it seemed farther away here, in this place, and sluggish to respond.

On the plus side, she was feeling considerably more…energized now. Smut as caffeine-replacement? If that was a side effect of fairyland, she could almost understand the appeal.

Martin broke into her disordered thoughts. "Remember what I just said about the wildlife?"

"Yeah…?" She turned her head enough to look at him, curious.

"Next time, tell me to shut up." He grabbed her elbow and hauled her backward, almost pulling her arm out of the socket just as something whooshed past them, a blur of black and dun. Jan's gaze flickered madly, trying to sort out what was going on. Three, no, five of them, low to the ground and turning in a pack, lean bodies and long tails. She thought at first that they were giant cats, maybe cougars, but they moved too fast, too clumped together, turning together more like a herd of horses, or—

One of them snarled, and it echoed—no, not an echo—there were more of them coming up from behind. And Martin and she were caught in between.

"Back to back," he told her, suiting action to words. Jan reached for the knife in her pocket, even as she wondered what the hell she could do with it. Sweat dripped down her back, and she could feel her heart racing, adrenaline screaming at her to run, even as her brain was telling her to stay put, stay still.

The not-cats wheeled around them again, as if she and Martin were the center of a Maypole, flowing almost like a school of fish, and the others came into her line of vision. These were different, slightly smaller, and their fur was almost the same color as the grass, flecks of brown and emerald green.

Scared as she was, Jan still could admire how gorgeous they were. She had seen enough nature programs to think that they used the grass as camouflage, probably slinking low to get up close to their prey and then leaping, while the others…

"Don't move. Stay very still."

"I can do that," she responded. That light, almost breezy tone was now recognizable as the same she used to deal with Steve, her boss, when he was on a cranky tear, and Jan decided that of all the default responses to abject terror one might have, breezy was probably as good as it got.

One of the dun-and-black creatures let out a scream that made her almost wet herself, and she could feel Martin tense against her back, the staticky feel of magic making her think that he was about to change.

Oh, god, not now, she thought. Now would be a very bad time for me to have to close my eyes!

There was a low cough-and-growl from one of the greenies, and then all hell broke loose, the greenies leaping forward—and bypassing the two figures entirely, landing smack in the middle of the black-and-duns.

Jan had never seen a catfight before, but she knew one when she saw it. She probably would have been standing there until it ended, openmouthed in fascination, except that Martin started backing away from the scene, taking her with him.

Only their legs moved, a step and then another step, never looking away, until suddenly it was all over, the black-and-dun cats fleeing the scene, leaving one corpse behind. The greenies, triumphant, likewise disappeared, as though they'd been absorbed by the grass.

She'd been right about where they came from and how well their camouflage worked.

"Shit. They're still around. Somewhere. Anywhere."

"I don't think they're interested in us," Martin said. "I think we were just in the middle of a turf war. The larger ones, they're probably from the mountains."

"Why would they come down here?"

He shook his head. "I don't know. I'm not really interested in hanging around to find out. You?"

"Not really, no."

He let go of her elbow, and they slowly turned around, facing the mountain again.

"So there are more of those big cats, up there?"

"You won't smell right to them," he said. "Neither of us does. That's why they ignored us. We didn't smell like food, and we weren't acting like a threat."

"Right." She was less convinced, but maybe if she believed that really hard, it would be true.

When they started walking again, they instinctively maintained a half-step distance between each other, the better to go back-to-back again, both of them scanning the landscape, half expecting another attack of—something.

Jan felt like an idiot now for thinking that this land was empty. Just because the dangers weren't obvious, like in the city, and just because there weren't warning signs she could read, that didn't mean the signs weren't there. They'd gone through a portal and come out somewhere utterly foreign, weird and dangerous. She couldn't afford to forget that. Neither of them could.

And that meant she had to stop just accepting things as "not-normal" and therefore unknowable, or something that Martin would know, or take care of. She needed to get more information. Jan coughed, more to clear her head than her lungs, and asked, "So, where exactly are we headed?"

"Don't you know?"

She shook her head. "If I did, I wouldn't need to ask, would I?"

He sighed, staring up at the sky as though some answers were going to fall down on them like rain.

"Where are we going?" she asked again.

"Under the Hill." He said it as if it should mean something to her.

"Under the mountain?" She looked up at it, looming ever closer on the horizon, and the massive bulk sent a shiver through her. "Under? You mean through, right? Or they've got an installation carved into it, like the military, caves, and elevator shafts, and…"

Her voice trailed off, unable to imagine elevators here in this world. Magical beasts, flying you from one level to the next, maybe. Or a spell that lifted you...

No, they didn't have spells. Not even the preters. But even if they didn't *do* magic, they *were* magic. She alone—all humans—were outside that.

Or were they? She had seen Martin and Toba shift, but you could almost find a logical, scientific reason for shape-shifters, right? There were species that changed gender, and species that went through several different forms, and...okay, it wasn't the same at all. But she could extrapolate, make it make sense. And the portals, those were physical, and, hell, maybe they were some kind of wormhole or black hole or digital time-space continuum timey-wimey whirligig-thing that totally made sense when you knew enough physics. Even Tyler changing shape, that could just have been a mind trick, another kind of glamour.

The really fantastical kind of magic, making things out of nothing, making people fly without engines... that would be harder. She hadn't seen anything like that. She had no reason to believe anything like that existed. She wasn't going to rule it out, though. She'd be on guard, ready for anything, be able to adapt to anything.

"Under the Hill," he said again. "It's the only thing that makes sense. If you're right, it's the only place she could be going. Especially if she knows, or sus-pects, that we're coming. She's taking him to the heart of her people, where she will be strongest—where there will be the most of them. The queen of Under the Hill, and her Court, and…"

He was blithering out loud, the way she had been in her thoughts. Driven by something she didn't understand but didn't question, Jan changed her stride so that they were walking next to each other, and slid her arm around his waist, tucking her thumb in the loop of his jeans.

His breathing eased, and his words slowed almost immediately, as though she had calmed him merely by the contact. She felt a smug, almost selfish sort of satisfaction in that, that she could make him feel better just by being there. And, weirdly, his reaction made her feel better, too.

They were walking uphill now, a steady rise, and the grass was taller, growing more in sparse clumps rather than the previous plush, a paler green than before. It was the first real change she could remember since they'd left the woods. She wondered if one of the black-and-dun cats were watching them somewhere.

"There are different rules there, Jan. The Court—the Unseelie Court, it's called in fairy tales. We don't have anything like it, our world is too fragmented, too independent. There's no law that binds us, the way there is here.

"If she's gone Under the Hill, I don't know what to expect."

Jan licked her lips, wishing she'd thought to bring a water bottle as well as her pack. She still wasn't hungry, but her mouth was dry. "So, what do we do?"

"I don't know."

She sighed and leaned against him, feeling his arm come up to drape over her shoulders, holding her closer. His body was warm, his smell familiar, the thump-thump of his heart slightly faster than a human one, but just as loud and—by now—reassuring.

"The thing to remember is that preters like order. Supernaturals thrive on a bit of chaos, and naturals, humans—you roll with changes. Preters don't. All the stories, all the legends, everything emphasizes that. They follow rules—their own rules, not ours, but they follow them."

"And how does that help us?"

"I don't know. Yet."

The terrain got rougher, and his arm fell away from her, each moving under their own power. Jan missed the weight of his arm, but she had to admit that it was easier to walk. They climbed over a particularly steep rise and were confronted with one last hill ahead of them, leading to their destination. Close. So very close. She wanted to turn and run—and she wanted to get it over with already.

Besides, where would they run *to?*

"Do you think we'll get out of this?" she asked.

"Kelpies are endlessly optimistic. Stupidly so, even. Just ask AJ."

She smiled, even though he hadn't answered her question. "I'll do that. Soon's we're home."

"You're not going home, human." The speaker appeared out of nowhere, making Jan yelp. Tall and skinny, like a bad wind could knock it over, the long wooden stick held in its hands suggested that they take the implied threat seriously. Two companions, likewise armed, appeared as suddenly and silently out of the grass as it had.

Of course there were guards. Why hadn't either of them thought about there being guards? Unlike the cats, they didn't look as if they were going to ignore the strangers, either.

Jan tensed, prepared to drop or dash as needed, if Martin started to shift or needed to fight. But when he merely stood and waited, she took his cue and studied the newcomers. Not preters. Not pretty, the way Stjerne had been, not as weirdly recognizable as not-human, but still exotic, alien. And her skin still prickled uneasily, when they came too close.

"Not human. It stinks," one of the newcomers said. Male and young, if the voice was anything to go by, which it probably wasn't. Otherwise, Jan couldn't tell gender at all; their hair was short, almost in a buzz cut, their faces were different shapes but all bone-sharp and blue-white, and they wore pale-colored pants and long-sleeved vests that highlighted their height without revealing anything else.

The look of disgust on their faces was universal, though.

The first one shoved one end of the burnished wooden stick at Martin's chest. He shifted closer to Jan, but otherwise stood there, motionless.

"A beast. Nothing to say for yourself, beast?"

"Nothing to you," Martin said. His voice was colorless, emotionless, and Jan got a very clear sense of warning: she was to say nothing, draw no attention to herself. Let him handle this.

The second guard, the one who'd mentioned a stink, sneered. "And who, then, do you think you're going to say it to?"

"Do you really want to take me on, children?" Martin's voice was still flat, colorless, but there was an edge of something inside now, like the warning flash of claws. "Do you know what I am?"

Jan held her breath, expecting them to retort, maybe hit him again, but instead there was silence. She recognized it: they were trying to think of a comeback and failing.

"Do you really want to challenge me?" Martin asked again, and the claws were out and visible in his voice this time. His body shifted position slightly, his feet planted, his upper body moving forward, his shoulders and elbows back. It looked awkward to her, but the three reacted as though he'd showed them a badge and gun.

"Go on, then," the first one said finally, letting the

stick fall back into neutral stance. "Go on, and you'll wish you'd stayed to deal with us, instead."

Martin didn't bother to reply but took Jan's hand in his own—it was shaking, she noted—and walked past them without a word.

When she worked up the nerve to look back over her shoulder, they were gone.

"What were those?"

"Greensleeves." His voice was still flat and cold.

"What?" Their vests had been sort of an off-white, the color of unbleached linen, sleeves and all.

"Greensleeves. They were human, once. A long time ago. That's what happens to the ones that are taken, but not kept. They wander, abandoned, trying to find some point to their existence, thinking to guard their abductors, to prove their worth…but they have no worth, anymore." He sounded as if he was retelling the end of a story, one he'd heard so many times it had become indistinguishable from history. And yet, she had seen them, and they were here, and…maybe all the stories were true, after all.

"That's what will happen to Tyler? If we don't rescue him?"

Martin wouldn't look at her. "If he's lucky."

Jan bit her lip and started walking faster. After a minute, Martin caught up with her. A few paces on, her hand slipped into his and felt the answering, re-assuring pressure.

"We can do this," he said quietly.

"They don't think so. They let us go because they think we're going to fail. They couldn't take you, but this Court can."

The rise they'd been on gave way to a plateau, and then the next hill started. The sky above was starting to darken and clear, but the quality of light hadn't changed—still silvery-gray, still giving her eyestrain. She scanned the grass in front of her, and something caught her eye, a faint indentation and shadow. There was not quite a path but an indication of where others had walked, leading up. People—beings—came here, on a regular enough basis to create a trail.

They were getting closer. She could feel it.

Panic hit her again, suddenly, a familiar and unwelcome companion. "I can't do this."

"Yes. Yes you can." He came up behind her, put his arms around her upper body, resting his chin in her shoulder. "You can. AJ saw it in you. You can do this. For Tyler." His breath ruffled her hair, warmed the tip of her ear.

The two of them, going up against a court of beings like the bitch? Martin's confidence was sweet, but stupid. Jan's eyes prickled, and her throat swelled, as though she were going to cry, but no tears came. All right. They would go, and they would do what they had to do, and then…

And nothing was certain beyond the moment. Okay, fine. Embrace the uncertainty. She hadn't sat quietly in her apartment crying because she had been abandoned. She hadn't hesitated, when Martin called her on her promise, pulled her into this impossible, terrifying, gloom-struck world.

All right, maybe she had hesitated. But she hadn't refused.

"Everything built up can be broken down," she said, quoting Glory on one of her more annoying motivational jags. "Everything that is broken down can be rebuilt."

"If you're not dead, you're still alive," Martin said in response.

"Let me guess: AJ."

He just squeezed her hand once, and they walked on in silence.

Chapter 15

If time was wonky in fairyland, it got wonkier the closer you got to the Court, or whatever was lurking under that mountain, Jan decided. Time and distance seemed to be dilating, or compressing, or something, because she would have sworn they'd only taken a few steps up the last hill when the mountain was suddenly in front of them.

"So." Jan tilted her head back to look at it. It wasn't a pretty mountain, up close. Squat and square-shouldered, mainly rock and random trees, occasional patches of shrubs… It looked unfriendly as hell. Or maybe she was projecting. "We go up that."

"Into it," Martin said.

"Right."

She waited, almost expecting some third challenge to show up, but nothing happened except the mist lifted a little more, showing more dark sky.

There was a real path now, distinct if not well-marked. They followed it, winding around boulders, rising slowly but steadily above the plains. The pale green grass gave way to dryer soil, then bare rock, as they went up into that last hill, looking for a way inside.

"There." Jan was the one who saw it first, although it was truer to say that she felt it before she saw the opening in the side of the mountain, like a cold spot in a room. Somewhere between a cave mouth and a doorway, it was nearly ten feet high and twice as wide, banded along the edges with some kind of white metal that held its own light, like a solar lamp.

Emergency lights, like in a plane, she thought.

They stood outside the mouth and waited. Jan wasn't sure what they were waiting for, but she counted off the breaths, making it to thirty before Martin stepped forward, and she followed.

The opening led to a cavern, smooth-walled and at least ten feet high, maybe more. There were brackets set into the wall, each of them holding a round shape that glowed softly. In that light, she could see that the cavern extended farther in, and at the far side there was a door, closer to normal-size.

"Ready?"

"That was possibly the stupidest question that has ever come out of your mouth," she told him.

"We could just stay here. I mean, eventually we'd starve to death, or someone coming in or out would find us and probably take us to the Court, anyway, but—"

A kelpie's danger was in his charm, his appeal. *He seduced by making you want to be with him.* Jan knew that and took his hand, anyway. "C'mon."

Inside. Under-the-hill, Martin had called it. Well, there was truth in advertising, because they went down a stone path, deeper and deeper, until Jan lost all sense of how far they'd gone. The air was still fresh, so there had to be some kind of ventilation system.... But why wasn't there anyone else? Was this the only entrance? No, there had to be others, even preters needed emergency exits, right? Maybe they were coming in the back door, and that's why nobody was here; it wasn't that they were waiting down there already, expecting them...

They didn't speak, fingers twined together like Hansel and Gretel heading into the forest, her breathing harsher than his. It was too dry, the air filled with dust, and she wanted to pull out her inhaler, but it was the only one she had, and she'd been using it a lot; she had the bad feeling she might need it more, later.

Just when she thought the hallway they were in would go on forever, or maybe just dump them on the other side of the mountain without actually taking them anywhere, the path opened into another chamber. She stopped, Martin beside her, and stared. Unlike the entrance chamber, this one was three times the size of her entire apartment, and at least two stories high. A single light floated overhead, giving enough clear white light to see everything below it perfectly. The chamber was ringed with stone benches, the seats carved with so much filigree, Jan wondered if they could actually support any weight, or if they were just for show. It was the first bit of design she'd seen anywhere, almost startling after so much bare wall.

There were no doors visible in those walls, their entrance the sole archway, and Jan wondered for a moment if they'd come to a dead end. Then Martin squeezed her hand and lifted his chin to indicate a single figure standing against the far wall, where the benches turned down and blended into the stone floor.

How had she missed that? Had it even been there before?

"Go," Martin said, his voice barely a whisper, and he let go of her hand. "Go forward, and claim what is yours."

She swallowed hard, already missing the comfort of his touch, and stepped forward. The preter—it was an elf, of course it was an elf, no matter what they called themselves they were elves—raised its head and stared at her.

She had expected it to be attractive. She had expected it to be unnerving. She hadn't expected it to be terrifying. Unlike the greensleeves, this creature exuded a real, if quiet, menace, even more than the bitch, because its attention was entirely focused on *her*.

Martin stayed behind, and for a moment she hated him intensely for abandoning her. But that wasn't fair. He'd told her before that he couldn't interfere, couldn't help. He didn't care about Tyler.

This was her battle.

She forced herself to study the preter. The high cheekbones and pale skin were utterly eclipsed by the eyes, which were round and large and a solid black, with no pupil whatsoever. Was it the lighting? Was it angry? Were their eyes always like that? It was stupid and pointless, but it was better to wonder stupid things than think about what she was about to do.

They stared at each other, Jan's heart thumping way too fast and too loudly, until she was sure everyone under the mountain could hear it. The guard showed no surprise at her appearance; it showed no emotion at all, beyond that impersonal menace.

They liked order, patterns, rules. They were bound by tradition and didn't deal well with surprises. Well, she was about to surprise the hell out of them. Hopefully.

"I am here to claim what is mine," she said. Her voice did not shake, did not tremble, but carried cleanly across the space, as though she were speaking of something of no consequence.

The preter stared at her and then stepped aside, and the wall opened into an arched doorway, a twin to the one they had come in through, as though the opening had always been there.

Guess she'd said the right thing.

It took every inch of spine Jan had—and the knowledge that going back wasn't an option—to step through that archway. She did not look back, but only hoped that Martin followed.

Inside, there was an even larger chamber, this one lit by many smaller, more blue-tinged lights, and filled with people.

No, not people, Jan corrected herself quickly. Preters. *Elves.* Dozens of them, some wearing bright, elaborate gowns and long vests, others in pants, shirts, and jackets that wouldn't raise an eyebrow back home. Some were pale, others dark, but they all had that tall, unearthly grace when they moved, and they were all—now—looking at her. They had been gathered along the walls to the right and left of the doorway, and were filling in the space behind her, even as she walked forward. It was almost as though they were driving her toward the end of the room, where a huge dais was set up with chairs—and figures sitting on those chairs.

There was a sense of panic, the herd beast surrounded by predators. Jan refused it, shoving it away.

She had survived the cats by being still, and they'd gotten past the greensleeves by being confident. This was just another test, and not even the scariest one.

But, oh, how she hoped that Martin had her back.

She listened, as she walked, and was reassured by the faintest echo of another set of feet behind her on the stone floor. Unless a preter was creeping behind her—don't look, she thought, don't look—Martin was there.

She and Martin, up against the entire—what had he called it? The Unseelie Court. They were outnumbered, something like twenty-to-one, and all she had on her was a knife she didn't know how to use, and Martin…well, he had hooves. If the magic worked the same way on them, maybe she'd be able to attack while their eyes were closed as he shifted? But then her eyes would be closed, too.…

She reached the center of the room and stopped, forcing her mind clear. She needed to be ready for what would happen, not what might. The problem was, she didn't know what would happen, either.

A stolen knife in one pocket, inhaler in the other, a kelpie at her back, Jan lifted her head and approached the preter Court.

The dais was directly in front of her now; five long strides would take her right up to it. She stopped where she was. The dais itself was made of the same stone as the walls, smooth silvery-gray and carved like the benches out front. Apparently it could support weight. A lot of weight.

She had thought, maybe, there would be two figures seated there; instead, she counted ten, seven of them standing, the other three seated on the slender-legged, high-backed chairs that had caught her attention when she came in.

They were all still, as though caught in various poses of conversation, and they were all looking at her.

Disconcerted, Jan's gaze flicked around the room once, taking impressions more than specific details, then she went back to the one figure that caught her eye.

Tyler, toward the back of the room, half hidden by others. How had she not known he was there, the moment she walked into the room? The preters and humans around him whispered to each other, flicking fans and raising their hands for privacy, but he watched her, his face still and tired, and she would have sworn she saw a flicker of something in his expression. Recognition? Hope?

She opened her mouth, not knowing what she planned to do—call his name, race to his side?—and then the figure in front of him shifted, spreading a deep blue cloak outward, blocking him from Jan's view.

No. Blocking her from his.

Bitch, Jan thought, knowing instinctively who it

was under that cape. The urge to confront the preter who had stolen Tyler surged in her, and she almost took a step forward, when then the figure in the left-hand chair lifted a hand, and a figure stepped out of the crowd, into the circle of space where she stood, drawing her attention away.

"So you are the one who has caused a disruption at the portal," the creature in front of her said. It—he—was as handsome as the bitch was beautiful, and just as disturbing, with skin that was too pale, and ears too sharp, and a voice that was empty of anything except a grim humor. "It is rare that a human comes to us, unescorted. And to bring one of the lesser breeds with you—does he bear your equipment or share your bed? Or, perhaps, both?"

The insinuating tone made it sound filthy, as though Martin were an animal.

Oh, no, you don't, she thought, after the first flare of anger hit. *Magic and weird animals and interdimensional physics-changing portals freak me out, but snide bullies? Those I was dealing with by the time I was thirteen.* Jan didn't say any of that out loud, just squared her shoulders and said, again, "I've come for that which is mine."

"Oh, Stjerne's pet?" The figure glanced lazily in Tyler's direction. "He does not seem to belong to you, human."

Jan didn't let herself look again to where Tyler stood, half hidden behind that bitch's cloak. Her heart ached, but only a little. Martin had said that they followed rules, abided by traditions. She had to focus on that, not her emotions. "I followed him here, between worlds, led by the tie between us. That gives me claim."

The guard raised his eyebrow and pursed his lips. "There is truth to that."

"No!" The bitch stepped forward, pushing her way through the others, stung into responding. "He is *mine*. This human would have taken him away, but he fought to stay with me."

"There is truth in that, as well."

"You've brainwashed him!" Jan said, trying not to let the desperation show in her voice. "His heart still knows me."

"Enough," the figure in the left-side chair on the dais said, drawing her attention back. Definitely male, for all that he was draped in a deep red brocade gown that flowed over his body like a dress, and his chestnut-brown hair curled down past his shoulders in commercial-perfect spirals. "What we take, we retain."

"Not always." She might not have known much about elves, or fairyland, or anything preternatural, but she knew that much. She thought of the legends AJ had mentioned, the stories of true love and determination. "Not if I can take it back."

The bitch shook out her blue cloak, looking smug. "You tried once, in your own lands, and failed."

Jan squared herself, ready for battle. "And here I am, to try again."

"Once there, once here. It seems fair," the guard said, and turned to the red-robed figure on the dais for confirmation.

"Yes. Let Stjerne, for her arrogance, stand against this human for possession of her pet. That should settle the question of her behavior, and how well she has performed her duties to this Court—or if she has, indeed, failed us."

There was a fuss of noise behind Jan, as though someone tried to protest and was stopped or silenced. Stjerne herself? Or Tyler? Jan did not let herself turn to look.

"Is that the royal 'us'? I thought there was supposed to be a *queen* of the preternatural Court." Martin's voice was odd: almost insolent, arrogant. It took Jan a moment to realize why he still sounded so familiar: he was channeling AJ at his worst.

She didn't let herself look but could sense him somehow, coming closer.

He didn't touch her, didn't speak to her, but she wasn't alone.

But he had said he couldn't help her fight for Tyler. What was he doing? Why was he trying to make them mad?

The male figure on the dais raised his chin and stared down his nose at them, but Jan hadn't missed the way the figures gathered around him shifted and muttered quietly. The Court around her was almost too silent, as if he'd slapped them. Something was wrong, here. What the hell was he *doing?*

"Where is your queen?" Martin asked, his voice, if possible, even more AJ-insolent. That wasn't Martin. He had either lost his mind or he was doing something…once she thought that, she could almost *feel* his intent: he was trying to irritate them, to distract them, to prod them into saying something they didn't mean to. "Why is there no queen of this Court?"

Silence, an angry, nasty silence, and Jan felt her skin prickle again. Danger. A shifting anger, rising from the crowd, directed at…them? No. If it had been aimed at them, she knew, they'd be dead already, it was that intense, that hard.

"Gone."

The voice came not from the dais, but the crowd below. A slender, jean-clad figure—and Jan couldn't tell if it was male or female, its long red hair caught in a simple braid, its features bloodless and severe—stepped forward.

"The Queen is gone. Into your world."

"Silence." The prince, or king, or whatever he was, snapped the word out so sharp it bled the air.

"The shame of it will not be silenced. She is gone, and will not return," the redhead said, undaunted. "She refuses her duty, rejects her obligations, for fascination. What is your world, that we should be so enamored of it?"

"Gone for a while, for them to be so angry, and so resigned," Martin said softly, meant only for her ears. "For one of their own, their queen to reject them? So very angry. The consort holds on with his fingernails."

"So that's what all this is about?" The pieces were starting to move under her hands, the colors and shapes finally creating something she could understand. "She abandoned you, so you want revenge?"

The crowd muttered, and the consort settled back in his chair as though Jan were no longer a threat, she hadn't proven herself worthy. Another shape shifted, and she shook her head, letting it fall into place. "No. That's not enough for you. Not as angry as you are."

She understood the anger, the mix of frustration and disbelief, the self-doubt and the fear, for yourself and for him, that something terrible must have happened....

"You want whatever captivated her, what took her. That's what this is all about. Not greed: anger. Fear. You can't stand that she wanted what was in our world, so you're going to claim it for yourself, all of it this time, so nobody can ever leave again." The entire world, and all the people in it.

If they were as rigid, as tied to rules and traditions as Martin said, a queen's abandonment must have thrown them for a whopper.

"Why did she leave in the first place?" Jan picked up what Martin had started; she couldn't manage that kind of arrogance, but disbelief worked almost as well. "What did you do to drive her away?"

She knew that making them angry probably wasn't smart, but she understood Martin's plan now, she thought: this was what AJ had sent them to find out. The reason for the change, why the preters were making such an almighty push now. But what were they pushing *for?*

There was an unhappy rumble from the crowd, silenced only by a raised hand from the figure in the seat next to the consort, a tall, hard-faced female who hadn't spoken or moved, until then.

"She felt something new in the wind," the redhead said, refusing to be cowed. "Some new twist in the worlds. She slipped away to follow it, and would not return."

"She must be brought home. And punished. We know how, now." The consort stood up then, glowering down at Jan—and, she presumed, at Martin, as well.

Elves, Jan decided, didn't glower well. Then he raised his hand again, and two others stepped forward with ugly, sharp swords in their hands, and Jan decided they glowered well enough.

They didn't like having their secret exposed—or having humans question them. Jan studied the blades, considerably more lethal than her own useless, pocketed knife, and tried to calculate the odds of her bolting, getting through the crowd, past the guards and the greensleeves…

Nope. She was dead.

"You agreed to a contest," Martin said, and suddenly he was between her and the swords, his body turned and his shoulders set. The two preters looked at each other, a sideways glance, as though trying to decide what to do, but stood fast.

"No matter that she is impertinent—she is human. Humans do that. You agreed that she might have the chance to win back her leman, to return with him through the portal, unmolested, undetained."

That was more than they had promised, actually. Jan clenched her jaw; now was not the time to be nitpicking. Three goals: win back Tyler, find a way to stop the preters from kidnapping in wholesale numbers, stop whatever they had planned. Get home safe.

"I made no such promise." The consort looked to the figure next to him, as though for confirmation, and it—she—nodded.

Martin kept talking, faster than she'd ever heard him go. "And yet, you will. Because the challenge is a good one, the contest fair but impossible for a human who had already lost once to win again, here, Under the Hill. You will agree, and agree to the terms, and let the challenge go forth. Because to do otherwise—" Martin let the silence draw out just a second longer than was comfortable, and then finished "—would imply that you were afraid."

They *were* afraid. Martin was right. They were terrified—of something. Had the queen leaving thrown their world that much off balance? Like a clay pot on a wheel, maybe, and when one of the hands guiding it slipped, the entire thing went misshapen?

Jan licked her lips, willing her lungs to stay calm, to not let her cough. Thankfully, the cavern was cleaner than she would have expected, as though magic kept dust away. She wondered if that, finally, was a spell, or if fairyland was just naturally dust-free. If so, it was the first positive point she'd seen about it.

She should have been terrified; she should have been shaking like a leaf, convinced she was going to fail, convinced she was going to die. Instead, she was wondering about the preter's housekeeping habits. Jan was pretty sure that everyone in this place was insane, including herself.

"No second challenge," Stjerne protested, her voice whip-sharp. "He stays here. He is mine!"

The consort did not even bother looking at her, but the figure in the chair next to him, the one who had quelled the crowd before, did, and she subsided. Jan averted her own gaze, not wanting to look someone that scary directly in the eye.

"Is this your word?" Martin asked. "Is this your word, to agree to one term, and then offer another? Can the bargains of the preternaturals be that degraded?"

He was goading them again, trying to push them into something. But what, and why? They'd already found out why the preters were acting this way—did Martin have an actual plan, or was he tap-dancing, trying to buy time? If so—time to do what? No cavalry was going to ride over—under—this hill.

Jan wished to hell that they'd had time to discuss this more, before being hauled into the Court. While she was at it, a handbook would have been nice, too.

"Nothing is as it was," the consort said. "All is askew." He smiled at them, and his smile was scarier than his glower, all thin lips and menace. "But we will right it, balance the sides and claim it all. We know the secret now. One human, less or more, will not change the inevitable result. We will prevail."

"The hell you will," Jan said to herself, stung. And then, louder, "The hell you will. You will return what is mine, and you will get the hell out of my world."

The consort's smile broadened into a grin, displaying unnervingly white and sharp teeth that reminded Jan of the gnomes. They weren't omnivores, and she suddenly wondered what happened to the changelings and bespelled humans who didn't become greensleeves or stay useful....

"The challenge," Martin said, reminding them both to stay on track.

"You accept the terms?" the consort asked Jan

Even if she ignored anything and everything AJ and Martin—and the others—had told her, Jan knew that preters—elves—lied. They were tricky by their very nature. She had learned that much in her web surfing. You couldn't trust their word, and you most definitely could not trust a contract with them, because there was always a loophole, always an exit clause. She had absolutely no idea what she was getting into if she agreed to this.

But she'd known, from that moment in the street, with Martin calling on her promise, that it would come down to this. Maybe even before, when Tyler had first disappeared, when she had learned what had happened to him and to others…

She touched her pocket, making sure that the inhaler was still there, felt the hard shape of the knife in her other pocket pressing against her hip, and nodded.

"I accept."

Meredith paced down the length of the side street, irritated and hyper-alert. Even days old, the scent led her here; there was no way to mistake the musky river smell of the kelpie. And there had been a muddle of something else, too. Dark and violent, still and cool like a night wind. She had never smelled it before, but she knew from the very fact that she did not recognize it what it must be. Preter.

The alley also smelled of over-ripe garbage, sweat and something that had died a long time ago, so long it was only dry bones now, but she could ignore all that. The two smells that were important lay on top, most recent. The kelpie—and, one presumed, his human—had come here. Had encountered a preter. Magic had been worked, not the clean, clear magic of her own kind, but something more complicated, smelling of meat and bone and blood and pain, until some part of her was uncomfortably excited by it.

They're evil. But that evil is part of their seduction, AJ had warned them back when this all began. *They speak to the darker sides, the selfish desires. You may be tempted. You may not see the harm. But they will use you, and give you only dirt in return.*

AJ was her pack leader; even if she hadn't agreed with him, she would have obeyed. But he was right; this was not a thing she should choose. So she looked at the excitement, accepted it, and then put it down.

She was *lupin;* instinct did not rule her, she ruled it. Her orders were to find the kelpie and report back on his progress. She would do that. She would not fail.

Sometimes, though, duty and responsibility were so *boring.*

Meredith looked around, sniffed the information again, and sighed. Whatever had happened here, it was over. Even the most recent smells of magic were going stale.

The old portals were tied to place, to season. AJ had briefed them, over and over again until they could repeat it in their sleep. *These have no such restrictions that we can find, but the preters we have hunted always return to a specific place; they do not simply disappear when we find them. Something draws them back to where they came.*

So if the kelpie and his human had gone through here, it seemed likely that this was where they had to come back.

That could take a while, though. Remembering the street vendor around the corner, she went back to buy a kebob and a soda, found a spot with a clear line of sight, and settled down to wait. Eventually, either the kelpie or a preter would come through, and she would have something to do.

Chapter 16

All the panic that Jan hadn't felt before flooded into her the moment she agreed to the challenge, and the chamber erupted into quiet but excited murmurs. Martin took her by the elbow, and she jumped, startled, even though she'd known he was there.

"What did I just get myself into? I can't fight, you know that. I'm—"

He stroked her arm, the way she might have touched his neck in his other form, and some of her panic ebbed away. He was here. She wasn't alone.

"You did what we came here to do. What needs to be done. We know why they're doing this, even if we don't know how. If we can get your leman home, then we can see what he remembers, what he knows."

"I'm crap at fighting," she said, her entire body trembling now. "You know that. I'm fast, but I'm not strong, I don't know how to use this damn knife, and the last time I hit someone, I think I was eleven. And the moment I get an asthma attack—and you know I will, that's the kind of luck I have—it's all over."

"It's not a fight. Not like that, anyway."

He drew her off into a corner, the preters who had been standing there moving away to give them the illusion of privacy. Apparently they were very polite, once you agreed to die.

"It's a fight like what, then? Because now I've got, like, Survivor-style matches in my head, and I'm not going to be any good at that, either. In fact, I'll be worse."

"Jan." He turned her, his hands on both arms now, gripping her around the biceps, his long, lovely face close to hers. He had very thin lips, she noticed. Nicely formed, but thin, just like the preter's. But he had good teeth, square and strong, and his breath was sweet; if his body smelled like green water and moss, his breath smelled warm and dry, and just a little sweet, like cocoa. She wanted to inhale him, all her senses wildly alert and hyper-focused.

"Jan. AJ chose you for a reason."

"Yeah, because my boyfriend was dumb enough to get abducted by elves."

"Listen to me." He cupped his hands around her

chin, forced her to look at him. "We didn't tell you everything."

"Of course not." She couldn't even be bitter; nobody ever told her everything, not clients, not boyfriends, not werewolves. And they expected her to play catch-up all the way down.

"The preters, they've taken a dozen or more since we've been watching," Martin said. "None of their lemans would do anything, with or without us. Tyler wasn't special. *You* were."

"Me." She stared into his eyes, seeing for the first time the flecks of gold and green deep within the dark brown depths.

"You. Smart, and quick, and clear-hearted. Stubborn when you knew you were right, but willing to listen, willing to hear. Brave. So very brave—Jan, do you realize how brave you are?"

Jan blinked at him. She had never felt brave.

"You refused to believe your lover had abandoned you. You listened to strangers—and we know how strange we are, to you—and followed us into impossible places. You fought—"

"I ran," she said. "I left Toba there, and I ran."

"You allowed Toba to do his job, and leaped out of a window, trusting us to protect you. You got on my back and trusted me to keep you safe. You walked into fairyland, because you had made a promise. To save not only your leman, but all the others who have been taken. Jan, if that is not brave, then what is it?"

"Suicidal," she said. "All right, all right. I'm brave. Or incredibly dumb. So, what do I have to do?"

He released her, but the feel of his fingers against her skin remained.

"You need to withstand."

"Withstand?" Already, it didn't sound good. In fact, it sounded worse than before. "Withstand what? I'm really not good with pain, Martin. I once avoided the dentist for four years because I can't handle getting my teeth cleaned."

The kelpie didn't take her bait, the seriousness in his expression making her attempt at humor even worse. "You have given permission for magic to be worked upon you. You must withstand. You need to resist what is done to you, and remain true to yourself."

Jan absorbed that, thought about it, and felt a chill grow in her bones, rising outward. Magic. "You mean…like what she did to Tyler, changing his form?" She had convinced herself that was just an illusion, glamour. "Can they do that? I mean, for real? I thought you said they didn't cast spells, or anything like that?"

Preters and supers both, they seduced, they didn't tell the truth…but did the supers instinctively, intrinsically lie, too? Or did they just misdirect and avoid? Jan wasn't good with words, not that way, but she thought there was a real difference between not telling the truth and lying. She looked at Martin with narrowed eyes, waiting for him to respond.

"Maybe. Maybe other things. I don't know." He lowered his head until their foreheads touched. "Their magic…we don't have it. Supernaturals just *are*. We don't mess with the universe, we exist within in. Preternaturals—"

"Mess with the universe. Yeah, I got that already. Holding open a doorway between worlds just to cause trouble was kinda a clue."

"Portal, not doorway. A doorway is a simple set, a portal—"

"Now is no time to get pedantic on me," she muttered. "So I just have to, what, be stoic?"

A crease appeared between his eyes, and the flickers of gold and green disappeared into the brown again. "You can't forget. Remember who you are, why you're here."

"Right." It seemed too easy, which made her suspicious. "Will it…will it hurt?"

Martin might not always tell all the truth, but he never lied to her.

"I don't know."

"Oh, joy."

Jan bit her lower lip and pulled away from Martin, needing space between them, away from his concern and his utter uselessness. He had never claimed to be the hero, never said he had the answers; she had no right to be angry with him.

Anger didn't do her any good, but it was all she had just then. She couldn't bear looking across the chamber, either, where Tyler was surrounded by other figures, their capes and dresses flowing and moving around him, flashes of bright color against the otherwise drab stone walls, and so found herself staring at her feet, her sneakers oddly implausible in this setting.

She shivered, crossing her arms around herself, wishing this were all over with, already. "I would have thought that the fairy kingdom would be, I don't know, prettier. They don't believe in paintings? Or rugs?"

"Preters aren't very creative," Martin said, falling in with her attempt at distraction. "I think that's another reason why they take humans. You create— we don't, either, really. I couldn't even imagine how to make something, visualize it and make it real."

Jan tried to imagine not being able to take an idea and translate it into a new site, a specialized design, and shivered again. She didn't think of herself as being particularly creative, but to not have even that?

"What do supernaturals do, then? I mean, other than steal cars and rescue kidnapped humans?"

"Mostly, we cause trouble too," Martin admitted. "We're not big on what humans consider morality, or honor. Sometimes we pick sides and help humans who amuse or interest us, but we—"

"Can't be trusted. Yeah. I got that."

There was a rise in the sound level from across the room, and his hands tightened on her shoulders, almost to the point of pain. She lifted her arms, putting her hands on his shoulders, letting them slide down his arms until their hands were clasped, as close to an embrace as they could allow themselves here, with an audience. In front of Tyler.

"It's time," Martin said.

She took a deep breath to reassure herself that she still could, and let it out slowly, the way her yoga DVD said to. "Be here for me, when I'm done?"

The shades of gold and green were back in his eyes, hot and sharp. "I'll be here."

To carry her home in victory—or bring her body home in defeat. Jan squeezed his hands once, then stepped away, his hands letting her go without resistance.

The space in the middle of the room where she had stood before was now larger, the crowd pushed back, the stone floor cleared of anything that might impede movement—or interfere with the sight lines of the audience, Jan thought grimly. All that was missing was the popcorn, and this could be a Saturday afternoon matinee. Or a day at the Roman Colosseum.

Stjerne was already there, waiting. The preter had taken off the cape and looked almost ordinary in her brown skirt and cream-colored blouse, brown leather boots rising to her knee, just a few inches under the hem of the skirt. As ordinary as anyone that striking could ever manage, anyway. She'd had time to change; those weren't the clothes she'd been wearing in the coffee shop, back home. In her mud-dried jeans and long-sleeved shirt, knowing her hair was a tangle and her eyes probably red-rimmed, her skin blotchy, Jan suspected she looked like a joke in comparison.

Tyler had been taken back into the crowd, half hidden by other bodies, but Jan looked over the bitch's shoulder and found him. His eyes were wide and his face was ashen, but she could not tell who he feared for.

Glamour could make you believe things. Could make you feel things. Were they real? Were they true?

Did it matter? You could love more than one person, and sex and the heart didn't always go together. Tyler loved her, and she loved him, and she was taking him home, where he belonged.

"And thus, now or never, do or die," Jan muttered under her breath, and stepped forward into the cleared circle. She found a spot that seemed comfortable, although it was no different from any other spot, set her feet the way she'd been taught in self-defense classes back in college, touched the inhaler in her pocket for reassurance, and lifted her chin. "Bring it, bitch."

There was no warning, no lifted hands or willow wand pointing, no incantation or sparkles, just a malicious twist to the bitch's mouth and Jan's body caught fire, agony whipping through every vein. Her eyes dried out, and the lining of her nose turned to sand, the moisture in her body evaporating as though she were in the center of a blast fire.

And inside that fire, the curling heart of it, the whisper *"Give in. let go. All this will end, if you only let go."*

"Bitch," Jan pushed out through gritted teeth, her fingers curling into her palms, giving her a real pain to focus on. "I don't think so."

The pain intensified, although she would have sworn that was impossible. Like lava chewing at her bones, destroying and renewing so that she could never actually die, never be at peace. She tried not to believe it, tried to reject it as illusion, but the pain was too much.

In agony, Jan thought of Martin, but the strange half guilt she'd been carrying turned on her then, lashing her with accusations and insinuations.

I wasn't. I didn't....

Her heart ached, so badly she thought it would crack, and she lifted her hands to her chest, as though to force it back in.

Her fingers touched the silver of her bracelet, slid against the cool metal, seemingly untouched by anything else, smooth and supple, like Martin's skin, splashed wet with sweat...

And she remembered being carried on his back through his riverine home, of cool water splashing over her, encasing her, and waking up wet but sound. Wet and safe.

She could trust him, even when he didn't trust himself.

Slowly, too slowly, the fire sizzled and went out, her sinuses dry and burning, but her skin soaked with sweat.

Jan wanted to say or do something to show her defiance, but here was barely enough time to breathe in relief before the next attack hit, twisting her arms and torso, bending her knees and sending her to the floor.

She looked up and saw the bitch staring at her, that cruel quirk of the lip now a full-blown snarl, like the one she had shown in the alley, before the portal. Jan had time for a fleeting thought—*she's not underestimating me anymore*—before something broke her spine and sent her facedown on the cold stone floor.

The pain was different this time, coming not from the inside, but out. Her body cramped and changed, fur sprouting from underneath her skin, her hands resting on the floor, her entire sense of self and gravity shifting until she had the urge to howl, to grovel to her pack master for release, to accept her role and let go....

A dog cowers, the pain whispered to her. *A dog heels. A dog—*

A dog was cousin to the wolf. Jan thought of AJ. Proud, fierce. Determined to do what needed to be done, no matter the cost.

"You are not my pack leader," she managed to force through jaws that felt odd and heavy, the wrong shape for speaking. "I do not give in...to you."

Pain flared again, forcing her eyes wide and her mouth open, gasping for air. The shape changed, twisting her around again, throwing her onto her back and making her legs spasm. Her spine arched in ways it shouldn't be able to, and her head hit the stone floor hard enough to make everything go silent.

Her arms sealed to her sides, her legs useless, Jan felt herself go cold as doubts sifted their way in. She was useless. Abandoned. Alone all day in a room, moving digits around for things no one would ever notice. Pale and too soft, too gentle, too needy. No wonder Tyler went elsewhere, found someone more exotic, more fascinating, more experienced.

Someone better suited to him, the doubts whispered, poison dripping sweetly. *You were never enough for him; let go, let him go his way, and you be on yours....*

Jan stretched, her muscles still working even in this new form, and lifted her head along the huge serpent's body, turning to stare at her opponent, lidless eyes unflinching. Her tongue flicked out once, twice, and caught the taste of fear. Her own... And her opponent's... And more.

The entire room was filled with fear.

It was a revelation for the bit of Jan still aware

within that massive form. All this, all their magic, their glamour, and they were afraid...of her.

They were afraid of humans. Of what humans could do.

The icy fog in her brain lifted, faded and melted, just enough. All right, Tyler had wandered. The lure of something different, something out of reach or forbidden, had been too much to resist. Maybe it was magic, maybe it was his own weakness, maybe she wouldn't be enough for him in the long run. But. Her tongue flicked out again and tasted memories of Tyler. She remembered his sleepy arms around her early in the morning, the way his legs tangled with hers while he slept, the look in his eyes when she glanced up and saw him studying her, intense and hot.

Her legs. Her eyes. Her hands, fixing and typing, touching and holding, creating and destroying. Her mouth, to speak, to sing, to shout.

She remembered them in the shower together, him singing, teaching her the words, while his hands moved over her skin....

Her throat couldn't form the words, but she remembered the song.

The snake's form shuddered and then cracked open, like shards of iridescent crystal shattering, flying across the room. The surrounding preters ducked, almost instinctively, even as Jan thought, in passing, distracted, "I must have been beautiful like that."

As though summoned by her own fleeting enjoyment, a blow hit her out of nowhere, this time nothing but rage, a heavy blow into her ribs, forcing her to double over. Nothing subtle, nothing transforming or delusional about this, only the very real pain, worse than before because there was no pretense, no distraction of a new form, only the searing, venomous rage.

And then another blow landed, this time from the backside, just above her hip. Jan fell to her knees again, not even aware of having stood up, tasting blood in her mouth. Had she bitten her tongue? Or was she starting to cough up blood?

Her throat closed up, her chest congested, all the warning signs of an asthma attack approaching. She could die here. She probably would die here. Tyler would be lost, Martin…what would happen to Martin?

AJ knew they had never had a chance.

You cannot win, the rage told her, a searing whisper like an iron clamped to her ears.

I will not lose.

Foolish mortal. Always foolish. Always losing.

Toba had lost. He had died, standing against the tide of turncoats, giving her time to escape. Giving her the chance to be brave when her time came. Was that really losing?

Only if she screwed this up.

"You cannot resist us."

Jan forced her eyes open, forced herself upright

on her knees, unable to do more, and stared at the woman who had stolen her lover. "That's not the way our stories tell it." And that wasn't how it had gone for their queen.

Stjerne's lovely face twisted in a snarl, as though she had heard that unspoken thought. Maybe she had. Maybe Jan had actually spoken it, not just thought it. The preter raised her hand for another blow, her knuckles already stained with blood. Jan's blood.

Jan was pretty sure that this blow would break something important, but couldn't bring herself to brace for it.

"Let go," the preter said, "and I will let you live."

Jan shook her head, remembering the terms. If she agreed to something else, anything less, she could lose everything. "I came here for Tyler."

The preter spat the words, the venom almost visible, the air trembling around her. "You don't deserve him."

Jan laughed at that, and blood dripped to the floor. "What makes you think love has anything to do with 'deserving'? What makes you think love has any logic to it at all?"

The pain relented just a little, as though her defiance had pushed it back to—almost—bearable levels. Jan got to her feet, slowly, one hand on the floor to push her up. Things crackled and popped, and a line of fire ran from her calves to her neck, reminding her that magic or not, the damage had been real.

She ignored the woman standing within arm's reach, fought down the desire to wring that beautiful neck, and instead turned to the figures on the dais.

Her breath came as though squeezed though lungs flattened like a toothpaste tube, but it came, and that was enough. She had resisted. Magic had been worked on her...and she remained herself, unowned.

"I'm not perfect," she said now, the words harsh out of a throat that felt as if she had been screaming for hours. "I'm maybe not even the right match for Tyler, even though I love him. I'm...angry at him. And scared. And...love is complicated." She swallowed and tasted blood. "But I know two things. One, that you have no right to hold him against his will, not if you tricked him, made him believe things that weren't true. And two, you have no right to be in my world."

Stubborn, that's what she was. That had been what AJ had seen in her, why he'd chosen her. Stubborn, not brave.

Jan thought that maybe, here and now, the two things were close enough to not matter.

Stjerne stepped forward, getting between Jan and the dais. "He is mine. I carved him out and created him anew. He is *mine*." She said the words as if they hurt her. Jan rather hoped they did.

"You deny the results of the challenge?" The consort sounded...amused? Jan had the sudden thought that, when there were no humans to abuse, the pre-

ternatural Court probably were just as happy to turn
on each other for entertainment value.

Without taking her eyes off the consort, Jan tried
to figure out where Martin was, if they could make
a run for it if needed. Then again, she could barely
stand, so running was probably out of the question.

"The creature was in the room," Stjerne said. "She
took strength from it. Kill it, and try again."

"What?" Jan's eyes widened, and pain or not, she
swung around with every intention of taking the bitch
out herself.

The consort looked to his side, to the preter who
had commented before.

"That is also…a fair point," the preter—some kind
of judge?—said.

"The hell it is!" Jan shouted. "Martin didn't do
anything, he just—"

"It's all right." Martin's voice, just behind and to
her right, and she turned to face him, still spitting
mad.

"Screw you and the pony you… Oh, hell, you
know what I mean." The slip made a faint smile appear on Martin's face, and Jan almost lost it at that,
a surge of affection—stupid but unstoppable—filled
her. She turned back to the dais and forced herself to
move up the steps, ignoring the pain. Stubborn. Oh,
yes, she could be stubborn. All *three* of them were
going home.

She had to pause at the top of the dais and take a

hit off her inhaler, and to hell with showing weakness. Not being able to breathe would be worse. The preters looked at her curiously but didn't interfere.

"I accepted the challenge, and I won. Adding additional terms and conditions after the fact is bullshit. More, it invalidates any existing agreement that might predate your sudden change in policy."

She was grabbing the memory of any disclaimers she'd ever put together for client websites, plus a smattering of the few warranties she'd ever actually read, tossing it together and hoping it sounded reasonable. If Martin was right and the preters had no creativity, if they were bound by rules, they might be taken in by linear double-talk that sounded plausible.

"And so you owe me not only my prize, but our freedom. To leave here, and to be unmolested." Tricky elves. Tricky. Not to be trusted. Get everything nailed down. The thoughts tossed through her head even as she was speaking, hoping to hell that she was doing the right thing.

"Stjerne." The consort looked over Jan's head, down at the preter still waiting on the main floor. "Your request is denied. The human resisted you, and stayed true. More… She amuses us."

He looked at her then, and only then did she realize that his eyes had the same golden rim as Toba's, although his face was fully, smoothly humanlike. Still, the way his hair moved in the nonexistent breeze, almost like feathers…she felt the urge to reach out and touch it.

Mind games, something whispered in her head. Seduction. It's what they do.

She stepped back, and the consort smiled again. "Yes. She amuses us, and so little has, in so many days. More: never let it be said we do not abide by our word, within the boundaries of this Court.

"You may go, human, and take your beast with you. Safe across our borders, and safe for…" He pretended to contemplate, but she knew he had planned what he would say before he opened his mouth. "Ten weeks and ten days and ten hours, you may have, for your audacity, and your honor."

Jan frowned. Something wasn't right. "Ten weeks and ten days…and ten hours," she repeated slowly. Here, or there? If time was twisty here…

"You wish it shorter, human?"

She had thought—she didn't know much, but everything she had read told her that seven was the magical number. As odd as that seemed, as worried as she was about the time distortion, that wasn't the real problem.

They said she could go and take her beast. That meant Martin. But…

"And Tyler," she said. "I fought to bring Tyler home. Those were our terms."

The consort's eyes glittered, and Jan had the uncomfortable feeling that there was something with sharp teeth and sharper claws standing just behind her, awaiting only a twitch to sink itself into her flesh. The sense of unreality that filled this land pressed at her, made her doubt herself and her right to demand anything.

Jan. A whisper of a touch, the soft gurgle of water over rocks, the singing deafness of deep water overhead, and then she could feel the slickness of her keyboard beneath her fingertips, taste the sweet, acrid sting of coffee, smell exhaust and rain on the pavement, and hear the slow, steady thud of a heart at rest under her as she curled in bed, rain outside and coffee beside her, and Tyler, safe and asleep and where he belonged.

"And Tyler," she said again, firmly. "You may not deny me that which is mine."

"If he in truth is yours, then you shall take him, and be gone." The consort smiled again, and Jan distrusted that smile that seemed to take immense pleasure in pain.

"Unleash your pet, Stjerne. Let us see where he goes."

Jan turned, not wanting to look away from the consort, but needing to see what was happening, too. She saw Martin out of the corner of her eye; he had moved to stand near the doorway, his long face worried and drawn. But when he saw her looking at him, he lowered his chin slowly, his shoulders easing, and she smiled. Whatever happened, he was ready to take her home.

Only then did she let herself look across the chamber, to where Stjerne had replaced her cloak, standing next to Tyler, a possessive hand on his arm.

Jan forced herself to look at him the way a stranger might. It was easier somehow, now; he was Tyler and yet, here, he wasn't. A slender, almost scrawny figure, his skin so much darker than her own, a color he said wasn't "true dark" but low brown, his close-cropped head covered in glossy black brush not yet long enough to curl. And his nose and chin as stubborn as her own, softened now with a sort of slackness that was unlike him—Tyler, who was always wound up, always going, even when she wanted to curl up and be lazy...

"Tyler. Ty, come with me," she whispered. She knew her voice wouldn't cross the space, not with such a high ceiling and the other preters muttering and shifting, but somehow he did hear her, his head rising and turning, his body straightening until he looked straight at her, and his eyes were awake, if not entirely clear. She could tell, even from where she stood, that Stjerne's spell was slipping.

He knew her. She could see it on his face. But he wasn't coming toward her, wasn't smiling in that sweet welcome, wasn't shrugging Stjerne's hand off his arm in disgust or shame.

Once before she'd tried to hold him, and failed. If

she failed now…he would be lost forever. Like the figures roaming outside, or…worse.

"Tyler. It's time to come home now."

"No. Stay. Here is pleasure and pain entwined, my pet. No cares, no worries, but only the simple act of being." The preter's voice curled around them like the swirl of oil in water, iridescently pretty but toxic if swallowed. Jan bit her lip and clenched her fist so tightly her blunt-cut nails dug into her palm, as she watched Tyler's eyes start to fade over again.

"Coffee," she whispered. "Listening to the blues. Dancing slow on the balcony, watching it rain. Pizza and the click of the keyboard, the hiss of the radiator." She was almost chanting now, pulling all the sensation she could remember, the ones she thought might pull him back. Real things. Solid things. Human things. Things she missed with a sudden lurch of yearning.

"Four-way online Scrabble," she said. "Yelling at the game on TV. Waffles with real maple syrup and cinnamon. Crossing against traffic and just barely making it, the way the number seven bus drivers yell when you bring your bike on, but you know they're not really mad."

His lips moved; it was almost a smile.

"Come home, Ty. It's time to come home now. To the real things. To me, Tyler Wash. Come home to me." Her cracked, hoarse voice broke, and all the pain she felt, all the frustration and the loss—the things she had gone through to get here, all dripped into her words, coating them with as much vinegar as honey.

And he stepped forward.

And then again. And he lifted a hand to his chest, curled his fingers around something, a chain of silver hidden under his shirt, pulling it over his head and dropping the chain on the stone floor.

"No!" the preter cried, and rage filled the room, but it could not touch Jan, not now. Her fists clenched to her chest, barely daring to breathe, Jan watched as Tyler took another step, then one more, and was almost halfway across the room, halfway to her.

There was a stirring in the crowd, as though someone might stop him, but it stilled, as though reminded that they dare not. The consort had said it: it was up to Tyler to decide.

Another step, and he looked up at her. His gaze was still clouded, his face scrunched as though he worried over each step. She wanted so badly to step forward, to reach out and bring him to her, but she was held by the same knowledge that restrained the preter: this was not her choice.

And then he took another step, and his hands reached up and she took them, feeling the chilled, trembling flesh under her own. Her chest clenched, but she turned to the consort, her back to the room, and said "mine."

The consort leaned back in his chair, his expression one of distant boredom. "Yes, yes. Go."

"Now." And Martin was beside them, although it should have been impossible for him to move that quickly. "Before something happens, or they set up another challenge, we have to go."

"Who?" Tyler still looked dazed, but his skin was starting to warm again, the chalky gray color easing to a healthier brown.

"No time," Martin said. "We're going, now." And, one to either side of him, they moved out of the chamber, feeling the gaze of a dozen or more preters on them, the hottest one from Stjerne, who paced them, stalking them, the full length of the chamber, although she dared not touch them with hand or magic.

And then they were through the door and into the antechamber, and Jan swore that the air rippled with some kind of weird time-distortion, quantum-folding, magic-shifting thing, because they were running, all three of them, up the passageway and out into the mist-filled world in half the time it had taken them to descend, as though the Hill itself wanted them gone.

She lofted her face to the clouded sky, breathed in the faint sunlight, and then bent over, hands on her knees, and started to hyperventilate.

"Do you need your inhaler?" Martin was at her side, worried, solicitous.

"No. Mmmokay. Just…"

His hand on her shoulder, warm and reassuring, helped. Slowly, the hysteria passed, and she got her breathing under ragged control. His hand withdrew, and she stood up, slowly.

"What…who are you?"

Jan's heart froze, then she realized that Tyler was looking at Martin, not her.

"A friend," the kelpie said, his voice tight. Reassured that she was okay, he was scanning the horizon as though looking for something, maybe more of the greensleeves who had accosted them before. Jan rubbed her chest, still aching, and worried about that, too. Was the consort's word binding on those who'd been cast off?

"A friend." Tyler sounded dubious, but Jan had other worries to deal with first. "Martin? How do we get home? How do we find the portal?" Worry threatened to turn into panic: had all of this been for nothing? Were they trapped here? Why hadn't they thought about an exit strategy, damn it?

Because neither of them had expected to survive.

Martin shook his head, still scanning the horizon, not looking at either human. "You have the pass from the consort; call it!"

Call it like a cab, raise her hand and have it come screeching to a stop at their feet? "You're sure?"

Martin let out a noise that was definitely a horsey snort. "No, I'm not sure. It would be just like preters to let us go and then leave us wandering here for the rest of our lives. But we're not going to know unless we try!"

"All right." She'd just taken on a preter and won, stood against magic and come out alive, if not unbruised. Calling a portal should be easy, after that, right? "Um. How?"

"Picture it in your mind." Tyler, not Martin, answered her and they both turned to look at him in surprise. "Picture it in your head, a doorway taking you where you want to go. Just picture it in yourself, and walk, keep walking." His voice was hazed again, but firm, as though he was speaking words someone else had told him.

"All right." She still held his hand in her left; she lifted her right and felt Martin's larger hand slip against her palm, fingers twining.

"I want to go back," Tyler said, his voice barely above a whisper. "I just want to go back."

"I want..." She almost said she wanted to go home, but the memory of the last time she saw her apartment, Toba's bloodied feathers filling the hall, the turncoats' mottled skin and sharp-filed teeth approaching on her...

"I want to go to the Center," she said instead, remembering the prickly velvet of the grass, the feel of clean water on her skin, the comfort of Martin's warmth next to her as she slept, and the knowledge that AJ was there, his eyes sharp on the sparrow's fall, like her grandmother used to say. Jan had never understood what the hell that meant, until now. "The Center of Everything."

And she saw it—no, she felt it inside her, and stepped forward, and kept walking until something shimmered just ahead of her, a match to the feeling in her brain, and then another shade joined it, like a campfire in shades from white to blue, and there was a sense of her, and a sense of Tyler, and she knew that this was right, this was the way home....

And then they stepped forward again into blindness and compression on her ears and nose and lungs squeezing her tighter than the worst-ever asthma attack, until she couldn't feel either man's hand in her own, and fought not to panic, not to let go.

Her first time through, she'd been on Martin's back; she hadn't realized how much that had shielded her. Like being shoved into a vacuum, icy cold and burning hot at the same time, twirling her around or twirling around her, vertigo making everything spin.

"Just the portal" she chanted inside her brain, focusing on those words and forcing her legs forward, step by step. "It's just the portal. This is the way home. Keep moving."

Her lungs collapsed on themselves, her eyes burst, and then they were out and through, and there was air again, and noise, and sight; she could feel her hands again, sweat-slicked and cramped from being crushed in a death-defying grip. Released, she fell to her knees, not on close-cropped, emerald-green grass, but pavement.

"About time you got back," a woman's voice said. "I was getting seriously sick of hot dogs."

Chapter 17

"Sorry we kept you waiting," Martin said. He didn't sound sorry. He sounded exhausted.

The portal hadn't taken them to the Center. They'd come back out where they'd come from. "I want to go back," Tyler had said, and not specified where. Had he been the one to open the portal, after all, not her? Or had they done it together? She thought about the feel of the portal itself as she looked around, taking in the so-familiar images of their world, and decided that either way, she was okay with the result.

"Typical kelpie," the woman said in response to Martin's crack. "I'm Meredith," she said to Jan. "AJ sent me— Oh!"

The realization that there were three, rather than

the two she'd been expecting, caused her to back up and let out a howl that shook the windows of the storefront—thankfully closed for the night. Jan didn't know what time it was, but it had to be late, based on how still and quiet the air was. But even in the small hours, there was more noise than there had been on the other side of the portal. Once the howl faded, she could hear cars honking and roaring in the distance, the occasional burst of music, someone's high-pitched screech of laughter, and a man's voice yelling, and underneath it all an almost audible humming of close-packed humanity that rattled Jan's bones and made her so relieved she wanted to cry.

When the *lupin*—Meredith—handed Jan her pack, saying, "This smelled like you, is it yours?" she almost did cry.

Electricity. Sweet, sweet electricity. She pulled her cell phone out of the bag and checked, out of habit. The power was almost gone—how long had they been over there?—but she had signal. Full bars.

Full bars, and nobody to call. Would Glory believe any of this, if Jan told her? Would anyone?

Would she have believed?

A sound drew her attention. At her feet, Tyler had gone down to his knees, clutching himself and keening. Meredith's howl, after the portal, must have been the last straw; whatever alertness he'd reclaimed when they'd left the Court was gone now.

Part of Jan wanted to help him, comfort him, and

the other was irritated at him—he was home! He was safe now!

"Janny."

Martin's voice, soft, behind her.

"Meredith's called for help—we need to get him out of here, before someone comes to investigate, or—and I need to talk to AJ. There's way more going on with the preters than he thought, this thing with the queen; if she's here, he has to know."

"Yeah. Yeah, I know." They couldn't stay here; they needed to report in. And Martin needed medical attention, and she'd kill for a hot shower and some food, and…

Her head was spinning the way it did when she'd had just that sip or two too much of beer and then lay down, and she wondered, sort of hazily, if she was going to throw up. She didn't think so; she was pretty sure they hadn't eaten or drunk anything the entire time they'd been in the other land, except maybe the water she swallowed, which meant…

How long had they been there? No wonder she felt weird. The craving for a hamburger hit her, and Jan's mouth watered at the imagined taste and smell. Pickles, and lettuce, and cheese, and red meat…

Maybe they could stop at a fast-food place.

She knelt down then and put her arms around Tyler. He shuddered but didn't draw away from her. Then again, he didn't acknowledge her, either, keening and rocking. She let him; maybe the movement gave him comfort, the way it did her when she was stressed.

Not that she'd done much of it recently, Jan realized. She hadn't been able to sit still long enough to try.

"I thought he'd be okay, once we got him home," she said, lifting her face to look at the supers. Martin's expression was worried; Meredith just looked irritated, her muzzle wrinkled as if she smelled something bad.

Maybe she did.

"You don't go with the preters and come back... the same," Martin said. "He needs help. Help we can give him. Come on."

A car pulled into the street, another sleek black sedan. Whoever Meredith had called, they'd been nearby. Or maybe the supers had people lurking everywhere, just waiting.

Jan put aside her annoyance and tried to make her voice calm and coaxing. "Tyler. Come on, Tyler, come with me, just a little farther, okay?"

Her voice seemed to soothe him a little. He let her pull him upright and shuffled forward, his body heavier than it should have been, leaning against her. It was a relief to slide him into the backseat, and she had a brief desire to close the door and walk away, to pretend that it was all over, that nothing more would happen.

Instead, she got in next to him, her arm sliding

around his shoulder, and waited for Meredith and Martin to join them. They got in, sitting on the seat opposite, and the car pulled away from the curb.

"Where are we going?"

"To meet up with AJ, to start. Then…" Meredith looked meaningfully at Tyler, who had stopped shaking but wasn't responding to anyone else in the car, leaning against the back of the seat with his eyes closed.

"It's not his fault," Martin said sharply. "You would not do so well, after a week or more in the hands of the preters."

A *lupin* face wasn't designed to look abashed, but Meredith tilted her head back, until her chin was practically pointing at the ceiling, and Jan understood that she was baring her throat to Martin in apology. The idea of it—a wolf showing submission to a horse—made Jan giggle, even as she knew that it was stress that made it seem funny. Stress and the sudden lack of stress, and exhaustion and worry and…

"Go to sleep," Martin said to her, as though he knew how close to cracking she was. Hell, he probably did. If anyone did, it would be him. "We'll be another half hour on the road, and a nap will help."

"But…"

"He knows you're here and the preters aren't. That should be enough, the condition he's in."

And there wasn't anything else she could do for

him, anyway, if it wasn't; she heard that, even though he didn't say it.

Jan closed her eyes and tried to relax enough to fall asleep, focusing on the feel and sound of Tyler, safe beside her. It didn't work. Her body was still overstimulated from recent events, exhausted but unable to let go.

The car rolled on, stopping and starting enough that, despite the dark-tinted windows, Jan knew that they were still in the city, and she wondered who— or what—was driving.

There were so many species of supernatural; was there only one kind of preternatural? If so, why? Martin might not know, but AJ would.

Then she wondered why it mattered.

"Looks like you had an…interesting time over there. What are you going to tell AJ?" Meredith's voice was soft, barely audible, and Jan strained to hear it almost instinctively, like a little kid trying to listen in on her parents talking below stairs.

Martin didn't hesitate. "The truth."

"All the truth and nothing but the truth?"

"All the relevant truth."

"Uh-huh." Meredith seemed amused by that but not disapproving. There was something under the surface of their words that Jan didn't understand. "You managed not to kill her. A lot of people are going to lose money on that."

"There were bets?" Martin sighed. "Of course there were bets."

He hadn't killed her. But he hadn't let her on his back, either. Except she had been on his back, hadn't she? The memory seemed foggy now, and Jan wasn't even sure that it had happened. Too much had happened, she couldn't remember what was real or not. She thought going to fairyland made you forget, but maybe part of it was passing through the portal? But Martin seemed to remember…and Tyler hadn't forgotten. Maybe it was just that she was so very, very tired all of a sudden….

There was silence as the car turned and then picked up speed. They must have left the city, heading into the suburbs, or maybe north. Jan tried to imagine where they were, but her sense of direction wasn't good in the first place and the time spent with the preters seemed to have made it even worse; she wasn't sure that she could have picked up from down just then, if asked. Were they going to the Center? Jan didn't think you could reach it by car, although at this point she wasn't sure of anything much at all.

"What are we going to do with it?" the *lupin* asked.

"With what?" Martin sounded like he had almost been falling asleep. He'd been awake as long as she had, and supernatural or no, he had to be exhausted, too.

"It. That."

"His name is Tyler."

"All right, okay. But seriously, it—Tyler, then— has been with the preters…how long? Weeks? That's as good as years, and you know it. That's damage you can't repair. Everyone knows that."

Jan, still exhaustion-fogged, waited for Martin to defend Tyler, to say that the *lupin* was overreacting, or wrong.

"AJ wanted someone who'd been in close contact with the preters. I brought him that. He didn't say it had to be in perfect mental health."

Jan tensed, shock running through her body. That hadn't been what she'd expected to hear at all. Hot tears prickled under her lids, but she refused to let them escape.

"And…" Martin hesitated.

"And?"

"We have to at least try. To help him, I mean. Humans can't help him. Not after what the preters did, whatever they did. They'd have no idea what they're treating, even if she told them. They wouldn't believe her. And she doesn't really understand, either." He laughed, harshly. "I don't, either. I was there, and I couldn't tell you exactly what happened. Parts of it are sharp and clear, and others are hazy, and I don't trust the bits that are sharp any more than the hazy. Less, even, because how do I know it was real?"

"What happened? What's it like, over there?"

"Beautiful. Like the stories say it was here, once. No cities, no smog, no…no people. It was beautiful, and very quiet. I can understand why the queen left; she was probably bored out of her mind."

"Wait, what?" Meredith sat upright, based on the sounds, and demanded, "What did the queen do? Where did she go?"

"No. I'm only going to tell that story once, and that's for AJ. But you'll understand then."

Meredith said something that sounded unpleasant, and then silence fell in the car.

Jan felt Tyler's fingers reach for hers, shifting in his sleep the way he used to when they lay in bed together. She slid her fingers against his palm and finally fell asleep, their hands clasped together, his head on her shoulder, and the sound of Martin's breathing in her ears.

"Jan. Janny. Come on, we're here."

The voice was calling her, enticing her out of the deep velvety darkness she'd crawled up in. She made a murmur of agreement but was too tired to wake up entirely; someone moved her body upright, out of the car, and her body protested, wanting only to snuggle back down and sleep for another week.

"Janny, come on. You have to wake up."

Martin's voice. Worried. Why was he so worried? Silly pony.

"Why is she like this?" Meredith, sounding annoyed. "She slept the entire way here. Her leman's awake, what's with her?"

"Shut up. Janny. Come on. AJ wants to talk to us."

She mumbled something again, trying to sink back, and the red-hot impact of a hard hand across her face jolted her forward instead. Her eyes opened, and she glared, tears finally spilling free.

"Wake up," Martin said, and didn't apologize, despite his hand raised as though to deliver another blow. "We need to report in to AJ."

"I'm awake." It came out more sulky than defiant. She turned her head, one hand coming up to rub at her face, avoiding the still-warm spot where he'd slapped her. "This isn't the warehouse." It wasn't the Center, either. It was a farmhouse, a real farmhouse, with a wide porch and two chimneys at either end, emitting white smoke, and in the back, not too far away, an actual barn painted red. It looked...bucolic, that was the word she was looking for. She could already feel her asthma waking up, too. Why had they brought her here?

"The warehouse isn't an option anymore," Meredith answered. "There was...a problem, there. We had to relocate."

"A problem?" Martin didn't know anything about it, either, obviously.

"AJ will tell you," she said, pointedly, giving him a sideways glance Jan couldn't read. "Come on."

By now, the front door to the house had opened, and there were figures on the porch, waiting for them. Jan stumbled forward, hoping against hope they would have coffee and maybe the cheeseburger she had been dreaming about. Or even just a steak. Something with a lot of protein, because she felt as if she'd been drained of every bit of energy she'd ever had.

"No. No no no no more I can't I won't I can't I won't!"

"Tyler!" Jan forgot everything else, swinging around to see what was wrong. He had backed up against the car, staring at the farmhouse with a look of horror…no, not at the farmhouse. At the figures, waiting.

Jan blinked, then realized what the problem was. He'd been too tired, too confused to react, before. But now, to him, they were all preternatural, all dangerous.

"It's all right, Tyler. They're…" Friends? No. "They're here to help us."

"No!" He seemed to want to say something else, but the words got tangled and stuck in his throat. "No no no no," and he threw himself backward, hitting his head against the car hard enough to hurt himself, until Meredith got him in a headlock and forced him down onto the ground.

"Yeah, your boy's going to be *real* useful," she growled. "Don't just stand there. Help me!"

And suddenly there were figures around them, and Jan found herself gently but firmly moved out of the way.

"But…" she protested, wanting to be the one who cared for him, needing to be the one holding him. They were supers, they were only going to scare him worse!

"He'll be all right." AJ was standing beside her, watching as Tyler was half led, half carried away. "We can give him something to drink that will calm him down, ease his fears. It's all right, Jan. We're not going to let him hurt himself. And then, once he's calmer, we can talk. But for now, you two, come with me."

Jan hesitated, her feet wanting to follow Tyler, to see what they were doing to him, to not lose track of him again, but AJ's words made sense. Much as she wanted it to be, this wasn't over yet.

The inside of the farmhouse was cozy, if crowded. Jan thought she saw Elsa in the living room, talking to someone, but AJ didn't pause long enough for her to be sure it was her. The *lupin* made a gesture at someone in the oversize kitchen, then led them through the house to a small room at the end that clearly once had been the TV room.

"Sit."

They sat. The sofa was battered, incredibly soft leather, and Jan's body—still craving the sleep she had been dragged out of—wanted to sink back into it. She forced herself to sit forward, instead. "Tyler— you can help him? What's wrong with him?"

"I warned you," AJ said. "They had him long enough to mess with his mind, change his loyalties."

"I know that—he thought he belonged to her—but when we put it to the challenge, when he had to choose, he came with me!"

AJ looked at Martin, who nodded. Jan was too tired to be pissed that the *lupin* wasn't just taking her word for it. "Is that how you managed it? I will want all the details, so we can keep complete records, not the crap and half-remembered legends we've been relying on. Well done, in any case—my estimations of you were dead-on."

Jan was pretty sure that he had meant that as a compliment. Maybe.

"As to your leman, preternatural mind games can be ugly. I have people looking him over, trying to sort out the damage, and as I said, we'll be keeping him calm, letting him see that we mean him no harm, that he can trust us. Odds are, the longer he's back in this world, the more he will recover. But…"

Jan looked sideways at Martin, his long face set, his gaze looking at something across the room. "He's never going to be the same again, is he?" she said, not so much asking as admitting to something she had wanted to, if not deny, at least ignore.

AJ's face really wasn't designed for expressions that weren't threatening, but she had learned to ignore his face and look in his eyes. They didn't have the flickers of gold and green that Martin's showed, but were only a deep, red-tinged brown that made her think of velvet and down.

"Are you?" he asked.

She dropped her gaze and looked at her hands, instead.

There was a knock on the door, and then it opened, and a slender young girl slipped in, carrying a tray. "Coffee, and milk, and kofta," she said, putting the tray on the low table in front of them. "Cook put *pignoli* in the meat this time, but you're not allergic, are you?"

That was directed at Jan, who shook her head numbly. The smell of whatever the kofta was hit her nose, hot meat and spices, and her mouth watered.

The girl flicked her gaze at AJ and then left, closing the door gently behind her.

"Eat," AJ said. Jan didn't need to be told twice, reaching for the round balls of meat, discovering toothpicks left to the side for lifting. The small meatball was warm and slightly greasy, and the moment it hit her taste buds she almost cried.

"Eat," AJ repeated. "It will resettle you in this world."

She wasn't sure what he meant, but she was too hungry to stop, anyway.

"What happened to the warehouse?" Martin had sat on the other end of the sofa, ignoring the food and coffee, his arms crossed over his chest, watching AJ intently.

"Turncoats. Something set them on us about the same time you crossed over."

"Coincidence?"

"You know how I feel about coincidence. But it might have been, they might have been tracking Jan, and found us. Or, they might have been set on us directly. However they came there, they were determined to keep us penned up, to not let us leave—as though they didn't realize you were already gone."

"So if they were sent, they were sent by someone who had incomplete information?"

"Or, what they thought was going to happen, did not. The timing of their approach…" AJ looked thoughtful but didn't explain further.

"So what happened?" Jan asked.

"They swarmed, eventually. They're not very patient, and rather single-minded. They destroyed the warehouse. We lost a lot of people." AJ's lips curled back in an unnerving snarl. "We made them pay, though. We put the bastards down. They won't come back from that any time soon."

Jan thought of the things that had attacked her, first on the bus and then in her apartment, and the food in her mouth suddenly tasted sour. She swallowed, then asked. "They won't just send more?"

"Gnomes are long-lived. They're also slow-breeding."

Jan had to think about that, then nodded. They

wouldn't have the numbers to send more. "But you lost people, too."

"We did. But we also gained a weapon. You. Your knowledge. You went through a portal—and came back. The information you have…" He stood, pacing to the single window in the room, glancing out, and then coming back to them. "Martin, eat something. And then tell me what happened. Tell me everything."

Jan blinked at him, not even sure what he was asking. "From…where?"

"From when you disappeared would be a good start, since you didn't exactly leave a note."

Jan licked her lips, trying to put her thoughts in order. "I was in the coffee shop…we'd set up a date, but he didn't show." God, it seemed like another lifetime. Maybe it was. "And then…she walked in. Stjerne."

"Who?"

"The preter who lured her leman," Martin said, having eaten the leafy greens presented alongside the meatballs and now in the process of fixing his coffee. He took an obscene amount of sugar, Jan noted.

"Right. And he was with her?"

"Yes."

AJ's muzzle wrinkled. "Interesting. I wouldn't have thought that they'd allow that, bringing him back here. Too risky. Usually they keep their humans wrapped up close until they're through with them."

"That must be why the consort was angry at her," Jan said, trying to ignore the rest of his comment.

"The consort?" AJ looked from one to the other, his nostrils flaring as though he'd picked up a new scent.

"Skipping to the interesting part, unless you really want the details of the Snake, or troll-bridges or what the stars look like, over there?"

"Another time, maybe. You went into the Court?" AJ sounded almost incredulous, without openly disbelieving, and not, Jan thought, a little jealous. She supposed, if you hadn't actually been through it, it would sound like an incredible adventure. If you were a little crazy to start, anyway.

"We were following them—following Tyler. It seemed a reasonable risk—if Jan could reclaim him, she'd—"

"Yeah, I get it," AJ said. "What happened when you were there?"

Martin opened his mouth, closed it again, shook his head, ran his fingers through his hair, and then tried again. "AJ, the queen is gone. She's abandoned the Court and come here."

AJ's entire body went still, and then he blinked and sat back in his chair, digesting that news. "The queen is here. In this world."

Martin and Jan both nodded.

"To quote humans, Jesus Christ on a pogo stick."

His expression should have been funny, but it wasn't.

"And they want her back?"

"They want to punish her. And us, for being more interesting, I guess." Jan picked up a mug of the coffee and sipped at it. The last of the fog left her brain, and she did, in fact, feel grounded again. Maybe the fairy tales about food in fairyland worked for your own world, too? "That's why they're coming in such numbers; you're right, this is an attempt at an invasion. Or not an invasion really. Maybe a resettlement. If we're so damn interesting, they're going to move in. I guess. They've been insulted, and I get the feeling that they're not really the bygones-be-bygones kind of folk."

"No. They're not. So if they can't take her away from her toy, take her toy?" AJ hrmmed deep in his throat. "But how? How are they opening portals at-will? Tell me you found an answer to that, too."

Jan shook her head. "I don't know. We— Tyler told us to visualize it, just *think* about it, and we opened one to come home, but I don't know what we did— and I don't even know if I was the one who did it, either. I tried to bring us to the Center, but we ended up back where we started."

"No technology?"

"I didn't see anything that looked like tech, no towers or wires or…I'd say that world hasn't gone much beyond basic industrialization, if that: water wheels, and muscle power."

"But they're connecting to your internet, some-how," Martin said. "Luring humans that way... They wouldn't have just stumbled onto it...."

"But that might have come after they learned how to establish portals on their own," Jan pointed out. "Once they were here, if they were among humans, then they were going to see people using smart-phones, computers, all that everywhere. If they're really peeved about their queen finding this world interesting, they'd want to know everything...."

"And they discovered a new tool. Great."

Jan sighed. All that, and they still didn't have an answer.

"We have time to find out how Jan—or Tyler—created the portal, though," Martin said. "AJ, when Jan won her challenge, she pushed the consort, made him extend terms. We have time before they'll try to come back here."

"We can trust him?" Jan asked, still dubious.

"You got very specific terms," Martin sad. "He has to abide by those, to the letter and number."

"You arranged a truce?" For the first time, AJ ac-tually looked impressed.

"Yes. I think. For ten weeks, or something like that."

"Good. No, better than good. You did amazingly well, Jan, thank you. And the queen is still here?"

"We think so," she said. "Yes. Unless there's a third world you guys forgot to mention?"

"Bite your tongue and swallow the thought," Martin said. "She's here, AJ. And I'm betting she's relatively close, if they've been focusing their efforts on this part of the world. Does that change anything?"

"It means if we can find her, we have a potential hostage."

Jan hadn't thought of it that way. From the look on Martin's face, neither had he.

"And you'll find her…how? Set every super in the country to sniffing?" She used his own words back on him, but the *lupin* just grinned.

"If I could, I would have, already. Too much world, not enough of us willing to play. But the fact that we haven't gotten reports of escalating disappearances outside this continent means that we can, like Martin said, focus our efforts here. And she may give herself away, may already have given herself away. She's cut off from her own home, as weak as you two were over there, but alone. She's going to need to rebuild her own Court. She might take a few humans, but she's going to reach out for the supers, too; we're more familiar, built of the same stuff, to her mind."

"The gnomes?" AJ had said he thought someone sent them to the warehouse…she had thought he meant the preters on the other side, but…

"Gnomes, and others." He stood. "I need to pass word along. I'll be right back."

* * *

The door closed behind him, and Jan put her coffee down on the table. "Are you okay?" she asked Martin, echoing her earlier words to AJ.

"I will be." He wouldn't look at her, though.

"Martin." He looked up, but his gaze was averted. "Thank you."

"You did the hard work," he said. "I was…"

"You got me there. Kept me alive. Kept me strong." She exhaled, feeling weirdly guilty, as if she was about to give someone the brush-off. But that wasn't what she wanted to do. Glamour, she reminded herself, the food and coffee letting her think more clearly again. Seduction and fog. As much as Tyler had been befogged, hadn't she, too? With Martin's touches, his voice, his smell…

She wanted to cry.

"And you got Tyler back," he said.

"Yeah." For all the good that did. They had warned her, over and over, and she hadn't understood. Whoever Tyler had been before, he wasn't that person now.

Then again, neither was she.

They sat there in an oddly awkward silence, until AJ came back through the door, a look of satisfaction on his face.

"Word's going out. Even the ones who wouldn't come to us…they'll pay attention to this. There are communities with a long grudge against the preter Court…."

"Not all of them known for using best judgment," Martin said.

"True. But they know what's at stake; they'll keep her intact, if they find her."

Jan had a momentary flash of sympathy for the queen, and then decided that, if she was anything at all like the preters Jan had already met, sympathy was wasted.

"Still, we can't focus all of our attention on her. We need to find a weakness. The preters of old were restricted by what they could do. These…we can't shut them down, we can't stop them from picking off gullible humans. Once your term of truce is over…" AJ sat down, his body language finally showing exhaustion. Had he slept at all, while they'd been gone?

"Short of shutting down the internet, we're probably hosed," Jan said. "And your earlier plan of finding them sucked. You may not like tech but they… Hey."

She stopped, things clicking into place the way they did when she finally saw how to redesign something, to fix a problem. Shift and drop, pull and push, and things became so obvious, it was embarrassing.

"What?"

Obvious, but impossible. "It's probably nothing, but…"

"Nothing is nothing, not right now," AJ said. "What?"

"The truce the consort gave me. Ten weeks."

"Yes?" AJ waited, as patiently as he could.

"Ten weeks, ten days, ten hours. Very specific. Ten, ten, and ten."

AJ looked at Martin, who shook his head. Neither of them got it.

"Wasn't the traditional magic number for elves seven? Seven years of captivity, that kind of thing?"

"Traditionally, yes," AJ agreed.

And they're creatures of tradition and habit, right? They don't like change, they don't break patterns. So why ten, suddenly? And three sets of ten? Or, if you look at it another way, one and zero, one and zero, one and zero. It was as though he was constrained to binary."

She'd lost the *lupin* totally, she could tell. "What?"

"Code. Computer code, at its most basic level, is binary. Ones and zeroes."

"Ten, and ten, and ten…" Martin was trying to parse it, then shook his head, too.

"It's how computers speak to each other," she said. "And now preters're using it, too, replacing the numbers that had traditionally been important? I mean, like I said, it might not mean anything…." She started to dismiss her thought as foolish, but AJ held up a hand to stop her.

"No. Any pattern around the preters is useful, and probably significant. The world is chaotic: we have learned to ride that—"

Martin snorted, and AJ talked right over him.

"—but the preters find their comfort in order and

pattern, you're absolutely right. That is why they are so tied to their word: a vow imposes order. They are uncomfortable breaking it, because it sweeps them back into chaos."

"We tend to be more comfortable with chaos," Martin said to Jan.

"I would never have guessed that," she muttered back.

"Children… But change comes to everyone. We change—we take jobs that blend with the human population, we interact and are influenced. Dryads work with environmental groups, half the centaurs I know have gone back into politics,"

Jan raised her eyebrows but didn't follow up on that.

"The point is, we change in order to survive. All of us. If this particular change is tied in to how the preters are suddenly able to control the portals—"

"Computers—code—is the most basic order. That would appeal to them— Oh. You don't do magic, you *are* magic. Binary magic?" Jan's eyes got wide, and her brain ached.

"I don't know," AJ said. "I don't know what that means, if it makes sense, and if it is true, if there's anything we can do to counter or stop it. But everything we learn helps."

Before Jan could ask any questions—before she could even think of any questions to ask, there was a knock on the door.

A stick-slender, rough-skinned supernatural poked his head in at AJ's "enter."

"Boss? We need you two. Kinda now."

He pointedly had not included Jan.

She had been hurt, for a minute, then practicality come to the fore: if they were coordinating with other supers, she would be less than useless, especially if they were dealing with the ones that didn't like humans.

"Go," she told them. "I may just curl up and take another nap."

Martin hesitated, as if he wasn't sure he believed her, but followed AJ.

Left alone in the small study, Jan finished her coffee, contemplated the inviting sheen of the sofa, and then went in search of where they were keeping Tyler.

Chapter 18

The farmhouse had been renovated at some point, Jan noted, walking through the rooms—the open space had clearly once been several smaller rooms. Unlike when they'd first come in, nobody seemed to be just hanging around or doing chores; in fact, the house was oddly empty. The first two supers she ran into shrugged when she asked them about the human male, giving her an odd look, as though they weren't sure they were even supposed to be talking to her. Disheartened, Jan wandered into the kitchen.

The woman standing at the table, stirring something in a massive metal bow, looked as if she had been carved out of a massive oak, down to the bark-like texture of her skin. She was wearing a chef's jacket and loose white pants, and had the expression of someone who tolerated no foolishness in her domain. Jan hesitated in the doorway, almost afraid to speak up.

She gave herself a mental kick: someone who'd stood up to the preter Court shouldn't be afraid of a single supernatural! Especially one who's an ally.

Cook looked up when Jan came in, gave her a once-over, and then, before Jan could even ask, pointed out the window to a small shed behind the house.

"The other human?" Jan asked. Cook just nodded.

"Thank you." Somehow that didn't seem enough to say. "Those meatballs, those were yours? They were very good."

The cook just turned back to her bowl, but Jan was pretty sure she heard a satisfied "hrmp-hpmph" escape the creature's lips.

There was a knot of supers clustered around a table in the main room when Jan went out again. They ignored her, and she returned the favor, going out the back door, down two steps, and crossing the yard to the shed.

Shed was a misnomer, really. It was the size of a one-car garage, with no windows and only one door set into the side. Jan stepped up to that door and hesitated. Should she knock? Just go inside? Turn around and walk away?

She has half a breath from doing the last, when the door opened.

"Oh, good," the being standing there said. "I was thinking we'd have to go find you. Come in, come in."

She went in.

Contrary to the expectations from the outside, the shed was actually clean and well-furnished, with carpeting underneath and a kitchenette against the back wall. There was a beat-up sofa and a couple of chairs and, oh, god, a beanbag chair. It lacked only a wide-screen television to pass for any suburban rec room from when she was a kid.

But the expressions on the faces of those in the room were anything but recreational. The man who had opened the door looked almost human, except that he had no ears alongside the narrow bones of his face, and his skin had a faint blue-green cast to it. Behind the sofa stood a figure that could never have passed for human: thick-chested, with the battered face of a pugilist and the body of a huge cat. He turned when she came in and then looked away, and she was struck by the similarity to pictures she had seen of the great sphinx, after its nose was broken off.

"Come in, please," a woman's voice said. She was sitting on the sofa, and at first glance she reminded Jan slightly of Martin—not physically, exactly, but the same comfortable quality. Her face was narrow, her cheekbones high, but she was homely rather than pretty, the birthmark on her forehead like a smudge

of soot. Jan only gave her a brief glance, drawn to
the figure sitting next to her, an arm's length of space
between them.

Tyler.

"Hi," she said.

"Hi," he said, his voice a little uncertain.

She wanted to ask him if he remembered her, but
she was afraid of what his answer might be. "How're
you feeling?"

"I…foggy."

His eyes were glazed, and his expression sagged
a little still; she recognized the signs from her college years: whatever they had given him to "calm him
down" had left him high as a kite. But he was calm;
no panic at being surrounded by supers, no stress or
trembling. So that was good, right?

"You see?" the woman said, her voice a low, sweet
noise. "Here's Jan, safe and well."

He looked at her again, as though he'd already forgotten she'd just come in. "You're okay?"

"Yeah." She wondered how much he remembered,
how much they were letting him remember. She got
the feeling that now wasn't a good time to ask. "I just
wanted to make sure everything… That you…" She
ran out of words. What had she wanted? To see if
he was suddenly, miraculously, returned to normal?

He looked at her, then his gaze fell, looking at
something else, and flinched. She looked down to
see what had upset him, but it was just her, just—she

moved her hand, and the silver at her wrist flashed, still bright despite everything it—and she—had been through.

"I want a pizza," Tyler said. "Do you think we could have pizza?"

Jan looked helplessly at the woman next to him.

"I think we could manage that, yes," she said soothingly. She didn't touch him, didn't even look at him, but some of the tension left his body, unmistakably.

"All right." Apparently, that was all he could focus on, because he looked down at his hands, folded in his lap, and didn't look up again.

"Right now, we're trying to resensitize him to this world," the blue guy said softly. "The sounds and smells and taste of things that are real, familiar, so he doesn't react to them like an attack. Then we can ease him off the *sophum,* and start to recall his memory of what happened."

"Do you have to? Can't he just…forget?" Forget, and have it be the way it was last month, when her world made sense, was content.

"We need to know what he saw, what he learned. It's—"

"I know. It's important." More important than the status of her love life. And unless they made her forget, too…nothing was ever going to be the same. She looked at him now and saw Tyler…and she saw the way he had looked at Stjerne. "Tyler?"

He looked up, and the expression on his face was so open—glazed, uncomprehending, but hopeful—that Jan felt something inside her, something that had held on until then, break.

"I gotta go. There are things I need to do. But I'll... I'll be here. Okay?"

He stared at her and then nodded, but she had the feeling that he wasn't really listening anymore.

"His attention...it fades. But he knows you came to see him. That's good, that's helpful. Thank you."

Jan found herself outside the shed again without any memory of having moved, the door shut firmly behind her.

She licked her lips, feeling how they'd dried and cracked, and felt a sudden intense urge for a hot shower, and the long nap she'd told the others she was going to take. And a drink. God, a beer right now...

Instead, she went looking for AJ.

She found the *lupin* the main room, a map of North America spread out in front of him, other supers gathered around. There were pins and markers in the map, and others layered underneath, although she couldn't tell what land masses they covered.

AJ looked up when she came in, and lifted a hand, some signal to tell the others to clear out. They did, except for Martin.

"Operation Queen Hunt's underway, huh?" She meant it to sound snarky, but it came out shaky.

"A good name for it. Yes." He watched her, solemn. "So, what now?"

"For you? Now…you go home."

"What?" Jan blinked, not having expected that.

"Go home," AJ repeated patiently. "Reassure your friends and family, your employer, that everything's under control, let them know that you're okay. The world isn't going to end tomorrow—not even next week. You need to pick up the pieces and go on."

That was exactly what she'd wanted. So why did she feel as if she'd just gotten dumped?

"Martin?" She looked at him, noticing how the skin on his hands and face had healed, only a faint scar showing any damage had ever been done. Either they had an amazing doctor, who hadn't been to see her, or—he'd shifted form, that must have been it. Once he was away from her, he could shift and the magic would fix him.

In contrast, she was still ragged and bloody and probably smelled like hell.

"You've done everything you can," AJ said, not letting Martin respond. "You've done more than anyone could have asked. We cleaned up your apartment— you've only been gone a few days, and part of that was the weekend, so you can catch up. You can recover."

Jan looked at him in disbelief, and then looked at Martin. "You think that's what I should do?"

The kelpie looked down at his hands, the same

way Tyler had, but he looked up again. "Jan, you were never meant to be part of this. Humans… humans aren't… You did what was needed, now you can go home, be safe. Isn't that what you wanted?"

Yes. Yes it was. Tyler home and safe—or at least being helped, and she could go back to her life, pick up the pieces and…

And do what? Stop by every now and again, be part of Tyler's therapy, while they took him apart for what he remembered? Wait by the phone, like a good girl, for updates? Or worse—for news that they'd failed, sorry, and wait for your new preternatural overlord?

"No. Oh, hell, no." She shook her head. "You need me, still. You need what I know. This isn't over. I'm not going anywhere." Stubborn, AJ had called her? He didn't know half of it.

"Human…"

"AJ." Martin stood up. "Give us a minute."

AJ looked from Martin to Jan and nodded. "Right. I'm going to take a walk. Get some fresh air."

The two of them stood there, frozen, until he left the room, the sound of the back door closing behind him. Then Martin rounded on her. "Are you insane? We're trying to keep you safe!"

His anger, perversely, made her feel better. "What am I supposed to do, go home and pretend none of this exists?"

"Yes!"

She stared at him, her eyes wide, until he looked away, blowing out his frustration in a huge, gusty sigh. "No. All right, I know you can't just…forget. That was stupid. But, yes, you should go home. Stjerne had to give up claim to Tyler, she won't try and take him back. No matter how…attached she thinks she was, they just don't work that way. They move on. So he's safe, and so are you."

"But they're still coming, still stealing people."

"Jan, they've always come. They will always come."

She was starting to get annoyed. She was the one who had won them a truce, however short. She was the one who'd maybe figured out the connection— okay, not figured it out, but put them on track to figuring it out. Her, a human. "Yeah, they've always come, humans don't know what's going on, etcetera etcetera ad nauseum. I got that. But it's different this time. They're not restricted, not until we find a way to keep them out, to close the doors forever. And you don't know how to do that. You don't understand what they're doing, or how. You didn't even recognize binary, and that's the only clue we have, right now."

She was no hacker, no tech genius, she didn't have the kind of brain that thought in code—but she was all they had. A thought flickered…she was all they had… but she wasn't all *she* had. Geeks with a puzzle…. She just hoped Glory was still unemployed—and still talking to her.

Martin was breathing heavily, like he was trying to keep his temper, and his black nails were digging into his palms.

"Even if we survive… You'll never be able to go back, if you don't go now. I don't know a lot, but I know that much. Nobody who chooses this, who chooses to walk among us…ever goes back. Not really."

Jan felt a shiver that told her he was telling the truth. "I know."

She'd just spent the past week or more—endless hours more, in fairyland—under one glamour or another. Martin's first, then Stjerne's, then…everywhere she turned, magic had pushed at her, gotten under her skin, manipulated her.

When she'd faced the preter challenge, Martin had told her to remain who she was. Only who she was had changed. Like AJ said—you had to, to survive. She was Tyler's lover. Martin's partner. Human. Part of this.

Glamour or not, whatever had happened before: before she'd met Tyler, before she knew about kelpies and *lupin* and preters and portals…she couldn't go back there. So she had to go on.

"It's my world, too," she said. "I'm not letting it go."

* * * * *

The story continues in SOUL OF FIRE

Sophie Littlefield

Of living things there were few, but they carried on

"Evocative, sensual, harrowing."
—*Publishers Weekly on Aftertime*,
starred review

Sophie Littlefield

AN AFTERTIME NOVEL

HORIZON

Cass Dollar is a survivor.
She's overcome the meltdown of
civilization, humans turned mindless
cannibals and the many evils of man.

But from beneath the devastated
California landscape emerges a tendril
of hope. A mysterious traveler arrives
at New Eden with knowledge of a
passageway North—a final escape
from the increasingly cunning Beaters.
Clutching this dream, Cass and many
others follow him into the unknown.

Journeying down valleys and over
barren hills, Cass remains torn
between two men. One—her beloved
Smoke—is not so innocent as he once
was. The other keeps a primal hold on
her that feels like Fate itself. And beneath it all, Cass must confront the
worst of what's inside her—dark memories from when she was a Beater
herself. But she, and all of the other survivors, will fight to the death for
the promise of a new horizon....

Available wherever books are sold!

Be sure to connect with us at:

Harlequin.com/Newsletters

Facebook.com/HarlequinBooks

Twitter.com/HarlequinBooks

HARLEQUIN® LUNA™

™ www.Harlequin.com

LSL354

C.E. MURPHY

YOU CAN NEVER GO HOME AGAIN

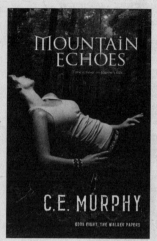

Joanne Walker has survived an encounter with the master at great personal cost, but now her father is missing—stolen from the timeline. She must finally return to North Carolina to find him—and to meet Aidan, the son she left behind long ago.

That would be enough for any shaman to face, but Joanne's beloved Appalachians are being torn apart by an evil reaching forward from the distant past. Anything that gets in its way becomes tainted—or worse.

And Aidan has gotten in the way.

Only by calling on every aspect of her shamanic powers can Joanne pull the past apart and weave a better future. It will take everything she has—and more.

Unless she can turn back time....

Available wherever books are sold!

Be sure to connect with us at:

Harlequin.com/Newsletters
Facebook.com/HarlequinBooks
Twitter.com/HarlequinBooks

HARLEQUIN® LUNA™
™ www.Harlequin.com

LCEM351

NEW YORK TIMES BESTSELLING AUTHOR

DIANA PALMER

IN THE VERY DREAM OF PEACE LURKED A MONSTROUS TREACHERY

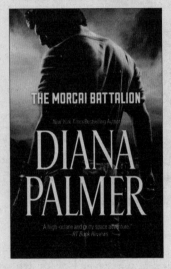

Available wherever books are sold!

Be sure to connect with us at:

Harlequin.com/Newsletters

Facebook.com/HarlequinBooks

Twitter.com/HarlequinBooks

Sophie Littlefield

The world's gone.
Worse, so is her daughter.

Awakening in a bleak landscape, Cass Dollar vaguely recalls enduring something terrible. Having no idea how many days—or weeks—have passed, she slowly realizes the horrifying truth: her daughter, Ruthie, has vanished. And with her, nearly all of civilization. Instead of winding through the once-lush hills, the roads today see only cannibalistic Beaters—people turned hungry for human flesh by a government experiment gone wrong.

In a broken, barren California, Cass will undergo a harrowing quest to get Ruthie back. Few people trust an outsider—much less one who bears the telltale scars of a Beater attack—but she finds safety with an enigmatic outlaw, Smoke. And she'll need him more than ever when his ragged band of survivors learn that she and Ruthie have become the most feared, and desired, weapons in a brave new world....

Available wherever books are sold!

Be sure to connect with us at:

Harlequin.com/Newsletters

Facebook.com/HarlequinBooks

Twitter.com/HarlequinBooks

HARLEQUIN® LUNA™
www.Harlequin.com

LSL352